the
wednesday
group

the
wednesday
group

sylvia true

St. Martin's Griffin ✠ New York

THE WEDNESDAY GROUP. Copyright © 2015 by Sylvia True. All rights reserved. Printed in the United States of America. For information, address St. Martin's Press, 175 Fifth Avenue, New York, N.Y. 10010.

www.stmartins.com

Design by Kathryn Parise

LIBRARY OF CONGRESS CATALOGING-IN-PUBLICATION DATA

True, Sylvia.
    The Wednesday group / Sylvia True. — First edition.
      pages cm
    ISBN 978-1-250-04892-9 (hardcover)
    ISBN 978-1-250-05188-2 (trade pbk.)
    ISBN 978-1-4668-5004-0 (e-book)
    1. Married women —Fiction. 2. Group counseling—Fiction.
I. Title.
    PS3620.R75W44 2015
    813'.6—dc23

                                     2014033797

St. Martin's Griffin books may be purchased for educational, business, or promotional use. For information on bulk purchases, please contact the Macmillan Corporate and Premium Sales Department at 1-800-221-7945, extension 5442, or write to specialmarkets@macmillan.com.

First Edition: March 2015

10 9 8 7 6 5 4 3 2 1

For Danny

the
wednesday
group

Lizzy

The wind howls, then quiets to a gray whisper. Lizzy pauses in front of the bedroom door holding a bottle of wine and two goblets. Her casual nightshirt shows off her long legs. If this marriage is going to survive, they need to reconnect.

She opens the door and stands at the foot of the bed. At fifty-two, Greg could still pass for thirty-five. He has a full head of dirty blond hair, a boyish grin, and healthy skin—no age spots, no circles under his brown eyes.

"Thought you might want some wine," she says.

"What kind?" He sits up a little.

"Chardonnay."

"I guess."

She senses his hesitation and begins to pour.

"That's enough." He holds out his hand.

There's still plenty of time. He's always been a slow starter, although she'd thought that would change after he confessed.

"What are you watching?" She slides under the covers, not too close, but close enough so that he can easily touch her.

"Antiques Roadshow." A woven tapestry, an elaborate depiction of an old church, is displayed.

"How much do you think that's worth?" she asks.

"Don't know." Greg yawns loudly, a signal that he is not in the mood.

The small rejections build on one another. But she's not about to give up. After a few more sips of wine, she inches closer.

"Want to just talk awhile?" she asks.

"Sure."

Finally, he turns off the TV. She reaches for the cord on the closed shade behind her. A little moonlight would be nice.

"Leave it," he tells her.

She does, although she'd like to look into his eyes, to see if he really does want her.

He finishes his wine. "Maybe I'll have some more."

Her vision has adjusted enough to see the bottle. She refills both of their glasses, and they drink in silence. If she's too assertive, he's only going to feel pressured and withdraw. Eventually, he places his glass on the floor, then turns to her and runs his fingers, stiff and tentative, along her neck.

He holds her face, kissing her forehead, her nose, her lips. Her shoulders relax as he grows more forceful and moves a hand down her nightshirt.

"That feels nice," she tells him.

"Why don't you take it off?"

She pulls the shirt over her head, glad to be rid of it.

He cups her breast, and she gently slips her hand below his waist. He sheds his flannel pajama top. They hold each other. She's missed his skin touching hers, but after a few seconds, she senses his loss of urgency. She kisses his neck and begins to slide down. His thighs tense and he stops her.

"I'm sorry." He sighs.

"It's all right," she says, and moves back up.

He grimaces and squirms as he shifts her head from his shoulder. "A cramp in my arm," he tells her, then sits and gropes for his pajama shirt. After he puts it back on, he lies on his side of the bed.

Her chest aches. "Do the guys in your group talk about how they deal with sex . . . after? I was thinking if it's an addiction, like alcohol, people have to talk about how they're going to deal with it when they're sober. You know?"

He responds by tapping the mattress with his hand.

She waits, trying to be patient. He clears his throat, as if that will help to dislodge the words that seem stuck.

"I thought," she begins, "when you stopped watching, you'd want me again."

"It's not that." His voice is tight.

She wishes she could do the wise thing, say good night and bring this up another day when he's not so defensive and vulnerable, and she's not on that boundary where rejection begins to harden.

"Then what?" she asks.

"It's . . ." He's stuck again.

"Do you want me?"

"Lizzy." He slaps the mattress. "I've told you I do."

There, it's out. What she was begging for—yet it's not enough. "It doesn't feel like it when it's so hard for you to say it." She sits up and gathers her long, curly hair. She'd worn it down for him. "You told me when you stopped watching, things would change. And they haven't." The words are hot; anger slips out.

"Christ, Lizzy, we go over the same shit. Things have changed. I'm going to my groups and seeing a therapist. It's not going to happen overnight."

She isn't looking at his face, but she imagines he is sneering. "So how long will it be?"

"I can't answer that."

"What can you answer?" Her voice is louder than she intended.

"This is going nowhere." He sits up.

She can tell he's getting ready to leave, to sleep in the guest room.

"I didn't mean to yell. It's just hard sometimes knowing you'd rather be looking at young women on the computer than making love to me."

He flips back the covers. "Why don't you tell me what exactly it is you want me to say?"

"That you love me. That you want me and not them. That you think *I'm* pretty." She detests that she's sinking this low.

"I do tell you those things."

"Only when you want me to shut up."

He swings his legs off the bed. "I can't do this anymore tonight. I have to get up early."

She wants to extend an olive branch, to tell him she's willing to work through this, that she loves him. But she doesn't.

He walks to the door.

"Just tell me you aren't watching porn," she says.

He shakes his head. "I'm sorry I'm not changing fast enough for you." The door slams behind him.

Every cell in her body feels as if it's about to burst. She wants to follow him, to keep fighting until they reach some sort of resolution. But of course she knows they won't.

She curls under the eiderdown. The room smells like stale wine. The beginnings of a migraine nag at her temple. He'll be asleep in ten minutes, relieved to be away from her. She listens to the wind growl, hating him, hating herself more.

Hannah

Hannah stirs an hour before her alarm clock is set to ring. Adam's snores remind her of a dolphin puffing as it comes up for air. She tries to fall back to sleep, but when she closes her eyes, she feels restless. A familiar unease weighs on her. The children are fine, life is good, but the sense of dread remains. In this state, neither asleep nor fully awake, she is less adept than usual at shoving away the feelings of despair. There is a leaky border between the subconscious and the conscious. A shower, a cup of hot coffee, and editing a few photographs will keep her occupied until it's time to get the kids up.

At breakfast, Hannah does Alicia's hair while she eats her Cheerios. Sam, who hates milk in his cereal, crunches. Hannah wraps an elastic at the end of Alicia's braid and kisses the top of her head. She has become skilled at knowing the right moment to slip in a squeeze or a pat.

She moves behind Sam, who inherited his thick brown hair from her dad. Hannah bends her neck, sniffing Sam's hair. The earthy scent reminds her of the first hint of spring.

Adam walks in, smiles at her, and pours himself a coffee. Until he's had two cups, he doesn't talk much. He's tall and well-built, with cropped red hair, and his light blue eyes are muted just enough so they always seem gentle.

He leans against the counter.

It's the fourth week in January, and the morning sun shines dully through the skylight. Hannah glances at her family, pulls up her shoulders and tells herself that she's going to stay positive and upbeat.

Adam smiles, softly, and she knows he feels the dip in her mood. He has mentioned she should get checked for seasonal affect disorder and believes the long New England winters are tough on her.

The kids finish their cereal, scamper off to get their backpacks, and head for the bus stop. Adam pours another cup of coffee, then reaches for Hannah, tugging at the arm of her sweatshirt to pull her in for a hug. She cozies into his chest and feels at home in his arms. She'd like to stay this way for a little longer, but he has to get to work, and she has things to do as well.

She steps away. "I'm fine," she says, as she picks up a couple of plates from the table.

After he leaves, she meanders to her studio and looks over a wedding album she has put together for a couple who are coming around noon. It's a good representation of her work, but nothing that really grabs her. In the last picture, the groom is carrying his bride as she waves to the camera. Funny, Hannah thinks, how this is what she ended up doing for a career, wedding photography, when her own wedding day had felt like the biggest farce of her life.

Leaving her studio, she walks through the roomy kitchen and down the hallway to the laundry room. Even this room has plenty of natural sunlight. She and Adam designed the house with lots of unique angles and dormers. A dream house, a dream life. And yet.

As she sorts the darks from the lights, she feels something, like a folded dollar bill, in a pocket of Adam's pants. She pulls out a business card, turns it over and sees a number with an area code she doesn't recognize. Certainly nothing alarming, yet her hands tremble. Even after all these years telling herself everything is normal, assuming those horrible episodes are long past, she can still think the worst. She reminds herself that his firm has clients from all over the country, but her heart beats erratically as she drops his pants into the washer and adds an extra cup of detergent.

In the kitchen, she picks up the phone. The dial tone drones. She begins to punch in Adam's number, but stops and hangs up.

The rest of the day passes in a hazy, panicked blur. Her clients come for their album, tell Hannah she's gifted, and write her a check. After they leave, she can't remember their names.

If he ever slipped again, she'd told him she would leave him. *Slipped.* What a stupid word for this. Slipped is when you lose your footing on the ice, when you forget your keys in the supermarket, when you hand in a field-trip form for one of the kids a day late. Slipping is not bulldozing your wife's life.

She calls her mother to ask if she can watch the kids tonight. After a few nosy questions, which Hannah evades, her mother agrees.

It's probably a futile plan. Actually, in truth, she hopes it's futile, and yet she finds herself dressing for the part. Old worn jeans, a heavy black sweater, her hair in a ponytail, and a modest amount of makeup, which she knows is ridiculous but can't help putting on.

She makes ravioli for the kids, helps with homework, folds the laundry. Adam's pants are at the bottom of the pile. Her mom arrives on time and raises her eyebrows when she sees how Hannah is dressed.

"I'm just hanging out at a friend's. No need to be fancy."

Hannah kisses everyone good-bye and slips on Alicia's furry pink Ugg boots, which are on the back doormat. In the car, she takes out Sam's Red Sox baseball cap from her purse and puts it on, along with her sunglasses, even though it's already dark.

Adam's office is down the hill from the State House. She drives around the block a few times before finding a space close to the parking garage he uses. She takes her phone from her purse and tosses it from one hand to the other. It would be so much easier, so much saner to just call. To ask. But what if he lies? And what if he tells the truth? Either way, she won't believe him. Trust is the most fragile thing in the world, and no matter how hard she's tried, or how hard they've worked, it's a canyon she can never quite make it across.

She slinks down when she spots him heading into the garage. Adam's car has a low, wide backside that's easy to follow. She stays a few cars behind. For a moment she's proud of her accomplishment, proud that she managed this whole scheme. Then the reality of why she's doing it intrudes, and her heart, which has been racing for the past hour, races faster.

It's fifteen degrees outside. The heat in the car is on low, and yet her palms sweat.

He turns onto Huntington Ave. He's not taking the Mass Pike.

What if he goes to some seedy hotel? Will she bang on the door of his room? She imagines his paramour, and her hand slips along the side of the wheel. She turns the heat down lower and opens the window. The air, dry and frigid, stings her neck.

The light ahead is yellow. She races through it. The car in front of her takes a right. Now there's just a VW between Adam and her. What if he sees her? She rolls the window down a little farther. *If he sees you, tell him the truth. You're not doing anything wrong.* But she feels wrong. Wrong, and confused, and scared. Scared to death.

It feels endless, the drive down Route Nine. Finally he takes a right into the Natick Mall and parks in front of Nordstrom. She shakes her head, smiling. He probably needs to look at some sort of structural thing for the new wing of the mall his company is designing. He's working, just not at the office. She's been hysterical. She's been following her husband's car, as if she's in some spy movie, on this freezing night in January, wearing her son's baseball cap and her daughter's pink boots because there was a phone number on the back of a business card. She's ready to continue on the path of how idiotic she is when she reminds herself that she's not really hysterical. After all, there is history.

She's about to drive home but decides against it. She parks three aisles over from him. He gets out of his car and walks quickly. She notices he's not carrying a briefcase. Actually he's not carrying anything, and his head is tucked down a little more than usual, something only she might notice.

In Nordstrom, she glances around. Without any customers, the sales people look sluggish. He takes the escalator to the second floor, where the women's clothes are. Maybe he's buying her a gift. But he walks through the department and into the mall, which is empty, a ghost town. Hannah tugs the brim of the hat a little lower and stays to the side, so if he does happen to look over his shoulder, she can race into a store.

Adam walks straight across, right to the public restrooms. He never slows, never turns his head. She stands at the end of the short corridor that leads to the bathrooms. This is a dead end.

She glances to her right, sees an elderly man heading toward Neiman Marcus. On her other side is a tall woman talking on her phone. No one is pushing to get into the restrooms. She takes a few steps, stops, and looks around. No one. A few more steps. She cranes her neck trying to see. If someone comes from behind, she'll say she's waiting for her son. No one is behind her. She hedges a little farther. Four urinals face the wall. The stalls are large with heavy wooden doors. She dashes into the last one, then looks down at her pink Uggs. Even though there are only a few inches of open space at the bottom of the door, she doesn't want anyone seeing her boots. She climbs on the closed seat and squats, her right hand against the beige tiled wall, steadying her. Adam is two stalls away. A faint odor, a combination of ammonia and cologne, makes her want to gag. She holds her breath.

Then the phone rings. But it's not just any ring. It screams the "Chicken Dance." Sam decided it would be funny if that was her ringtone, and she didn't have the heart to change it. He put the same silly ring on Adam's phone, and clearly he didn't change it, either.

"I'm here," he whispers.

Her stomach pitches and reels. *Breathe*, she tells herself, *don't lose it now*.

Someone comes in the restroom and goes into the stall with Adam.

Sweat drips down her forehead, but she can't wipe it off, afraid she'll lose her balance. Her thighs ache from squatting.

There's unzipping and unbuckling, followed by a crinkling of foil. Then Adam moaning.

"Don't stop," he grunts.

Although the stalls are large, semi-private, and divided by granite walls, the wooden door tremors, as if there's an earthquake.

Hannah's stomach spins. She's dizzy. The palm that rests against the wall slips, and she loses her balance. She tries to break the fall by twisting sideways. Unsuccessful, her purse clamors to the floor. Her legs give out. Her head hits the wall, and her pink boots poke into the neighboring stall.

Adam and whoever is with him stop.

"Hello," Adam says. "You okay in there?"

She pulls her feet back in, picks up her purse, and sits on the toilet seat. She's not okay. She feels seasick and puts her head between her knees.

"I'm getting outta here," the other man says.

Hannah jumps up and opens the door of the stall. She has to see what he looks like. On his way out, he glances over his shoulder. He's tan, wearing a tight T-shirt that shows off his muscles. His leather jacket is slung over his shoulder. He looks directly at her, and she thinks he must know who she is. He's young and handsome and doesn't wait around for any drama.

Adam rushes out of his stall and stares at her.

She touches her cheek and is surprised to feel tears.

"Hannah," he says, then stops.

She drops her purse and turns to the sinks. They have sensors, and she waves her hand, trying to get some water. Nothing comes out. Adam joins her, and with one swift motion the faucet runs.

She splashes cold water on her face, and for a second she feels better. Her face dripping, she picks up her head and gets a whiff of body odor.

Adam's eyes look cloudy. With his hands shoved in his pockets, he emanates shame, and she finds herself feeling bad for him, awkward and embarrassed.

"So this wasn't some sort of business meeting?" she asks, sarcastic, her voice raspy, her throat still pushing down acid.

"What?" he asks.

She covers her mouth, because she suddenly has the giggles. It's that funereal, inappropriate laughter.

"Hannah, this isn't funny."

She shakes her head no, as a chuckle escapes.

"Hannah, stop," he says.

"Sorry," she sputters, and goes back to the sink. But again she can't get the damn thing to work. She glances in the mirror and sees him looking at her, then her gaze drops. His belt is twisted. She holds on to the white porcelain as her knees buckle. He catches her so she doesn't hit the ground, but not in time to stop her from throwing up all over the floor.

They stand there, together. He holds her as she looks at the mess. She pulls away from him and yanks out a wad of white paper towels. On her knees, she begins to wipe.

"Leave it," he tells her. "Let's get out of here."

The paper scratches lightly on the floor. She can't leave it. She puts the dirty paper towels in the trash, then grabs more to finish the job.

Adam tugs at her arm. "Come on. Let's go home so we can talk."

The word *home* sits like a boulder in her empty stomach. How can they live under the same roof? How will she tell her mother, her children? What will she tell them? When?

"I wish I were dead," she says.

"Hannah, don't say that."

She grabs her purse and runs out of the bathroom. Adam stays a step behind.

In the parking lot, she climbs into her SUV and slams the door. Adam pounds his fist on the window. She starts the engine and backs up. There is nothing to say.

She arrives home before him. The kids are in bed. She thanks her mother, tells her everything is fine but she has a slight headache, so she's going straight to bed.

For the next two days she throws up the way she did when she was pregnant. Adam offers to stay home, and she shakes her head violently, no.

Exactly one week after the incident, after Adam's numerous pleas to talk, she agrees to go with him to his therapist. Hannah's been two other times, once a few days before they married, and again when the children were toddlers.

Nancy Baron, a small gray-haired woman, with clunky earrings too big for her face, sits on her hands when she listens. For most of the first forty minutes, Hannah cries as she retells last week's event.

"It sounds excruciating," Nancy says. "If you decide to stay in this marriage, Adam has a lot of work to do."

If she wants to stay? She should leave. But she can't. Not yet. She feels weak and pathetic. Her hands cover her face.

"You need support," Nancy says. "A friend of mine has a doctoral student who is starting a group for spouses of sex addicts. I think you may find it very helpful."

Hannah shakes her head no, but Nancy hands over a card anyway.

Hannah slips the card in her purse. The thought of telling random women about Adam's supposed addiction feels intolerable.

Bridget

The hangers clack as Bridget browses through the post–Valentine's Day sale racks of corsets and garters at Victoria's Secret. It's not likely that anyone she knows will be here, but still it would be totally fucking embarrassing.

She chooses an all-black getup, extra small. Forget anything with bows, or the ones that resemble what a French maid might wear. Nor is she into any S and M games. Truth is, she's not really into sex at all right now.

She doesn't try anything on, and she doesn't look at the cashier as she pays. Instead she glances at a mirror to her right. For a second she doesn't recognize herself. About a week after she found out about all the shit Michael was into, she dyed her hair red and started wearing thick eyeliner and leather shoes that look like combat boots. The soft, innocent Bridget had disappeared.

At their two-bedroom rented home in West Roxbury, she puts the groceries in the kitchen, then goes up to the bedroom. The corset pushes her small, pale breasts together, making it seem as if she actually has cleavage. She fumbles trying to press the hooks of the garter belt onto the stockings. It takes ten minutes. Finished, she glances at herself, spins around, and likes the way her butt looks. She pulls on a pair of jeans and a sweater, then heads downstairs to make dinner—steaks and potatoes, Michael's favorite.

"Something smells good," Michael says when he opens the front door. He walks into the kitchen, but stays a few feet from her.

"Just dinner." She smiles and opens the oven, pretending she has to check on something, because if she looks at him for one more second, she'll call him a fucking asshole.

"For us?" he asks. Even though he's six four, with scruffy hair and broad shoulders, he seems timid.

"Yep. For us." She closes the oven door.

"What's the occasion?"

"Nothing special. Just thought we could have dinner together."

"That's nice."

She watches him, her big, burly work-boot guy, the man she thought she knew.

"It will be ready in five minutes. There's a bottle of Jack over there. Can you pour us each a glass?" she asks.

She brings out the food as Michael places their drinks on the table. His movements are halting, as if he's overthinking his manners. Another whiskey will smooth out the discomfort.

"This is real nice." He sits and begins to cut his steak.

"Figured we needed it." She glances into his eyes, which used to make her think of beaches and warm summer days.

He finishes everything. She has two bites, her stomach feeling tight and small, her appetite gone. She refills their drinks and downs hers, hoping a buzz will give her more courage.

"Not hungry?" he asks, looking at her plate.

"I guess I have other things on my mind." She does her best impression of sultry.

"God, I've missed you." He reaches over and runs his fingers through her hair.

She takes a deep breath and leans toward him. They kiss. His mouth tastes salty, and despite it all, a part of her is coming alive.

She tries to pull away. "You go ahead upstairs. I'll take care of the dishes and meet you in bed."

He doesn't let her go. He keeps kissing her. She has to push hard against his chest to free herself from his grip. "I'll be up in a sec," she tells him.

"I love you so fucking much," he says.

"Go, or I might change my mind."

She takes the dishes into the kitchen, then drinks another shot of Jack, giving him enough time to undress and get under the covers. She's tipsier than she'd planned to be. In the bathroom, as she hangs her jeans and sweater on the door hook, she sways and bumps into one of the cabinet drawers. In it, there's a brand-new container of lubricant. Michael brought it home over a year ago last Valentine's Day. That, a pair of edible underpants, and a vibrator. They finished making love before any of the packages were touched. Now she opens the tube and puts in a dab.

It's only three steps from the bathroom to the bedroom, yet it seems like a long trek across a hot-tar parking lot. She tells herself she can do this, then breathes deeply and walks into the room.

"Get over here," he says.

"We're going to take our time," she tells him. "Roll over."

He does as he's told. She climbs on top of him, her knees pressing against his muscular upper body, as she massages his shoulders.

He tries to turn, to reach for her. She pushes his hand away. "No, not yet."

"You're wet," he whispers. "Just let me look at you."

"You'll have plenty of time for that."

She teases him, keeps him on the edge, does all the things he likes. Finally, he's on top of her and she knows he can't last much longer. She wraps her legs around his waist and holds him close. She didn't need the lubricant. She hates that she's still so attracted to him, that even now she wants him.

"Bridge, I love you. I fucking love you."

She turns her head. If she looks into his eyes, she'll be right back to square one, feeling hurt, in love, used, and betrayed.

He holds her. "You're amazing," he says.

She slips out of bed and stands in front of him, hand on her hip. "Take a long look, because that was the last time you'll ever get to fuck me. Go after some of those sluts you chat with online. See if they're half as good."

"Is this a joke?" he asks.

"Absolutely not." She feels strong, victorious.

He stares at her, baffled. Then sits up, reaches out to her. She backs up.

"I want you to remember what you took for granted," she tells him.

"But I never took you for granted. It was never that."

"Yeah, well, maybe you should have thought more before you did all that shit." The victory is exhilarating.

He stands. "Bridge . . . please."

"You never get to touch me again. Get out of my bedroom." She picks up a gold chain on her bureau. It slips, like water, through her fingers, and she feels herself break. Just a little.

"Can we talk?" he asks.

"There's nothing more to talk about." The necklace drops. The victory fades. She breaks a little more. "Go."

"If you didn't want me, you wouldn't have been so wet," he says.

"I had help."

His face turns hard. "You're messed up."

"Oh, really. That's the pot calling the kettle black." She keeps her head high.

"Bridge, if that was all an act, that's a sick fucking thing to do." He pulls the sheet from the bed and wraps it around his waist.

"You're one to talk about sick fucking things to do."

"I have an addiction. I'm working on it. I didn't go out of my way to—"

"To what? Lie, deceive, and manipulate? Yes, actually, you did."

He glares, then turns to leave.

After he's gone, she rips off her corset and stockings and puts on sweat pants and a T-shirt. She tries to convince herself that this worked, that she won, that he'll know what he's missing every time he sees her. But she doesn't feel victorious. She feels dirty and sad and, worst of all, lonely.

Kathryn

❦

Kathryn Leblanc checks her cell phone. Five minutes to three. She sits on one of the two wooden chairs in the hallway outside of her supervisor's office. She hopes Dr. O'Reilly will not be late for their final interview with Gail, a prominent Boston judge.

A woman, sixtyish, wearing a long beige raincoat walks down the hall and stops in front of O'Reilly's door.

"She's not here yet," Kathryn says. "She's running a little late." O'Reilly was also late for the previous candidate, Hannah, who chose to sit with Kathryn and talk about the weather.

The woman, whom Kathryn assumes is Gail, checks her watch, then looks warily at the other wooden chair, as if she's unconvinced it will hold her. Kathryn wonders if Gail's substantial weight has emotional roots that might play into her staying with a sex addict.

Gail places her bag on the chair and takes off her Burberry raincoat.

"Do you have any idea when Dr. O'Reilly will get here?"

"I'm afraid I don't." Kathryn stands and gestures to her chair. "Would you like to sit?"

Gail's bright red lipstick is a stark contrast to her pale skin and gray hair. "With my rheumatoid arthritis, that chair looks unsuitable." She adjusts the large ruffle on the front of her white blouse.

"I'm Kathryn Leblanc." She extends a hand.

"Gail." She shakes with a confident grip. "You are Dr. O'Reilly's assistant?"

"I'm actually a graduate student. She's my supervisor."

"And you will be running the group?" Gail asks.

"I will be."

"I have only an hour before I have to be back in court. Can you call her?" Gail asks.

"I'm afraid I only have her office phone number." They both glance at the door as if it might magically open.

"I see. Perhaps while we wait, you can tell me a bit about yourself and why you're qualified to run this group."

Kathryn absorbs both the query and the tone. "I'm in my last year of my clinical degree program. I see patients in Brighton as well as at an office in Jamaica Plain, where the group will be held."

"And you do have experience with spouses of sex addicts?" Gail asks.

Kathryn pushes aside her bangs, an old nervous habit. "I've worked with addicts and partners of addicts. I've done a lot of research on sex addiction, but no, I've never worked with spouses before."

Gail's hazel eyes narrow. "I see. And what type of members are you looking for?" she asks.

"Not any type, really. Women who are feeling betrayed and—"

Dr. O'Reilly arrives, out of breath, her coat hanging off her arm, her large bag bursting with papers.

"So terribly sorry," she tells Gail. "Back-to-back meetings."

Gail shakes her hand. Kathryn thinks they could be sisters. Not that their features are that similar. It's more their age, their status, their ability to convey authority with a few words, a slight hand wave, and an assured glance.

Dr. O'Reilly unlocks her door, holds it open for Gail, then walks in before Kathryn.

Three chairs sit in the room. One is O'Reilly's, behind the desk. The other two are made of soft red leather. Gail chooses the one closest to O'Reilly, who sits at the desk and fluffs her short, black-dyed hair. "Again, please forgive my tardiness."

Although O'Reilly routinely apologizes for being late, she is rarely so emphatic. Kathryn guesses it's due to Gail's distinguished position.

Gail takes a water bottle from her purse. "I must head out in about thirty minutes."

"I can see you've met Kathryn." O'Reilly folds her hands.

Kathryn glances around at the large office, filled with bookshelves, African art, and small Buddhas. The first time she was in this room, she had been nervous, afraid O'Reilly, chair of the psychology department, would consider the proposal for the group trivial. Instead she had been intrigued, and Kathryn was sure she had landed a fantastic mentor. But as they have been conducting interviews, some of O'Reilly's questions have been staid and old-school, and Kathryn has found herself uncomfortable with the fact that she often disagrees with her supervisor.

"My therapist assured me that you have an excellent reputation," Gail says to O'Reilly.

"Please give her my regards and thank her for the kind words."

"She also told me that you might be a candidate for the next university president. Very impressive."

O'Reilly smiles, then tucks her head down as if this conversation were unsettling. "I really haven't given it much thought."

Kathryn knows she must step in before O'Reilly finds a way to weave in her publishing credits.

"Gail," Kathryn says, opening a notebook. "May I ask how you discovered your husband was a sex addict?"

Gail repositions herself. "I was at my office." She speaks softly, each word demanding the listener's full attention. "My administrative assistant opens my mail. Barbara prioritizes and discards as she sees fit. I trust her immensely." She places a manicured hand on her chest and sighs. "You must excuse me. I have asthma, which at times affects my breathing."

"Take all the time you need." O'Reilly glances at the small gold mantel clock, whose face is hidden amid stacks of papers on the desk.

"It was about a year ago, on January thirteenth. I have never been one to believe in superstitions, but since that day, I find myself avoiding the number thirteen. But I digress." She fans herself with her hand, even though the office is hardly warm. "The letter my secretary opened was from one of Jonah's graduate students. My husband teaches philosophy, with the odd dip into theology, at Harvard. In the letter, the woman wrote that she thought it best to lay the cards on the table, an expression I dislike. She wanted me to know that Jonah was in love with her and not me. I read it as Barbara stood at my side, and then I assured her it was some sort of prank."

Kathryn writes down everything as she thinks Gail's focus on her assistant is a way to avoid pain.

"Did you have any support?" Kathryn asks. "Anyone else you could share the letter with?"

"I think what Kathryn means is, did you convey the contents of the letter to Jonah?" O'Reilly asks.

Kathryn glances at her notes. No, she meant what she asked. She wanted to know if Gail had friends, a family member, her therapist maybe, someone she could talk to. But at this point in the interview, Kathryn won't openly disagree with O'Reilly.

Gail sips her water. "I did share the contents with my husband. In truth, I just didn't think much of it. I was so sure he would say it was a hoax, or from a student who was mentally ill." Gail shakes her head. "Instead he sat on the edge of the couch and cried as he told me that he couldn't stop." Creases fan out from the sides of her eyes, and Kathryn wonders about the age difference between Gail and the woman who wrote the letter.

"Do you think there might have been clues along the way that you missed?" O'Reilly asks.

"I think of that all the time," Gail answers. "What should I have seen?"

"Would it have made a difference," Kathryn asks, "if you did find some sort of evidence that you missed a clue somewhere along the way?"

Gail's shoulders drop slightly as she seems to relax. "No, actually, it wouldn't. Nothing would have really changed. I suppose it's easier at times for me to do an inventory of my flaws instead of blaming Jonah."

Kathryn jots a few notes as she formulates her next question. O'Reilly jumps in first.

"I find it admirable that you are willing to be so introspective about this. It takes many people a long time to get past the anger stage."

She sounds obsequious.

"I am determined to move forward." Gail holds her head high.

"We are glad to hear that." O'Reilly looks at Kathryn, expecting her to concur.

"If you wouldn't mind," Kathryn says, "I'd like to get back to the issue of support, and if you have any?"

"Kathryn poses an excellent question," O'Reilly begins. "But since our time is limited, I think it's best we stay on track and make sure certain requirements are met."

"Of course," Gail says.

"Can you tell me why you believe your husband is a sex addict and not simply a man who wants to have affairs?" O'Reilly asks.

Kathryn cringes at the question but is careful not to let her feelings show.

"His therapist diagnosed him." Gail, once again, sits stoically. "Do you need some sort of document that states that?"

"No," Kathryn replies. "If both you and your husband believe he is a sex addict, that's really all that matters."

"He is in treatment," Gail adds.

"Is he finding it helpful?" Kathryn asks.

O'Reilly clears her throat. "I think it's best, Gail, that we focus on you for the moment."

"Well, what I can tell you about myself is that I am committed to working through this with my husband. I am not the sort to feel sorry for myself; rather, I'm the type to face the problem head-on and do everything in my power to fix it." Her red nails toy with the ruffle on her blouse.

"Very good," O'Reilly says.

"Will you be overseeing the group?" Gail asks.

O'Reilly places her hand on the large amethyst that hangs from her bold necklace. Her gesture seems to mirror Gail's, and perhaps she does it consciously. But she's missed the crux of it, Kathryn thinks. She does not fiddle. "I will be supervising Kathryn, but I will not be in the room. I do not want to intrude on her work. It is common protocol for me to send surveys to clients, and sometimes I make check-in calls."

"When will I hear from you?" Gail asks.

"You are the last person we are interviewing, so I'm hoping we'll have the group put together sometime next week," Kathryn tells her.

"I'd like you to know how grateful I am that someone is starting a group of this nature," Gail tells O'Reilly.

"Well, if it's something you want, we'd be pleased to have someone with your life experience and knowledge." O'Reilly turns to Kathryn, expecting her once again to agree.

"We haven't finished the process, so I'm afraid I can't promise anyone a spot at this point," Kathryn says. "But I'm pleased to hear that you are committed. That's extremely important." She smiles.

"Kathryn is very new to this, and wisely cautious. I think you'll find her a good group leader."

"I can sense that from some of her questions. I look forward to beginning." Gail stands, shakes O'Reilly's hand, and leaves. Kathryn feels dismissed.

"I'd like to talk for a few moments about your need to contradict me," O'Reilly states.

"I don't think I contradicted you. I was only telling Gail we haven't finished the process."

"This was our last interview, and I feel adamant that Gail should be a member of the group."

Kathryn collects her thoughts. "It could be because I'm relatively new to this that I'm just not convinced at the moment that Gail would be a good fit."

"She has experience. Just think what sort of knowledge, from a legal perspective, she could bring."

"I don't know that we'll need legal advice."

"With some of the situations that these women are in, of course you will. We've already interviewed candidates whose partners have had trouble with the law."

"But would it be fair to put Gail in a position to be a legal advisor?"

"No, of course you wouldn't do something like that. I'm merely saying she has a lot of wisdom, and I think you might find her a good balance to some of the other members."

Kathryn nods. "I understand, but . . . well . . . in all honesty, I found something about her a little arrogant. Perhaps it's a way to avoid her pain, but I think it may deter others from opening up."

"She is knowledgeable and committed. That is different from arrogant. And I believe it will be one of your challenges to get all these women to reveal their pain. That is a part of the process."

Kathryn closes her journal. "I will go through all my notes and e-mail you the seven people I think would be best suited for the group."

"Casting a group is much more difficult than reading one's notes and coming up with names. We've been interviewing for six weeks—it's hardly wise to rush the next step. And you will not have seven. I was thinking four would be good for you, considering you don't have much experience with groups. And Gail will be one of them. She has age and insight."

And power, Kathryn thinks. "Is choosing the members my decision or yours?" She looks directly into O'Reilly's eyes.

"I am your supervisor. So it is up to both of us."

"In the spirit of collaboration, then, I think four is too few."

O'Reilly glances at her watch. "I have an appointment with the dean of graduate studies," she says.

"I'd like to call the women next week."

O'Reilly grabs her bag and coat. "You can have five members at the most, and one of them must be Gail."

"I think this warrants more discussion." Kathryn tucks her notebook into her briefcase and stands.

O'Reilly is at the door. "No. Five will be good, and except for Gail, you decide who to include."

As Kathryn makes her way down the hall, she notes that Gail was the only one who didn't cry. Outside, the cold air feels refreshing, liberating. She hikes to the subway, debating silently with O'Reilly. By the time she gets on the train, her thoughts have shifted to the women, to their broken lives. It will be difficult to choose. She will need to research best practices for smaller groups. Earlier today she had a different group in mind, but now as she begins to visualize where the women will sit and the questions she'll ask, she feels energized again—excited to finally begin.

SESSION ONE

The first group happens to coincide with the first day of spring, although snow still covers the ground. There hasn't been a day above freezing for months.

Hannah tells herself to get a grip as she parks at the back of the small lot across from the rambling Victorian that has been turned into offices. A solid ten minutes early, she looks at herself in the rearview mirror. Her lipstick is even; the neutral tone seems appropriate. She's grasping for familiarity in what feels unfamiliar and terrifying. She reminds herself she doesn't have to stay; she can excuse herself at any time if she feels too uncomfortable.

When Kathryn called two weeks ago to tell Hannah she'd been chosen, Hannah felt honored, as if she'd won something. Kathryn sounded pleased that Hannah agreed to join. It was all so removed from the reality of actually exposing the shameful secrets that have become the skin of her life.

Instead of putting her keys in her purse, Hannah shoves them in her pocket. They will serve as a reminder that she is not trapped. Kathryn asked that Hannah think about what she wants from this group. *Support* was the first word that came to mind, but the more she thought about the word, the more literal it became. Support beams, support bras, support hose. Other words—*empathy, understanding, coping skills, friends*—came to her. None felt quite right. She finally decided that what she wants is relief from the panic that comes in the middle of the night, and the floating anxiety that plagues her most of the day. She wants to stop snapping at her children, stop obsessing about what Adam may or may not be doing. She wants to start living again—a tall order for a therapy group to deliver.

The place feels deserted. She climbs the stairs to the second floor and knocks on the door, wondering if she got the time wrong.

Kathryn greets her.

"Hi," Hannah says. "Am I too early?"

"No, but you are the first." Kathryn smiles.

Hannah has read somewhere that group leaders are sensitive to the early birds who try to sneak in one-on-one time.

"I'll wait out here," Hannah says.

"No, come in. Please." Kathryn looks younger than Hannah remembers. She has her hair in a ponytail, and her brunette bangs hit just above her well-defined eyebrows.

Hannah steps into the room, where mismatched chairs are arranged in a circle.

"Take a seat." Kathryn smiles again, and Hannah senses that she is also nervous.

Hannah decides on the wooden Windsor chair, the only seat without padding. She doesn't want to sit on the loveseat and risk being too close to someone else. And she's not going to take an armchair since she probably won't come again.

"There's water on the coffee table," Kathryn says. "Help yourself. I'm just finishing up some notes."

Hannah could use some water, but right now she's afraid her hand will shake if she actually tries to pour a glass.

It's too quiet. She digs her phone from her purse and reads the last text from Adam, informing her of the time he left work, traffic conditions, and estimated arrival. This is what her life has come down to—his reporting his every move. It's supposed to build trust, but it doesn't. She powers off her phone.

"Knock, knock," a voice calls.

"Gail," Kathryn says. "Come in."

The woman is already in, and Hannah wonders if it's because Gail is older that Kathryn seems too eager as she takes her coat. Gail has on bright red lipstick and no other makeup. The circles under her eyes have a plum-colored hue.

She looks around, nods as if the room is acceptable, then sits in the armchair next to Hannah. She shifts, trying to get comfortable. Her sneakers stand out against her tailored slacks and peach silk blouse. When she finds a position that seems suitable, she turns to Hannah and introduces herself. Hannah does the same and is stumped as to what to say next. Does one ask, *What did your husband do to mess up your life?* She settles on, "Did you run into a lot of traffic?"

"It wasn't as bad as I thought it would be," Gail replies, "although there isn't an easy way to get here from Cambridge."

Something about the way she says *Cambridge* reminds Hannah of people who need to drop in that they went to an Ivy League school. Gail pours herself some water and takes a sip with steady hands.

Two other women walk in. They are both tall. The older one, fortyish, has thick auburn curls thrown into an updo. She sits on the loveseat, clinging to the side, making sure there is enough room for someone to join her.

The other woman also sits on the loveseat. She is younger and striking, with brown hair, nearly black, that comes to her slender waist.

Hannah wonders why men would cheat on such beautiful women. Then she reminds herself that *cheating* is the wrong word, that she is supposed to think *illness.* Disease with a capital D. Yet *cheating* is what sticks.

Kathryn walks to the door and closes it most of the way. "We are waiting for one more member, but I think since it's seven, we should begin."

The woman with the auburn curls smiles. Gail takes a sip of water. Hannah's palms sweat. A panic attack is not far away. She grasps the wooden seat of the chair.

Kathryn passes out confidentiality forms, and Hannah signs hers without reading it.

"I'd like to look mine over," Gail says.

"Of course," Kathryn replies. "Perhaps we can begin by introducing ourselves and telling the group a little bit about what brings you here."

Everyone nods. No one looks comfortable.

"I will try to stay on the sidelines as much as possible," Kathryn explains. "If I think the group is getting off track, or if I sense someone isn't getting to share when she wants to, I will intervene." The words are well placed, formal.

The room is silent. Hannah wants to talk, if only to fill the emptiness. She lets go of the chair, ready to raise her hand.

"I'll begin," Gail says. "My name is Gail, and I'm here because I wanted a private group in which I could find support. As far as I know, there are no others in the area that address the issues that partners of sex addicts face." She looks around to make sure she has everyone's attention.

Hannah is impressed by how easily she can say "partners of sex addicts."

"I have a very high-profile job," Gail continues. "I can't risk the chance of the papers getting ahold of my story."

Hannah imagines Adam being arrested in some seedy bathroom. If that ever happened, and it wound up in the news or on some Web site, she would change her identity and flee to Argentina. With the children.

"There is often a lot of shame and humiliation around sex addiction," Kathryn says.

"Yes, well . . ." Gail says, sounding a touch irked that Kathryn cut her off. "Jonah is my second husband and my soul mate. From the moment we met, we both knew that we were meant to be together. We discuss everything, from what we perceive God to be to the latest state referendums."

Her words flow smoothly, unrushed. At this point, Hannah would be stammering.

"One afternoon at work, my assistant asked to see me. She was clearly distraught as she held a piece of paper. It was a letter from a graduate student of Jonah's. He teaches philosophy at Harvard. His concentrations are normative ethics and personal identity." She pauses, chin forward, head high.

Odd areas of study for a sex addict, Hannah thinks.

"In this letter, the student claimed my husband was actually in love with her, but he was too frightened to tell me. I brought the letter home and showed it to him. He crumpled as he sat on the couch." She takes a moment to bow her head.

Hannah gets the sense that the real Gail, whoever she is, is buried under well-practiced orations.

"He admitted that she wasn't the only one. There had been another." Gail bows her head again. This time with more solemnity. "Another? Was that better? Did that mean he didn't care about them and still loved me? I—"

The final member, a woman in her twenties with brassy red hair and shoes that look like combat boots, traipses in.

"Sorry I'm late. Traffic, and I hit every red light."

"Please, Bridget," Kathryn says, "take a seat." She gestures to the empty armchair at her right.

Bridget sits, takes off her jean jacket lined with faux fur, and places it next to her feet. She has a small, compact athletic body. Her eyes, a bright Irish blue, are heavily made up, and her lipstick is deep purple.

"I was just telling the group," Gail says, "about the night I discovered my husband was having affairs."

Bridget snaps her gum. "Asshole," she murmurs.

"I think it's best," Kathryn says, "that we refrain from making judgments."

Gail purses her lips.

"Would anyone else like to share?" Kathryn asks.

"I thought this wasn't one of those sharing twelve-step groups," Bridget replies, then yanks a tissue from the box on the coffee table and spits out her gum.

"No, this is not a twelve-step group. In here you are free to comment and give feedback," Kathryn explains.

"Because when I went to an S-Anon group, they tried to tell me I was a co-addict. I asked someone what that meant, and she told me there was no cross talk. I said that I just wanted to know what I was addicted to. She told me that perhaps I would discover that if I attended a few more meetings." Bridget twirls a finger in her hair. "Well, I wasn't about to go back there so I could get some ridiculous label."

Hannah guesses that pushing the boundaries comes naturally to Bridget.

"My name is Lizzy," the auburn-haired woman on the couch says. "I went to one of those groups, and I had the same question. I wasn't brave like you, though." She smiles broadly. "I waited until after the group to ask about what I was addicted to, and I was told I was an addict because I was choosing to stay in my marriage."

"Do you think that makes you an addict?" Kathryn asks.

"An idiot maybe, but no, not an addict. I don't understand what that word means anymore."

Hannah likes Lizzy.

"Perhaps this is a good time to talk about what addiction means," Kathryn suggests.

"Number one," Bridget says, raising a finger with a chewed nail, "addictions escalate. And number two"—she raises another finger—"addicts have withdrawals when they stop. I'm a nurse in a psych ward. I've seen it all."

"I don't think my husband had withdrawals," Lizzy says.

"Do you believe he's stopped?" Kathryn asks.

Lizzy tugs at a thread on the couch. "I want to believe he has."

"Not all people have withdrawals in the classic sense as we know them," Kathryn tells her.

"And," Bridget speaks up. "Addicts lie. They are con artists, and bullshitters." Her voice is abrasive, and Hannah believes fear courses beneath Bridget's tough exterior.

Gail draws in a deep breath. "I do not believe my husband is any of those things."

"Then maybe he's not an addict," Bridget tells her.

"I don't think that's for you to judge," she replies. "Addicts are individuals and behave in different ways. We can't generalize."

"I didn't say they weren't different." Bridget scuffs her boots on the carpet. "I just think that addicts have some similar characteristics. And one of those is lying."

"Lying is often part of an addict's behavior," Kathryn adds.

"Well, I know that Jonah has been working hard in therapy, and he has been vigorously honest with me since the discovery."

Bridget rolls her eyes. A taut silence falls. Hannah would like out.

"Bridget," Kathryn says after a few moments, "would you like to tell us why you're here?"

Bridget glances around, then focuses her gaze on Hannah, whose first instinct is to turn away.

"We're telling what our husbands are into, right?" she asks.

Hannah nods and tries to imagine telling these strangers about Adam. It feels impossible.

"Michael is into the chat rooms." Bridget's foot bounces. "Porn too."

"That must be difficult for you," Kathryn says.

"He gets off on the chase. He likes to know all these women get hot for him. He's on every dating site known to man, and he sends pictures of himself." She pauses. "It's fucked up. But if he ever crossed the line and slept with someone else . . ." Her small hands ball into fists.

"I don't think it matters what the exact nature of the addiction is," Gail says. "It comes down to feeling betrayed."

"Oh, it matters to me," Bridget tells her. "I'd kick his ass out if he slept with anyone."

"Does it frighten you that your husband might be doing more than he's telling you?" Kathryn asks.

Bridget twirls her finger in her hair again.

"Listening to other stories can be terrifying," Kathryn says. "Considering the betrayal you have all already experienced, it would not be surprising to start wondering if your husband was doing more than he is saying."

If Hannah finds out more, she will shatter.

Bridget bites her bottom lip, then glances at the women on the couch. "So, what about your husbands?" she asks.

The striking young woman gathers her hair and ties it in a knot behind her head. She scoots forward a little. "I am Flavia. My husband, his name is Demetrius. He is from Greece. I call him Dema." Her face flushes. "First I must say that, although I live in this country since five years now, my English is not always so good. Excuse me please. I am from Brazil."

"Your English is fabulous compared to my Spanish," Bridget says.

"I believe she speaks Portuguese," Gail interjects.

"Actually, I speak both."

"Sorry, didn't mean to interrupt your story," Bridget says as she glides a cool glance in Gail's direction.

"It is fine." Flavia smiles. "It is not something I like to tell, so stop me when you like."

No one speaks. No one stops her.

"This is how I find out," she begins. "I work for two years in the Boston Library. One day, not too long ago, one of the janitors brings me an article from the newspaper. He thinks it is my husband's name he sees in the paper. It tells he was arrested for groping on the subway. I nearly fainted. On the way home, I think of all the ways that Dema will tell me that the article is not about him. By the time I walk into my house, I have convinced myself there are many other Greek men in Boston with the same name. But when I show him the newspaper, his head sinks.

My heart felt like it explodes, and little glass pieces of it swim through my arms. I never have this feeling. Not even when my father died." She stops and rubs her arms.

Hannah thinks of the politically correct anti-groping posters she's seen the few times she's been on the subway.

"Then." Flavia shakes her head, and her hair falls out of its knot. "The library finds out, and I have no more job. Not because of my husband, they make sure to tell me, but because there is no more funding."

"Yeah, right," Bridget says.

Flavia re-knots her hair. "Yeah, right," she says with an American accent.

"Did you think of suing?" Gail asks.

"I cannot afford a lawyer, and I also do not want more attention put on this."

"He lives with you now?" Bridget asks.

"Yes, but I do not have the sex with him. That is the limit for me." She slices her elegant hand through the air.

"You need to make boundaries in order for you to feel safe," Kathryn says. "You will all make different ones. What's important is that you learn what works for you." She looks at Hannah. This is her cue to talk. Her palms are damp, her heart races. She glances at the rug as her face heats.

"Lizzy," Kathryn says, sensitive enough to move on. "Are there any boundaries you've made that have helped you?"

"I don't think I'm good at that. I think . . . well . . . . it's more like I've made anti-boundaries. The thing is, I probably should say I won't have sex with him, but I want him to prove that he wants me and not some porn star dressed in a Catholic schoolgirl uniform with pigtails." She hesitates. "He won't have sex with me."

Now Hannah feels the need to speak. "You could be Angelina Jolie, and he'd still watch porn."

"I know." Lizzy smiles. She has a round, warm face. "I try to tell myself that, but I'm not exactly young anymore, and I don't have time to work out at the gym every day. I have cellulite on my thighs."

"It is important," Kathryn says, "that you begin to understand that your husband's addiction isn't about you."

"How the hell is she supposed to believe that?" Bridget asks. "He's jerking off watching other women and not having sex with her. How is that not about her?"

"Of course she's affected by it," Kathryn says. "It can take a long time for it not to feel so personal."

"It's always going to feel personal," Hannah says. She may not be able to talk about herself, but having lived with a sex addict for years, she has learned a few things. "Sex in a relationship is the most intimate and vulnerable way we express ourselves, and when we've been made to feel as if our husbands want something or someone other than us, it's very painful." She pours herself a glass of water, believing she can now drink without her hands shaking.

"I disagree," Gail says. "Jonah doesn't want other women, and I recognize that. It's a compulsion with him. A disease."

Bridget grimaces. "I fucking hate that it's labeled as a disease. It's such a lame excuse. And then there's all the childhood emotional reasons. Poor Michael, his parents were alcoholics and didn't give him enough attention. My mother died when I was thirteen, and I didn't become a sex addict."

"Well, I happen to believe it is a disease," Gail says. "And since Jonah has also recognized it as that, he feels less stigmatized and has been more self-reflective. In turn, he's been healing."

"I get why alcoholism and drug addiction are diseases. They actually change body chemistry," Bridget says.

"That also happens with sex addicts. Neurotransmissions in the brain are altered. Essentially, it's the same thing," Gail replies.

"There has been quite a lot of debate in the psychiatric community about just this issue. Some people think of addictions as illnesses. Some believe they are compulsions," Kathryn says.

"Well, this is what I think," Bridget says. "Sex releases endorphins. I feel kind of high from it too. Doesn't make me an addict."

"It's when you can't stop. When it gets in the way of your everyday functioning, when you withdraw from your intimate relationships. Sex addicts lose their jobs, their spouses. Everything. Just like any other addiction." Gail glances around the room, satisfied she's won the debate. Lizzy and Flavia nod.

"Does your husband go to meetings?" Bridget asks.

"Yes. He's gotten a lot from them. And your . . . partner?"

"Husband. He goes, but sometimes the twelve-step stuff seems like a load of crap. Like he has to learn from a group that he's not supposed to lie to his wife." She huffs. "Seems like shit. That's all."

"Hannah," Kathryn says, "is there anything you'd like to add?"

Hannah's mouth goes dry. She knows she's supposed to share something about herself. It's not only her turn, it's her obligation. She rubs her hands along her jeans.

"My husband seems to get help from those groups," she says. "But I understand what you mean, Bridget. It does seem as if some of the things they talk about are pretty basic. I think for them it's about applying those guidelines to their addictive personality. For me it feels like I have two husbands: the one I fell in love with—he's thoughtful and kind; and the addict—he's narcissistic and self-centered."

Bridget nods. "I'm just so angry."

"Do you know the serenity prayer?" Gail asks.

"I hate that prayer. I mean, think about it, we're just supposed to sit back and wait for them to change? Not get involved? It makes no sense."

"Only they can change themselves," Gail replies.

"Then think of this," Bridget snaps. "If we hadn't caught them, you think they'd be changing or going to those groups? Probably not." She holds up her chin, mirroring Gail.

"I don't think you understand the prayer." Gail squares her shoulders. "It's about surrendering to a greater power."

"No, I don't think you understand. I'd love to just toss in the towel and tell Michael to fix himself and figure this all out, but he's not about to do that unless I help him. We've decided to stick with these men, and that means we're tied to them. Change doesn't happen in a vacuum."

"I think she has a good point," Lizzy says. "I doubt Greg would be getting help if I hadn't caught him. I think we're often the catalysts for change."

"Yeah." Bridget points to Lizzy. "We're the catalysts."

"Before Jonah and I leave for work in the morning, we kneel together and say the serenity prayer." Although Gail is at eye level with Bridget, she appears to be looking down on the younger woman. "It helps remind us to stay vigilant."

"I sure as hell will never be kneeling and praying with my husband," Bridget mumbles.

Kathryn leans toward her. "I think part of being in this group is learning to accept the different ways people choose to struggle through this."

"And I think some husband-bashing might do us all good." Bridget kicks up her leg and grins.

Hannah smiles.

Gail clenches the armrests of her chair. "I'm afraid," she says, "this is not the right group for me. I would prefer not to listen to someone denigrate my husband. Kathryn, I thank you for letting me come, but I will not be returning."

"I understand," Kathryn says. "But I would like very much if we could all try again next week. We will disagree about many things, but that's part of what being in a group is about. What we need to do is agree that we will try to withhold judgment of other people's partners." She looks at Bridget.

"Yeah, all right." She pauses, then bites her nails. "Gail, I'm sorry. You can keep on praying."

"Well, I thank you for your permission," Gail replies. "But I need to think about it. I might be looking for something that is structured a little differently."

Hannah sits taller. "If you want the twelve-step structure where you can't really talk to anyone, why not go to one of those groups?" Her question sounds more aggressive than she had intended.

"I don't want a step group. I'm just looking for something a bit more serene. A group where people have reached another level, that's all."

"What level?" Hannah shoots back.

"I've been doing a lot of work in therapy, with my husband and on my own," she says. "I think I'm at a different place. I've been through the anger and the grief. We're in the healing stage, and I don't think it will be good for me to go backward."

"If some of the things Bridget says will make you slip backward, maybe your footing isn't as strong as you think," Hannah tells her.

"Gail," Kathryn says, "we circle around with our feelings. Sometimes we think we're over the anger, and it comes back. Sometimes we find ourselves forgiving even if there's more grief to live through. It's a cyclical process. I think having people at all different stages is what makes this a powerful group." Kathryn places her hands firmly on the arms of the chair. "It is through your shared experiences that you can all find the courage to move forward."

"I respect everything you're saying. It's just that sometimes a personality conflict might get in the way," Gail says.

"So then I'll fucking leave." Bridget picks up her jacket and stands. "You can sit around and preach to everyone else. I don't need this."

"Don't," Hannah says. "Please."

Bridget sits. "As long as I can say whatever I want."

"No one has stopped you so far." Gail picks up her purse.

"No one has stopped anyone," Lizzy points out.

Good for her, to speak up. Hannah feels better about her own outburst.

Kathryn clears her throat. "When Dr. O'Reilly and I interviewed you, we knew there would be some differences and some conflicts to work through. That's part of the process. It's important that you all give this a few weeks. Often, what is bothering us outside the group we bring to the group, and it manifests in relationships we form in this room. When we work through those, we can work through some of the troubles we're having in the real world."

"I'll be back," Lizzy says.

"And me," Flavia chimes in.

"Thank you," Kathryn says, and looks at Hannah.

There is a hitch in her throat. She wants to say yes, but this was so much harder than she thought it would be. "I have to think about it."

Kathryn takes a breath before speaking. "When I called each of you, I asked if this was something you'd be able to commit to, and you said yes."

"I am committed to being part of a group," Gail says. "But this just might not be the right one. If I went to a therapist and it wasn't working for me, I wouldn't keep going."

"Yes, I understand. Please think about it then, and call me if you don't plan on coming back."

Hannah smiles briefly. "I just want to say that this feels like a good group. That's not why I wouldn't come back. When I left home tonight, I realized that I didn't want to give up a night with my kids. Especially since it's my husband's problem. I resent giving up this time."

"Many partners of addicts feel as you do," Kathryn says. "But they often find the support to be really helpful."

There's that word again. *Support.* Exactly how is she supposed to get that here? She doesn't need anyone to hold her up. Hannah nods, pleased at least to have set a valid excuse on the table.

Flavia puts on her jacket. Gail is the first to stand.

Outside, the temperature has dropped. It feels as if spring will never arrive.

"I hope you come back," Lizzy tells Hannah as they walk through the parking lot. "But I understand what you mean about it not really being fair that we have to give up a perfectly good night because of the stuff our husbands did."

"Thanks. I hate to make promises I can't keep." She pauses. "Unlike my husband." Hannah shudders as she realizes this is the most personal thing she's shared about Adam.

Bridget

✴

"Hey," Bridget calls out from across the parking lot. "Do you have a sec?"

"Of course," Hannah replies, opening the door to her SUV.

Bridget jogs over. "I— Can you explain what just went on in there?"

"I doubt I can explain everything, but if you have a question, I might be able to help," Hannah tells her.

"I guess what I'm wondering is, do you think it will help?"

Hannah touches Bridget's arm. "There really isn't a guidebook for this," she says. "See how you feel next week. Talk about what's going on. That's the most you can do right now."

"Does it get better though?" Bridget looks up at the office. The light is still on. "You know, the pain? Does it go away?"

"Time helps," Hannah says.

"Has it been a long time for you?" Bridget shoves her hands in the pockets of her jean jacket.

"From before we were married."

"So . . ." Bridget hesitates. "I mean . . . why?"

"It's okay to ask. I wouldn't have said anything if it wasn't."

Bridget shivers.

"If you want, we can get in my car, and I'll put on the heat," Hannah says.

Bridget climbs in, and Hannah starts the engine. The car smells like Cheerios.

"I just don't know if I can do it. Listen to all that shit. My head spins when I think about it."

"It's traumatic and overwhelming." Hannah grabs two Diet Cokes from the back and hands one to Bridget. The cans make a sharp slicing sound as they open.

"But it gets better. Right?"

Hannah leans her head back. "It never really goes away. It's like any addiction—it lurks."

"But lots of alcoholics get better. Don't they?" Bridget runs her finger along the edge of the can.

"They do," Hannah says flatly.

"How did you find out the first time?" Bridget asks.

"I was young and in love. My husband, Adam, was charming." She grins. "I used to joke that we sounded like those cheesy personal ads. You know, walks on the beach, back rubs, late-night talks. A regular old fairy tale."

"That's what I thought me and Michael were. The perfect couple. I had no idea."

"Most of us don't."

Bridget doesn't want to be in the *most* category. "How did you find out?"

"A week before our wedding, he told me he was an addict." Hannah shakes her head. "I still can't believe it, even after fifteen years. At the time, his therapist told me it had nothing to do with me. I believed her. I was in a state of shock on my wedding day. People said I had that glazed look of love in my eyes." She chuckles. "Little did they know."

Bridget glances at Hannah's thick hair and perfectly shaped mouth. She could have had anyone. And she ended up here.

"That's what I'm afraid of. Being naive. Like, I want to believe Michael, and I do, but what if he's still lying? Then what?"

Hannah takes a sip of Diet Coke. "There is just so much about this we have absolutely no control of."

"You think that woman up there, that Gail"—Bridget points to the building—"think she's a control freak?"

"Maybe. It might be a way to deal with some of the stuff that really hurts still."

"Yeah." Bridget smiles. "I use anger. Probably kinda obvious."

"It's normal to be angry when you've been lied to."

"First, Michael swore he was just consoling a friend. Then there were more calls, plus porn and this other shit, like married-hookup sites, fucked-up stuff. When I think that there might be even more I don't know about, I feel sick to my stomach." She pauses. "I still can't believe it. Any of it. That I'm here, going to a group because my husband is a sex addict. It's . . . degrading."

"The initial discovery is shocking," Hannah says. "It's like you get thrown into a different reality."

"That's exactly how I felt when I found the first text on Michael's phone. I kept thinking it was some sort of mistake. Then when I asked him about it, he got all defensive and said it was just a new singer they hired in his band, and she was going through a tough time. I fucking believed him. Not only that, I was relieved." She ducks down when she sees Kathryn, looking all professional in her black coat, walking to her car.

"We don't have to hide," Hannah says.

But Kathryn seems like the kind of person who has it all figured out, and it makes Bridget feel like an even bigger loser. "Think she can help?"

"She seems nice, but young, and this issue is a lot to handle." Hannah sips her Coke. "Has anyone ever mentioned doing a full disclosure?"

"Isn't that what we just did?"

Hannah sits taller. "You do it with a therapist, but you have to prepare. You both go in, then Michael tells you everything. It's awful, but at least you know all the facts and what you're dealing with."

"Did you do that?" she asks.

"No."

"I think I'd die if I found out more details."

"No, you wouldn't, even if you felt like you wanted to." Hannah nods slowly. "We just readjust. I don't mean that in a simplistic way. But we figure out how to keep going."

Bridget's eyes fill with tears. "Think I'm going to have a breakdown?"

"No. That's not what I meant at all."

"It will be all right. Right?" Bridget wipes her cheek with the back of her hand.

"God, I wish I could promise it will be. I'm going to give you my numbers. Home and cell. If life feels too horrible and you need to talk, call me." She rips the corner off an envelope and jots down her phone numbers.

Bridget gets in her car, starts the engine, and turns the fan on high. Cold air blasts out. She waits for Hannah to leave, then peels out of the parking lot. She hates Michael, hates her life, hates the road she's driving on.

"Fuck you," she screams to no one as she remembers the morning she came home from her night shift and found that first text. She'd been looking forward to snuggling with Michael.

Bridget pulls into the driveway and parks behind Michael's pickup truck. Maybe he will be asleep. But that will piss her off too. How can he sleep when their marriage is cracking?

Gradually, she makes her way upstairs.

"How was it?" he asks, and pushes himself up so that his feet are no longer hanging over the edge of the bed.

"It sucked."

"Sorry." He pats the bed as if she's supposed to hop in next to him, to talk to him as if she just went to a book club.

"It stinks that on my night off I have to drive to Jamaica Plain to listen to a bunch of women whose husbands have fucked them over." She sits on the edge of the mattress, as far away from him as possible.

"Sorry." He sounds like a broken record.

"And stop saying you're sorry. Or at least say you're sorry for the right thing."

"Bridge." He gets up and walks around to where she's sitting. "I'm sorry for all the hurt I've caused."

"Just tell me now if there's anything else you haven't told me," she says. "I want it over with. I don't want to look through any more phone bills or see on the computer that you're still chasing after women."

He sits and places his large hand on her back.

She shrugs him off. "Don't touch me."

He obeys, and yet she misses him.

"What do you want me to do?" he asks.

She thinks of something Hannah said. "I want you to give me a full disclosure," she tells him.

"Okay," he replies.

"You know what that is?" she asks, surprised.

"I've heard guys in my group talk about it."

"Did you ever think to bring it up, that it might be helpful for me?"

"I thought it would happen when you were ready. That's all."

"So what else haven't you told me?" Her veins feel twisted.

"Bridge." He slaps his hand on his thigh. "I've told you everything."

"All the details?" she asks.

He stands, walks to his closet, and tugs on a T-shirt. "It's not like you think," he says, backing up so that he's nearly at the door.

"What is not like I think?" The question comes out tight, whispery and terrified.

"I mean . . . what I mean is . . . There was this guy in group the other night. He said that you can't really move forward unless you've sort of . . . you know . . . put it all out there."

Her body feels like it's on fire. "But you just said you told me everything. Right?"

"Um. I told you most of the stuff. But this guy, he says that it's, like, important not to keep secrets. It's one of the steps," he explains.

"You had to learn that from some guy in a sex addicts' group? You don't know it's not okay to keep secrets from your wife?" Her voice rises.

"It just happened once."

"*It?*" She stares at him. His back is against the door.

"I can barely remember. I hated it," he mumbles.

"Remember what?"

"It wasn't good. I mean, it was awful. I didn't tell you because I didn't want to hurt you."

"Did you fuck someone else?"

"I . . . I had sex with her."

"Who's 'her'?"

"Vivian," he whispers.

"The one you first lied about? The one who was supposedly a singer in your band and just needed some comfort?"

"I'm so sorry," he says. "I'm so fucking sorry. But I had to tell you. It's like the guy in group said. You have to start from a place of honesty."

"Do you even know how stupid you sound? A place of honesty? You don't know what the word means."

"I'm trying, Bridge, that's why I'm telling you this. I want us to have an honest, open relationship. I want to work toward that." He runs his fingers through his hair.

"And if I don't?"

"I won't blame you," he says.

"Ha. How fucking generous. You won't blame me. And who will you blame? Your alcoholic mother? Your father who didn't pay enough attention to you?"

All she wants to do is fight. She doesn't want to think about him sleeping with Vivian. About how he felt her tits and her cunt.

He takes a step toward her. "Stop," she yells. "I don't want your filthy hands near me."

"I only want to help."

"Too late for that. Tell me, were there more?"

He looks like he's pondering the question.

"Uh . . ." he stutters. "I mean . . . Well, yeah, I guess. There was one. A while ago. They didn't mean anything. If I cared about them, it would be different. But I don't."

She stands, walks to her closet, and takes out an overnight bag, which she tosses onto the bed. From her closet, she yanks a shirt, then a pair of underwear from her dresser. In her head she hears her mother, counting. That's what she used to do to help Bridget fall asleep when she was a little girl. Thirteen, fourteen, fifteen . . .

"Bridge, listen. You got to listen. I didn't want to have sex with them. It was the chase, but it led . . . Shit, there's no good way of saying this."

She drops her hair dryer into the bag and zips it up. Then she counts her way down the stairs. When she's near the door, Michael charges down, pushes her aside, and stands, large and solid, in front of her.

"Bridge, I love you," he says.

The words are pellets, pieces of hail that bounce off a metal roof.

She slips past him and counts her way to her car, out the driveway, all the way to Huntington Ave where she finds a Holiday Inn.

The hotel receptionist gives Bridget a key card to room 135. Once inside, she paces, pulls at her hair, and kicks the foot of the bed. Her toe throbs. She has no idea how to get through this. In her pocket she feels the slip of paper with Hannah's number and hopes it's not too late to call.

Kathryn

❧

Kathryn sits on the red leather chair farthest from O'Reilly, who fumbles through the mess on her desk, trying to locate the folder on the group. It's already three-thirty. O'Reilly was half an hour late, and right now Kathryn would like nothing more than for this appointment to be over. If O'Reilly spends another few minutes searching her desk, all the better.

Finally, she sits back without the folder. Kathryn smiles politely.

"So how was it?" O'Reilly rubs her hands as if she's expecting some juicy gossip.

"Fine," Kathryn says. "They began to open up and tell their stories."

"That sounds rather flat. Was there more emotion than you're relaying?" O'Reilly asks.

"Yes, there were some emotional moments, but we only have about fifteen minutes so I thought it would be better to just stick to the facts."

"I can be a little late for my next appointment. Don't worry about time. I'm all ears."

"Gail didn't like the choice of some of Bridget's language." Kathryn chooses her words carefully.

"I'm not surprised those two would be at odds. I would have never recommended them being together." O'Reilly gives her hair a quick fluff.

Kathryn swallows. "Well, they may not be together much longer."

"And why is that?"

"I think Gail had a different sort of group in mind. Something more like S-Anon. I know she said she would like a private group, but I don't think she really wants feedback. I was worried about that during her interview." *Gail was your choice*, she thinks.

"My, my. A few moments ago you told me everything was fine. I would hardly call this fine, having a member wanting to drop out on week one." Her small brown eyes open wider. "Can you describe exactly what happened?"

"I think Bridget is frightened. I believe her fear came out as anger and was directed toward Gail."

O'Reilly nods as if she agrees, which might be a first.

"Did you get Bridget to acknowledge that her anger was based in fear and being projected?" O'Reilly asks.

"I tried. But I don't think she was ready to see that, and Gail said she was looking for a group that wasn't so contentious."

"An opening group certainly shouldn't be contentious. It's the time to go over ground rules and make sure everyone feels safe. Naturally that's what you did?"

"Of course." Kathryn takes her notebook from her bag and flips through it, stopping when she sees the summaries she wrote just an hour ago.

Gail: *Needs control. Is her life more out of control than she wants to admit?*

Flavia: *Brave. Beautiful. Seems like a risk-taker.*

Bridget: *Young, raw. In shock.*

Lizzy: *Uses her husband's desire for her as a barometer of her own self-worth.*

Hannah: *A good listener. But holding back.*

"I'd rather you not turn to your notes at the moment. I think it would be best if you just answer my questions. Did you explain that the group wasn't a place to judge others?" O'Reilly asks.

"I did. But I think Bridget felt judged by Gail, and that's what sparked her anger."

O'Reilly rubs her chin. "You know, after Bridget's interview I said I thought she was volatile. I doubt I would have recommended her."

"I chose her because she seemed to be in a lot of pain, and she doesn't have a therapist or anyone to really talk to about all this."

O'Reilly takes a deep breath. "Perhaps it would have been better to have told Bridget that individual therapy is generally suggested before diving into a group. Of course it's too late now. But it might be worth considering if a situation such as this arises in the future. And"—she wags a finger—"if Bridget is the reason Gail leaves, it's likely she'll pin her anger on another member."

"She seemed to get along with the others."

"Yes, because she had Gail. But really, you must understand without Gail, she will find someone else to target. Perhaps I should call Gail and speak with her," O'Reilly suggests.

"I think we should wait and see if she returns." Kathryn looks at the clock on the desk. It's already five past four. This session needs to end.

"No, I think a check-in call would be good. I don't see what harm it could do, and Gail did have confidence in me. Perhaps I could reassure her."

Kathryn pushes aside her bangs. "I know she likes you and has faith in you, but I'd like to see if I can build a relationship with her on my own. So, if you wouldn't mind . . ."

O'Reilly nods enthusiastically. "Yes, I see your point. Why don't we see what happens next week then, give you more time to form a bond."

"Thank you," Kathryn says.

"But if Gail does come next Wednesday, it's imperative that you provide a safe environment for every group member."

For the moment, Kathryn feels relief that her supervisor won't be calling Gail, who might report that Hannah was having doubts about returning as well.

"I'll do that," Kathryn says.

"If she is not there, I'd like you to call me first thing Thursday morning. Then I would need to contact her and see what's going on."

"All right." She looks at the clock again, then stands. "I'm sorry, but I'm meeting someone in half an hour." Just last week, she read an article about how lying to your supervisor is a form of denial. It's probably true, and Kathryn promises herself she will think about her behavior, but at the moment, she only wants out.

Gail

Gail is fifty-nine today. She doesn't remind Jonah of her birthday when he makes the coffee and she cuts the cantaloupe.

"Well," he says, after he finishes breakfast, "I'm off." With his gray eyes set too close, his ears too large, and his thin lips, he might not be the most objectively handsome of men, but he has what Gail loves—an intelligent, thoughtful countenance.

He walks to where she sits and places a light kiss on her cheek. The touch is electric. Magical even. But then he's gone, and she's left with her lukewarm tea and a body that feels lethargic.

Slowly, she pushes herself up from the table and takes her cup to the sink. Just a simple "Happy birthday" would have been nice. Then again, she isn't the type to want any fuss. But if he had made her breakfast in bed, she would have been so happy. She opens the pantry, reaches behind the tins of soup for a hidden candy bar, and hurriedly eats it.

At work, Barbara, who has been with Gail for seventeen years, has left flowers on her desk and a sweet card. There are a few meetings with ADAs in the morning, and then the afternoon is free. Jonah doesn't teach classes today, and as Gail looks over her calendar, she decides she will be spontaneous. She will stop off at the store and make a gourmet picnic lunch to bring to his office. It will be a sort of inverted birthday surprise.

She's back home by noon. In the kitchen she whips up a cucumber, mustard, and dill salad and packs it with a bottle of cabernet and the fresh éclairs she just bought. She glances in the mirror. Her suit is a boring, boxy nondescript gray. To spice it up, she throws on a purple scarf.

Walking across the quad carrying the basket, she keeps her head high, reminding herself that she's a distinguished judge and needn't feel that she's somehow not good enough to be strolling along the green at Harvard. And although she knows how hard Jonah works, she can't escape the thought that somewhere on this campus he was meeting up with April.

Then there was the other student. The one he didn't sleep with. The one who gave him a confidence boost, five years ago, when he hadn't been promoted from associate to full professor. It was understandable that some young, doe-eyed graduate student who fawned on his every word would make him feel better. Gail was much more devastated than she let on. She blamed herself. She was so busy, having just been appointed a judge. If she could have traded her promotion for his, she would have in a second.

Her therapist has told her to focus on the present, and that's what she's determined to do today. People who have survived hardships together can come through them, sharing a deeper and stronger bond.

A student holds open the heavy wooden door. She thanks him and pauses in the entrance. Two young women flit by, chatting gregariously. She pictures them in Jonah's office, enthralled by his every word. Couples separate over much less than what she and Jonah are working through. But that's exactly the point, she thinks as she attacks the stairs. She and Jonah are choosing to make their marriage work.

Winded by the time she reaches the third floor, she sets down the basket and composes herself. After a few moments she takes small steps, wishing the wide wooden floors wouldn't creak so loudly. Jonah's light gait probably barely makes a sound.

His door is closed. It's likely that he's not in, that he's in the library or having coffee with another professor. She knocks.

"Yes," he calls.

"It's me, Gail," she says, relieved to hear his voice.

A few seconds later, the door opens. He greets her with a bemused smile.

"I brought you lunch." She gives the square picnic basket a small swing.

"I hope that's not all for me," he says as she walks in.

"It's for us." She glances around his office, at the overflowing bookcases, his desk stacked with journals, papers, and manila folders.

She walks toward the small oval table that sits between two tattered armchairs.

"I wasn't expecting you." He runs his hand over his thinning gray hair, which he brushes over his bald spot, his one vanity.

"I know. It was just something I wanted to do."

"It's very nice of you." He watches as she unpacks the plates.

"I brought your favorite." She holds up the bottle of cabernet.

"That's nice. But . . ." He glances at his watch.

"I know it's still early. But sometimes a glass for lunch can stimulate the brain." She smiles.

He clasps his hands, as if he's sorry he has to say no. "I'm afraid it would make me tired."

"Well, at least have something to eat. I made cucumber salad."

"I . . . uh, well, I have a meeting in half an hour. I would have canceled had I known about this lovely surprise."

"Of course." She feels humiliated. But what did she expect? "Just have a bite then."

He perches on the chair and has a small forkful. "It's excellent," he says, but she can see he doesn't want more. He's been looking too thin lately, and his spine seems more curved.

"No court?" he asks politely, formally.

"No. I took the afternoon off," she tells him.

"Good for you," he says, too exuberantly.

"Well, it's March twenty-third, and I thought I'd treat myself."

"You thought I forgot?" His face brightens. He looks young, and she is reminded he is four years her junior.

"I thought you might have been busy."

"Gail, I would never forget you." He puts down his fork and stands. From his desk, he pulls out a small turquoise Tiffany's bag.

"You didn't have to." She feels giddy.

"For my darling wife, who is forgiving, and thoughtful, and kind beyond measure." He hands her the bag.

She accepts the gift, unwraps the small box, and takes out one of the earrings inside. She doesn't wear silver, and long, dangly earrings are for younger women. But he remembered, and he tried, so she's not about to criticize.

"They're beautiful." She puts the earring back in the box.

"You can return them if they're not your type."

"No. They're perfect." She smiles up at him.

He leans down, kisses her forehead, and rests a hand on her shoulder. She savors the moment of closeness. This is all she really wanted.

"Thanks for coming by," he tells her.

She doesn't want to leave yet. "I don't mind if you have work. I can wait around here, organize the bookshelf. Then after your meeting, we can go to the art museum."

He sighs and squeezes her shoulder, then draws away his hand. "I would like nothing more, but I just can't. I'm sorry."

"Who is the meeting with?" She glances in the basket, at the unopened wine and éclairs, and tries to mask her disappointment.

"A research assistant. She's due any minute." He looks at his watch.

"Is she new?"

"She's been working with me for a couple of months. A grad student."

He makes it sound so normal, just everyday procedure. But April was a grad student, and so was the one he dallied with during his despondent period. Then there was number three, who came after April, but keeping count is hardly productive. Sex addicts are bound to have multiple partners.

"Well, at least eat a bit more of your salad," she tells him.

"Would you mind if I saved it for later?" He rubs his flat stomach. "I've been a bit off this morning."

"No, of course I don't mind." She's about to wrap it up when there's a knock at the door. A second later a young woman pokes her head in.

"Camille," he says, taking a step toward her. "Come in."

"I'm not interrupting or anything?" she gushes. Her long, thin legs are clad in tight jeans. Her hair, thrown up with a clip, has that casual sexy air of a fashion model.

"No, of course not. Meet my wife." Jonah gestures. "The Honorable Judge Larson."

Gail smiles politely, wondering if he's compensating for her not being thin and pretty. Camille begins to sort papers on Jonah's desk.

He rubs his hands together. "Well," he says to Gail, "it was nice you came by."

She doesn't make a move to get up. There's the beautiful picnic lunch she made for them, almost untouched. A pair of Tiffany earrings on her lap, and a young woman wearing cowboy boots, who seems much more at home in this office than Gail ever has.

"Camille," Gail says. "I brought some éclairs. Would you like one?"

She stops sorting for a moment and looks at Gail. "No, thank you, Judge Larson, but thanks so much for offering."

"We really have work to get through," Jonah says.

"I suppose I should have phoned first." Her tone is acerbic. She stands.

Jonah cradles her elbow. "No, of course you shouldn't have. You're always welcome here. It was a magnificent surprise. I wish I didn't have so much to do." He kisses her on the lips, right in front of Camille. He knows just what to do when her insecurities get in the way.

"So, I'll see you this evening?" she asks.

"I'll be home at the usual time. We can go out and celebrate."

"Nice meeting you," she tells Camille on her way out.

Jonah carries the basket as he walks her to the elevator.

He presses the button. "I wish I had more time."

"It's all right," she tells him.

"Just this morning I received an invitation to dine at the Harvard Club. It's in a few weeks. I know it's only some stuffy professors, but I would like it if you came."

The elevator door opens. He holds it for her.

For a second she wonders if he's asking her out of guilt. If he's trying to make up for having Camille in his office. Then she tells herself to stop doubting. They are past that. They are a couple, partners, with a long, healthy relationship ahead of them.

"I would love to join you." She brushes her fingers along his cheek. He reaches for her hand, then skims it with his lips, kissing her as if she's royalty.

On the way out of the building, she passes a vending machine. She stops, puts the basket on the floor, and buys a bag of salt-and-vinegar potato chips.

Hannah

When Bridget called last week, it wasn't a surprise, at least on a rational level, to hear that her husband had been keeping more secrets. But each time Hannah thinks about the late phone call last Wednesday night, she feels as if she's just been punched. Bridget could barely talk. It took forty minutes for her to explain, in stops and starts and gasping breaths.

Hannah will help Bridget get her feet on the ground before she extricates herself from the group.

Seeing as she'll be out in the evening, Hannah has decided to make sure the kids get her full attention this afternoon. They should not have to suffer because of the trouble she and Adam are going through.

For two consecutive days the temperature has finally climbed up and hit sixty. The result—soggy lawns, wet sidewalks, and Sam soaked, proud to announce he has jumped in every puddle. Hannah finds him dry clothes as Alicia hurries to her room.

"Alicia," Hannah calls. "Come to the kitchen for a snack."

No reply. Hannah goes to her daughter's room and opens the door. There is a lump under the purple polka-dot quilt. She walks to the bed, sits, and puts a hand on the cover.

"Are you feeling sick?" she asks.

Alicia kicks her legs. "Get out."

"Don't speak to me that way." Hannah is sharp.

"It's not like you care." Alicia stays under the quilt and turns so that she's facing the lavender wall.

"Of course I care. Tell me what's wrong."

"You'll just yell at me. That's all you do. You're a big, fat yeller."

It's true, she's been short-tempered lately about their rooms not being tidied, about homework not being finished before the TV goes on, about hair and teeth not being brushed.

"I'm sorry. I don't mean to yell. Can you just poke out that pretty face of yours and tell me what happened?"

"I'm never going back to school again."

"Did you get into trouble?"

Another leg kick, but with less force, a sign of defeat.

Hannah pulls down the covers. Alicia claps her hands over her face.

"It can't be that bad," Hannah says.

Alicia keeps her hands over her eyes. "I don't want to talk to you."

"Sometimes when we feel embarrassed about something, the best thing we can do is talk. I promise you'll feel better when you get it out." She leans in and kisses the top of Alicia's head.

"It was Tori's idea. She said if I didn't do it, she'd tell everyone I copied her spelling test."

"You need to tell me what it was you did."

"We put on makeup."

Hannah tugs Alicia's hands from her face. Glittery blue eyeshadow is smeared over her eyelids. "Whoa." Hannah laughs.

"I hate you," Alicia says.

"Honey, I didn't mean to laugh at you. I guess I'm relieved. I thought it was something worse."

"It wasn't the makeup we got in trouble for," Alicia mutters.

Hannah feels a twinge in her chest. "What was it, then?"

"I didn't want to do it. I told Tori we shouldn't."

"Shouldn't what?"

"I'm only telling Dad."

"No. You will tell your father when he gets home, but now you are going to tell me."

"Fine." She pouts. "I said that Peter was gay."

"Why would you do that?" The twinge deepens to an ache.

"Tori made me."

"Stop saying that someone else made you. If you said something like that to Peter, you need to own up to it. What anyone else said or told you to do doesn't matter."

"Peter likes boys."

"He is allowed to like whomever he wants to without you saying anything. How would you like it if someone called you a name?"

Alicia glares. The blue shadow shimmers. "You think you're so perfect."

"We're going over to Peter's house as soon as you wash off that makeup, and you will apologize."

"You make everything worse. I knew you would. It's not better to say something."

Hannah stands. "Get out of bed and wash your face. I'm calling Peter's mother."

Alicia stomps out of the room. Sam is in the doorway, tears in his brown eyes. Hannah scoops him into her arms and kisses him.

"What's the matter?" she asks.

"No one is nice anymore."

"Hey, little man." She tugs at his nose. "How about after we stop at Peter's house, I take you to the bookstore?"

He dives his head into her shoulder for a hug.

At five-thirty, they return from the bookstore. Alicia had begrudgingly told Peter she was sorry and that she didn't mean to hurt his feelings. She managed to slip in that Tori did it too, which made Hannah furious. A terse lecture on accountability followed. Of all the frightening, awful things Hannah has imagined happening to her children, she never thought that one of them would be a bully, especially Alicia, who has always been so sensitive.

It's nearly six, and Hannah is in her bedroom, getting ready for group. She picks out a gray cashmere turtleneck, then puts in a pair of gold hoops. With everything that happened today, there is no way she'd be going to group if she hadn't promised Bridget.

Gabby, their babysitter, is due any minute. The one good thing about tonight is that Hannah will not have to see Adam. By the time she gets home, probably nineish, maybe later if Bridget needs her, he will be in the guest room. The rules are simple but firm. In the morning Hannah takes care of the children. After they leave, she goes to her studio. Adam cleans the kitchen, showers, and heads to work. They do not see each other. In the evening, after they eat politely as a family, they split home-work chores and story-reading duties. By nine, he is in the guest room, and she is in what used to be their bedroom. The only time they spend alone is during the car ride to couples' therapy. Hannah has debated taking her own car, but their therapist is on Newbury Street, and it's dif-ficult enough to find one parking spot, let alone two.

Her phone, which sits on her long mahogany dresser, vibrates. It's too early for Adam to be texting. She hurries across the room, guessing it's Bridget.

Am almost home. Don't worry about getting a sitter. A

Goddammit. She's already made the plans. What does he not under-stand about needing to stick to the schedule? She types furiously.

Gabby is on her way. You weren't supposed to be here until seven.

She wants to tell him not to come home until then, but the thought that he'll have over an hour of free time frightens her. She presses send.

I'll still pay Gabby.

That's not the point.

Wanted to spend time with kids. Knew you had group.

She whips the phone onto the bed.

"Mumma," Sam shouts as he races into her room. "Gabby is here."

Gabby is in the kitchen, handing Alicia a headband. Sam bounces as he waits for his surprise. It's a kid's place mat from a restaurant. His eyes light up.

"Adam is coming home earlier than expected," Hannah says.

"Can Gabby still stay?" Alicia asks.

"She can. But she certainly doesn't have to. Either way, we'll pay you."

"It's fine, Mrs. Jenkins. I can't take money for not working. Really."

Hannah takes a twenty from her wallet anyway just as Adam walks in through the back door.

"Dad, we want Gabby," Sam says.

Adam's laugh is gentle, and as he stands smiling at his son, Hannah feels a familiar draw. After everything that's happened, he's still the man she's attracted to.

"I'll come again soon." Gabby zips up her blue parka.

"Can I watch TV?" Alicia asks Adam.

"It's up to your mother," he tells her.

"No. Not tonight. You need to wait in your room and then tell your father what happened."

With red cheeks, Alicia runs off to her room and slams the door.

Gabby lets herself out. Sam scampers off to the den, and Hannah is left in the kitchen, holding a twenty-dollar bill.

"What happened?" Adam asks.

"She'll tell you."

"Was it so bad that you had to embarrass her that way in front of Gabby?"

"Yes, actually, I think it was that bad. But it's better Alicia tell you.

And I also don't appreciate your changing the schedule." She grabs her purse from the counter and a scarf from the rack next to the back door.

"Have fun," he tells her.

Really? Have fun?

She glances over her shoulder at him. "Go fuck yourself," she says, and walks out.

SESSION TWO

Kathryn's door is open. Hannah pokes her head in and sees that once again she is the first to arrive.

"Hannah." Kathryn swivels around and stands. "I'm so pleased you decided to return."

Hannah sits on the same hard wooden chair and looks through her purse for her phone. Damn. She left it at home on the kitchen counter.

A few minutes later, Lizzy walks in. She takes her corner of the couch and pins up a loose curl.

"I'm so glad you're here," she says to Hannah. Her smile is honest.

"Thanks." Hannah glances away, feeling guilty that this is going to be her last group and that she only came for Bridget.

Flavia, wearing a scoop-neck sweater that complements her long neck, strolls past and also sits on the couch, same as last week. Kathryn folds her hands on her lap.

Lizzy smiles broadly, warmly, and Hannah wonders again why men married to these women would ever jeopardize their relationships. She reminds herself that, as in her case, the addictions have nothing to do with the women. But still.

Kathryn glances at a small oval alarm clock with bold black numbers. "It's just about seven. I haven't heard from either Bridget or Gail, so I assume they're coming. I thought perhaps you could each take a moment to think about what you want to get from this group."

Hannah tugs at the sleeves on her sweater. Last week she came here hoping the group would magically enable her to start living again. Now all she wants is for Bridget to show up so she can somehow make her see that coming here will be beneficial. She recognizes the hypocrisy of her goal, but it's the best she can do.

"I would like to find out what it is I really want. Do I want to stay with Dema?" Flavia holds out her hands as if they are the scales of justice.

"We can—" Kathryn starts to say as the door opens.

Hannah is ready to jump up and greet Bridget. But it is Gail who stands, out of breath, on the threshold.

"Gail." Kathryn beams. "We're so happy to see you."

She fans herself. "Am I late?"

"We were just getting started." Kathryn gestures to the chair Gail had taken last Wednesday. It is obvious, at least to Hannah, that Kathryn is pleased her group is living to see another week.

Gail places a hand, with long, manicured nails, on her chest.

Kathryn taps a pencil on her knee. "We were just talking about what people hope to get from the group, but before we continue, I'd like to quickly review the norms. It's essential that we all understand that everything said in here is done so in confidence. Please be mindful of allowing others to speak and, if possible, refrain from giving advice."

Gail clears her throat. "Are we expecting Bridget tonight?"

"Yes, I believe so," Kathryn answers.

"I think that punctuality should be a norm. Personally, I find it difficult when people come late to meetings and topics need to be repeated."

Flavia raises a hand. "I do not intend on being late, but I know there are times when we cannot help things. A broken bus. If she can make it only for five minutes, and that will help her, I would not want to take that away." She dips her head and glances at Bridget's empty seat.

"I suggest," Kathryn says, "that we agree we will try our best to get here on time, and we will also finish on time."

Gail and Lizzy nod.

Kathryn turns to Flavia. "You said you would like to find out if it's your husband you really want. Do you want to say more about that?"

"Only that I am not sure the way I once was."

"What about anyone else?" Kathryn asks.

Lizzy brushes her hand along the knee of her black jeans. "I believe my husband this time. But we still don't have sex. I'd like to understand why."

"It could mean," Gail says, "that he's going through an anorexic phase. He's quit pornography, and maybe he wants to stay away from everything. It's not uncommon."

Hannah has never heard of sexual anorexia. She wants to tell Lizzy that she's beautiful and attractive, and that her husband is a moron for not showing her affection.

"Why do you think it is?" Kathryn asks Lizzy.

Lizzy's neck and face redden. "He's not attracted to me."

"But you are a beautiful woman," Flavia interrupts. "It cannot be that."

"What if it is?" Her eyes are moist. "I mean, what if, for whatever reason, he's just not attracted to me? What if he finds out through going to groups and therapy that he's really gay?"

Hannah's heart races. She knows that fear all too well, even though Adam has sworn that isn't the case.

"I don't really know who he is anymore," Lizzy says. "Who knows, tonight might be the night I go home and he'll tell me that he's never really loved me."

Lizzy takes a tissue and wipes her eyes. The room grows quiet.

Hannah still wonders where Bridget is.

Flavia scoots forward. "I will speak. I have a different problem. Dema, he cannot sleep unless he is in the bed with me. I say okay. Then at night he comes closer. One thing, it leads to another, and then . . . we have sex. I know I said I would not, and now I do not know. Was it okay to do that?"

"Did it feel okay to you?" Kathryn asks.

"I suppose, yes," Flavia answers. "I am shy to say this, but it is nice."

"I remember," Gail says, "when Jonah and I made love the first time after I learned about his disease. It was difficult for me not to think of other women. But we took it slowly, and we meditated beforehand. The key is that you have to trust your instincts and—"

Bridget stands in the doorway. She looks thinner than last week, almost gaunt. Her hair is stringy, her eyes puffy. Hannah jumps up but stays next to her chair, sensing that another sudden movement might make Bridget bolt.

"Come in," Kathryn says.

She doesn't move. No one speaks. Flavia grabs the tissue box and tiptoes over.

"Would you like one?"

Bridget pulls out a tissue and stuffs it in her pocket. "Thanks," she mutters.

"Do you want to come in?" Hannah asks.

Bridget scans the room. Her gaze rests on Gail for a second or two, then she turns and leaves.

Hannah hurries down the stairs, opens the front door, and sees Bridget in the parking lot.

"Hey," she calls. "Wait up."

Bridget stops but doesn't turn.

Hannah jogs over. "I was so worried about you."

"I don't think I can go back up there."

"You don't have to talk. You can just sit and listen."

Bridget takes a step away and shakes her head. "I'm not feeling so good."

"I noticed you look thinner. What's going on?"

"Nothing." She shrugs. "Just don't know how I'm going to deal with all this crap."

"I hate this saying, and I'm going to say it anyway—one day at a time. You don't need to know how to deal with it all right now. It's a process. A long one."

"What if I want out?"

As Hannah looks at Bridget, she thinks that's probably the best option. She has no children with Michael, she's young, there aren't any permanent ties.

"There are so many things you have to consider. You need to figure out if you love Michael enough to want to go through this with him."

"Did having kids change things for you?" she asks.

"I love my children more than anything, and yes, kids make it more difficult to leave."

"I hate my fucking life."

"Come on inside. It may help."

"Nah, I can't. Not after last week, after I said if my husband did the kind of shit Gail's husband did, I'd leave. I lasted one freaking night at that hotel and then ran home. I'm a hypocrite."

"No." She puts a hand on Bridget's arm. "We've all been there. We've all made threats we don't end up carrying out, and it's not because we're victims or weak. It's the opposite. It's because we care for and love these men."

"I hate Michael."

"Of course you do now. And you might always. That's fine too. You need to figure out what's best for you, and listening to what other people are going through can really help."

"Fine. I'll go in."

As soon as they enter the room, Gail stops talking.

"Thanks for joining us." Kathryn speaks calmly.

Bridget sits and stares at the carpet. "Sorry for interrupting."

"It is so good that you decide to return to our circle," Flavia says. "Some days, they are more difficult than the others."

"That's for fucking sure," Bridget replies.

"We were talking about how people resume their sex lives after they've discovered their husband is a sex addict," Kathryn says.

"Not a smart move." Bridget shakes her head.

"Some of us may want to," Gail replies.

"Yeah, well, from my limited experience, it was the stupidest thing I ever did."

There are a few moments of silence, then Kathryn turns to Lizzy.

"You spoke earlier about your husband having difficulty making love. Do you think he might have performance anxiety?"

"That used to be one of his excuses. But now I'm not sure. What if it was because he was watching porn all the time, and he didn't have anything left for me? He says I should have more patience."

"For real?" Bridget snaps. "You? *You* should be more patient? I can bet my life that you've done nothing wrong."

"I'm sure I'm not always right, but I get your point." She grins.

"Jonah used to be like that. Saying he didn't want to aggravate my rheumatoid arthritis, or he was worried about my high blood pressure. He made it sound as if he was being thoughtful, but really it was just a way for him to come up with excuses." Gail takes a tissue and blots her face. "Lizzy, perhaps if you show your husband that you understand how hard this is for him, he'll be more willing to open up about his fears."

"I am so fucking sick of this being all about them." Bridget glares at Gail. "First it's their addictions, now it's their recovery. And then they get chips for good behavior. How about if we got some chips?"

"Those sobriety chips are an important symbol. Jonah just received his nine-month one."

"Since you and he have it all worked out, why do you even need to come here?" Bridget asks.

"As I was saying when you stepped out, I think it's wise to talk about the experience with other people who understand."

"Well, I don't understand anything anymore. All I feel is rage. No rational thoughts go through here." She taps a finger on her head.

"How do people deal with their anger?" Kathryn asks.

"I've learned to surrender," Gail says. "That's when the battle ceases."

"Or maybe it's when you kill your opponent," Bridget adds.

"I smashed the heel of a shoe into Adam's dashboard," Hannah says. "I threw a chair at him once too. They might not have been the most mature actions, but they felt good at the time."

Flavia raises her hand, then cups it to the side of her face, as if she's trying to hide. "One night when I was so angry, I took Dema's best pants and I cut little tiny holes in the back of them."

A few of them laugh.

"I think I'll try that one," Lizzy says.

"Anger is something that we will be discussing a lot." Kathryn pauses, then looks at Flavia. "You asked earlier if it was right to have sex with Dema. Now that you've heard what other people have to say, do you have any other thoughts or feelings?"

Flavia's fingers move deftly as she braids her hair. "I understand that Lizzy needs to know her husband still has desire for her. I admit that I was happy also to know Dema felt this for me. I also understand what Gail says. That she medicates before she is with her husband. I think I should try this medication. Yes?"

Hannah watches Bridget smirk as she turns to the older woman. "You medicate before you have sex?"

"I meditate. I think she may have misunderstood. I find it keeps us in the moment so I can let go of the anger that he has been with other women."

"I will never let go of the fact that Michael has fucked someone else." Kathryn tilts her head. "When did you learn this?"

Bridget bounces her knees. "Last week."

"That must have been very hard," Kathryn says.

"Not as hard as what I learned today."

"What?" Hannah asks.

"I'm pregnant. And it's my fault. I slept with Michael after I found out about his chat room crap. On purpose. To show him how good I was, and what he'd never have again." She holds her head in her hands. "I don't know what the hell I'm going to do now."

"I'm sorry," Gail says.

Bridget wipes away a tear. "Thanks," she whispers.

"Have you told your husband?" Kathryn asks.

Bridget shakes her head and reaches for a tissue. She cries, looking at Hannah.

"It will be okay." Hannah moves across the room, kneels beside Bridget, and takes her hand. As she does, she realizes she will have to come here again, at least one more time.

Hannah

Two square black armchairs sit in front of the tall windows in the Newbury Street office. Hannah enters the room first and decides to sit on the chair that Adam usually occupies.

"This is different," Elias, their couples' therapist, notes as he closes the door. He's a slight middle-age man, with thinning white hair and quiet, unobtrusive movements.

Hannah looks at Elias, then her husband, then across the street at the Church of the Covenant.

"I guess I'll get current." Adam keeps his gaze on his hands.

She flinches at the phrase.

"I haven't acted out. I've been going to my meetings. Aside from an episode we had Wednesday before Hannah went to her group, it's been a smooth week."

Elias shifts his gaze equally between the two of them. "An episode?" he asks.

"I thought it would be nice to come home at six before Hannah left. I wanted to spend a little extra time with the kids." He looks at the bookcase as he speaks.

Two minutes in, and she already feels enraged.

"He didn't follow the schedule." She looks into Elias's eyes. His slight nod tells her he understands, and for a moment that calms her.

Adam shakes his head. "It was never clear that I couldn't come home at six. Granted, I normally get home around seven, but I knew she was leaving so I didn't think it mattered."

"You knew I hired Gabby to come at six, so how could it not have been clear?"

"Yes, I knew Gabby was coming, but you were leaving and you didn't say anything about me not being able to come home early. I didn't think it would hurt to see the kids an hour sooner."

She sighs, exasperated. "But that wasn't the plan."

He smacks the arm of the chair. "I know it wasn't the exact plan, Hannah, but can you bend just a little?"

"Oh, right, because I'm so inflexible." They haven't even been here five minutes and already the battle is gearing up to bloody.

"Do you feel like the boundaries your wife has set are unreasonable?" Elias's voice is soft.

"Overall, not really. I understand why she needs them. But I don't think I was breaking a boundary on Wednesday."

"But you were," she says. "It was clear you weren't supposed to come home until seven."

"Hannah, I get that now. It was also clear that you were going out. So I'm sorry if I just don't understand what difference it made."

"I know I probably sound like some sort of control freak, but you both know why I need these rules. It isn't exactly how I would have chosen to live my life."

"I think what your wife is trying to say is that she needs you to understand her," Elias says.

Adam glances at his hands. "It's not as if I've been breaking the rules. I've been respectful of what she wants."

"I can't do this," she says. "I can't keep getting into these bickering matches."

"This can feel like slow work," Elias replies.

Adam shifts so that he faces forward. "Maybe it would help if we spent more time together. Without the kids."

His request might sound kind and sympathetic to an outsider, but to her it feels like an assault.

"I'm not ready."

"I know you're not ready to be alone with Adam at home," Elias says. "What about meeting somewhere more public? Would that feel safer?"

"Like a men's room?" Her words are quiet, so it takes a moment for the dig to sink in.

"And you wonder why we're not getting anywhere?" Adam says.

"I'm not ready for a public place," she tells Elias.

"Understood. But it might be something you want to consider in the future."

Adam's brow is creased. He keeps shaking his head as if he can't believe how unreasonable she is.

"I come in here wanting to work through things, to make them better, but instead I feel . . ." She takes a water bottle from her purse and opens it. "More out of control."

"Is that how you feel when Adam doesn't follow the rules?" Elias asks.

She nods, takes a sip of water, but has trouble swallowing. She doesn't want to cry.

"I'm sorry," Adam tells her. "I'm trying."

She glares at him. For a second their gazes meet. "Trying what exactly?"

"I'm going to therapy and groups. I've been doing a lot of writing with the steps. I call my sponsor twice a day. I tell you every move I make."

"Except when you don't, and you come home when I have a babysitter planned." Hannah feels tears welling. She takes a deep breath. *Control*, she tells herself.

"I think what your wife is asking isn't so much about Wednesday night but more to do with understanding how frightened she is."

"I'm asking that she understand that I'm trying as hard as I can," Adam replies.

"Okay." Elias looks at Hannah. "Can you hear what he is asking for?"

She slams the bottle on the small table that sits between the chairs. Water spills. "What I need you to understand is that I feel anxious all the time. Nothing is the same. I go out with my friends, who don't know any of this, and they tell me I have the perfect life. I want to laugh in their faces. It's such a farce. But I smile and pretend that I'm as lucky as they think I am. I can't look at my mother without wanting to cry. But I'm not about to tell her what's really going on. She'd never speak to you again."

Adam doesn't shy away from looking at her now. "I get it," he says.

"No, you don't. What you don't get is that every little fucking rule you break, however well intentioned, feels like you're breaking our marriage vows again. That's what you don't get. If this were a normal marriage it wouldn't be a big deal, obviously, if you came home an hour early. But it's not a normal marriage, no matter how much I wish it were." She dabs her eyes with a tissue.

"It's upsetting for you not to feel understood," Elias says.

That makes her cry harder. She hates that the man she still loves, who's only two feet from her, doesn't reach over to hold her hand and tell her he understands how alone and ashamed and petty he's made her feel.

Lizzy

❧

It's the kind of weather that sets off migraines—a thirty-degree shift in temperature. One day it's forty, the next seventy. If Lizzy didn't have medication for her headaches, she'd probably have to move to a climate that wasn't so variable. But she loves it here, especially the small hamlet she teaches in.

She erases the whiteboard in her classroom as a few students meander in for the third-period class of the day.

"Hey, Ms. Nickels," Bryan says. "Guess what I did last night?"

She turns and smiles at him and the capricious tuft of bright red hair sticking out above his ear.

"What did you do?" She expects a wisecrack.

"Homework." He holds up a hand for a high five.

She swats the air, purposefully missing.

"Aw," Bryan whines. "You can do better than that."

"Not in my skill set."

A few others walk in, and she feels herself come to life. The classroom is her sanctuary.

Kathryn brought up the word *safe* a few times in their group, and although Lizzy wouldn't exactly consider her home unsafe at this point, she can say with certainty that she feels most at ease, even peaceful, in a room full of teenagers.

The bell rings. A few students are chatting. Most are sitting, staring blankly. Lizzy writes a few notes on the whiteboard. A couple of students read it and giggle. She is going to begin teaching limiting reagents today, and she likes to start using the analogy of "Ms. Nickel's Brew."

"I need five spider legs, one toad, and two student eyeballs." She jots that down. "Here is what I happen to have. Eight eyeballs, twenty-five spider legs, and only one toad. Which one," she asks, "will limit my brew?"

Bryan shoots up a hand. Lizzy nods for him to answer.

"You have a broomstick?"

"Of course. But which ingredient will limit how much I can make?"

"The toad," Bryan says. "That's kinda easy."

"Right. It's no more difficult when you use formulas and equations." Her right temple aches. It's the first sign of a migraine. She puts up a problem.

"Work on this," she tells the class, then opens the drawer where she keeps her bag. She reaches in for the blue Imitrex bottle and shakes it. There's no noise. She rummages around in her purse and realizes she doesn't have another bottle.

It's eleven-twenty. She'll have to call the main office and ask them to find someone to watch her class for forty minutes while she runs home.

The dean of students is in Lizzy's room within five minutes. She explains what the class needs to do and what her next class should get started on, then she races out of the building.

Home is thirteen minutes away when all the traffic lights are green, seventeen when she hits red. She pulls out of the school parking lot, massages the spot above her eye that is starting to pulse with more force, and feels frustrated with herself for coming to school unprepared.

Passing the old town hall, she glances at the daffodils that are starting to shoot up and begins to think of the group. She likes everyone a lot, and even after only two weeks, she'll miss them, but she's decided it isn't the right fit for her. She can relate to all of the women, but her own situation just doesn't feel nearly as critical. Later today, she'll give Kathryn a call.

On top of the pain above her right eye that is growing steadily sharper, her body is beginning to feel listless, another symptom.

She turns onto Rolling Hill Road. Their yellow colonial is a few houses away, and she squints when she thinks she sees Greg's green Toyota in the driveway. Why would he be home? He works eight- to ten-hour days at a software company right down the street from the high school she teaches at.

She parks in the driveway, closes the door carefully, quietly, not wanting the sound to pierce through her head. She hurries up the front concrete steps, opens the door, and calls for him.

There's no answer. In the foyer she looks up at the chandelier. It shivers slightly. Odd. It must be her headache offsetting her vision. She calls to Greg again.

Still nothing. Maybe he didn't feel well and came home for a nap.

"Greg," she calls yet again. "I just came home to get some Imitrex."

She climbs the stairs, then stops on the landing. Is that rap music? She glances down the hall at the doors of the four bedrooms that were once intended for the children who never happened.

The noise is definitely coming from his study. She knocks. He doesn't answer, and she imagines him lying on the carpet, unconscious from a heart attack.

She barges in.

"Oh God." She covers her mouth. There on the computer screen, which happens to be in her direct line of sight, is a girl on her hands and knees, with one man penetrating her mouth and another man forcing himself in from behind.

Greg glances over his shoulder, sees her, and hurries to shut off the computer.

She stares as the screen goes black and he zips up his pants.

He turns off the music. "I'm sorry," he whispers.

"I was getting a headache, and I didn't have any medicine at school. I thought you'd be at work." She speaks robotically, as if she's ordering food from a drive-through window.

He stands and walks toward her, then stops when she glances at the crotch of his pants. The last thing she wants right now is for him to touch her. She thinks of sticky white semen.

"I didn't think . . ." he begins.

"No, of course not. Why would you? I mean, I never come home during the day. I mean, I didn't think to call. I didn't think you'd be home. I . . . Why were you listening to that awful music?" she asks.

He fidgets with his belt, looking around the room at everything but her. "I like it sometimes."

But she's already forgotten the question. That girl on his computer, she looked younger than the students at her school. She was blond and petite, and her breasts were small, peachlike. She had been moaning, as if she enjoyed what they were doing to her.

Lizzy points to the computer. "Do you think she really likes it?"

"What?" He avoids her gaze.

"The girl you were watching. Do you think she really likes it?" She feels strange. Not crazy, or enraged, or upset. And her headache, it's still there, but it's oddly disconnected from her, as if it's a few feet away, pulsing healthily.

"Lizzy, look, I'm sorry. I—"

"How old do you think she is?" she asks.

He backs up. "Look, I know you're upset."

Except that's not how she feels. At least not in the way he's thinking she is. No, she's worried about the girl.

"Do you think she's eighteen?" she asks.

"Of course she's eighteen." His words come out squeaky, defensive. "She has to be. They can't hire younger ones."

"But she didn't look it."

"It's against the law for them to be under eighteen." He finally looks at her, his face red and angry. "They have to be," he shouts.

"Don't talk so loudly." She puts a hand to her head. Why is he yelling? She just wants to know how old the girl is. That's all.

"It's just that your questions seem so . . . so . . . off the point."

Her head feels as if it's filled with wet concrete. "What is the point?" she asks.

"Oh, for Christ's sake." His face is redder and sweaty.

Somewhere in her brain she receives a message that she should be hurrying to the bathroom, grabbing her medicine, and rushing back to school. But she doesn't move. His eyes dart.

"Work, what do you tell them?" She watches him. He looks at her for a second but can't hold her gaze.

"Sometimes I work at home where it's quieter." He speaks to the wall.

"With that music?" The neurons in her brain begin to light up, to connect again. Her headache is back, tenfold. "How often do you come home?"

"It's not like I keep track. I don't have a time card."

Her chest swells and burns as if it's filling with poison gas. She holds on to the wooden door frame. "Why are you getting so defensive?"

"I'm not getting defensive." He stiffens. "It's just that I feel like you're the Spanish Inquisition."

She glances around the room. The blinds are down, which she feels grateful for. Not that anyone could see in on a bright day like today, but if the mailman, or . . . She sniffs. The air is musty, and she guesses the windows haven't been opened for a while. She walks to the bookshelf and picks up their wedding picture. In it they are smiling at each other, glowing, as if nothing but the other existed. She places it facedown.

"I'm not the Spanish Inquisition," she says, emotionless. "I'm your wife. The one you don't want to have sex with."

"It's not about you," he says.

"You know, I used to think you were shy, inhibited, self-conscious. I used to think that's why it was difficult for you to have sex. But it's because you'd rather look at other women."

"Lizzy, please. It's not about you or us."

It feels as if there's a knife going through her right temple. She has to get her medication, but she can't, not yet.

"But it is about us," she says. "It's about you choosing to have your sex life without me. So it is about me. And us." She thinks someone in her group said this, and it didn't really click then. It does now.

"Whatever." He shakes his head. "I can't deal with all the philosophical stuff. I have to get back to work."

"I don't think this is exactly philosophical." There's an awful taste in her mouth, like sour milk. More neurons connect, yet not enough for her to fully engage. *Is this shock?* she wonders as she watches him touch his belt, his hair, move his feet, as if he's skulking around in a cage. He's free to leave.

She sinks to the floor. "I don't know what to do." She tugs out her bun. Her hair falls into large ringlets.

He sits a few feet away and reaches to touch her, but stops himself. "You have a bad headache. You need to take your medicine and lie down."

She flicks a tiny scrap of paper on the rug. "I just don't understand. I mean, it's okay if you watch a little porn. I'm not a prude. It's that . . ." She wraps a lock of hair around her finger and pulls it as hard as she can. "It's that . . . you don't want me. That's all. Really, I'm not a prude."

"But I do want you. I've told you that." He taps his hand on the carpet, frustrated.

She takes a deep breath. *Get it together*, she tells herself, yet she's cracking, and every time he talks her arms prickle, and her blood surges.

"Stop," she shouts, even though it makes her head scream to raise her voice. "You not having sex with me is about me."

He grabs her arm. "Come on. Get up and take your medicine."

"This is not about my medicine. I'm not crazy. Don't treat me like I'm crazy." Although even as she says that, she realizes that she's not looking like a picture of mental health at the moment.

"I'm not treating you like you're crazy. But you need to stand up. I'll get you a glass of water."

She bats his hand away. "I don't want medicine or water. I want you to have sex with me, now. Here in this room, where you watch other women. That's the least you can do." She glares, daring him.

He grunts and shakes his head. "You're not rational."

"I come home. You're watching porn on the computer, which means you must be horny. You tell me you want me, and here I am, ready and willing. How is that not rational?"

"I can't do it on command."

"Then I'll help you." Her fingers tremble as she begins to undo her blouse. Her hands feel as if they're in oven mitts. She'll be here until midnight if she keeps trying this way. She rips open her blouse, hears the buttons pop off. One of them pings as it hits the bookshelf.

"Stop," he tells her.

"I'm not stopping." She takes off her camisole and unhooks her bra.

He stands and walks to the door.

She gets up, glances at the strewn clothes on the carpet, then approaches him. She pushes him against the wall. "So tell me, aren't my breasts good enough for you? Or am I just too old?"

He looks away. "Liz, stop. I can't do this. Get dressed."

"So I'm right, you don't want me. You can't even stand to look at me." She grabs his chin, turns his face.

He tries to nudge her away. "You need to get control of yourself."

"No, you need to show me you want me."

"Don't do this." His words are tight, his eyes small and mean.

She looks down at herself, at her breasts that sag, and suddenly it's not him she hates anymore. It's herself.

She runs out of the room and locks herself in the master bathroom. She finds her medicine in the cabinet and takes two.

"Are you okay?" Greg calls through the door.

She turns on the faucet to the bath to drown out his voice, then begins to yank open the drawers. There isn't anything in particular she's looking for. Pill bottles, nail clippers, bobby pins, barrettes, and razors go flying. She picks up a lipstick from the floor and writes on the mirror.

You ugly, crazy bitch.

She empties a few more drawers. An old, unused pregnancy test and another pill bottle clatter on the tile floor. She picks up the bottle— Klonopin prescribed a few years ago by a fertility doctor who said there was nothing wrong with either of them, that she just needed to relax. He also told them that Greg should save up, not have too many orgasms before she ovulated. What if they couldn't have a baby because he was masturbating all the time?

The pills expired ages ago. Still, she opens the bottle, tosses three little green tablets into her mouth, and swallows. She pulls a towel from the rack and sinks her head into it.

She cries. The bathwater runs. Greg knocks.

Eventually either the crying or the Klonopin exhausts her. She curls on the floor, closes her eyes, and imagines being with the group, telling the women what a crazy person she became. Soon she is fantasizing about going on a retreat with them. Maybe to Mexico. They will drink margaritas on the beach and laugh at their ridiculous lives.

Somewhere far away she hears the banging on the door. *Go away*, she thinks, as she imagines the sun warming her skin. She pulls her knees in closer, then takes her cell phone from her pocket and texts the school, telling them she's too sick to return today. Finally she begins to drift, feeling pleased that she didn't make that call to Kathryn.

SESSION THREE

This Wednesday Adam clearly knows he's not expected until seven. Gabby is due any minute, and as Hannah gets ready she tells herself this will really be the last Wednesday that she deserts the children. Yes, she likes everyone, and of course she'll keep in touch with Bridget, but she's been dealing with this much longer than the others, so her needs are naturally different.

She is pleased to walk into Kathryn's office and see that Bridget is there before her. Her face has more color, and her eyes sparkle again. They chat about morning sickness, traffic, and the weather.

Flavia and Gail come in at the same time, and Kathryn starts at seven, even though Lizzy is absent.

The women glance around, making sure not to jump in if there is someone who might need to go first.

Flavia finally begins. "This week is the week Dema must go to the court. He begs that I go with him. I cannot say no, but I am very nervous. I feel it in the stomach."

"Can you talk about why you feel nervous?" Kathryn asks.

She purses her full lips, then lets out a long breath. "I am afraid he will have to go to jail. That is my worse fear. I am also afraid of the newspaper. I think they want to make Dema to be bad, partly because he is different. Then they can say it is not their own kind that does these types of things, but the dark foreigner."

"Does he have a good lawyer?" Gail asks.

"The one they give to us."

"And when do you go in?"

"Tomorrow I go."

"In Cambridge?" Gail asks.

"Yes."

"Is this his first arrest?" Gail's questions are proficient, mechanical.

"It is."

"Does he go to therapy to get help for this?"

"Yes."

"Then you must tell the lawyer to make it very clear he is getting help." Gail points a finger, making sure Flavia understands the importance of what is being said. Hannah guesses she is some sort of lawyer.

"Thank you." Flavia bows her head. "It is also hard because I believe what Dema did was not good, but when you know the person who does this type of thing and you understand that they cannot help it, it makes it all confusing."

"It's a horrible position to be in," Gail says. "But I will say this: if it happens again, no judge is going to be lenient." Her long nails click.

Hannah is sorry she won't be back next week to find out what happened. She is about to wish Flavia good luck when Lizzy walks in with her head lowered. She sits on the couch, hunched, clinging to her corner. She doesn't glance up or smile or apologize for being late. Her skin is sallow. She has aged ten years since last week.

Flavia picks up the tissue box, makes a move to hand it to Lizzy, then withdraws. They all know what's happened. Not the details, but the sum of it, the discovering of more lies.

"Lizzy." Kathryn leans toward her. "Are you all right?"

Lizzy's fingers grip her sweater. "Just a little tired."

That's not the truth, of course, although Hannah wishes it were. The room is quiet, reverent.

"Sometimes," Hannah says, her voice just above a whisper, "it helps to talk."

"Thanks," Lizzy mumbles. Silence again. "I . . . maybe . . . I feel like such a fool." She rubs her palm on the seat of the couch. "I really believed him this time."

"They know what to do to make us trust them," Hannah says.

"It hurts." Lizzy's voice cracks as she reaches for a tissue. "I go between hating him for doing it and hating myself for being stupid enough to believe him."

Gail shakes her head slowly. "Not one of us is stupid."

The small oval clock on the desk ticks. Bridget glances around nervously. Flavia touches Lizzy's arm. Hannah watches.

"What happened?" Kathryn asks gently.

"I came back home in the middle of the day. I needed some medication for a migraine. He was home, watching . . . I thought he'd be at work." Her breath catches.

"Sex addiction can be a harder habit to break than cocaine," Kathryn says.

Flavia hands Lizzy another tissue. She places one on top of the other, then folds them into squares.

Kathryn waits a few moments. "Are you going to be all right?" she asks.

Silence shrouds the room.

Slowly, carefully, Kathryn begins. "If anyone is open to it, I have an exercise some of you may like to try."

There are a few nods.

"The first part requires that you rate your marriage on a scale of one to ten, ten being the highest." She folds her hands. "If you feel comfortable telling the group . . ."

"A fucking zero," Bridget jumps in, awkwardly loud, in an attempt to break the mood.

"I'd like you to think about what would make it a one," Kathryn says.

"Nothing."

"I know it's hard, but can you think of anything that might bring it up from a zero?"

"If he took a lie detector test and passed."

"Good," Kathryn says. "Is that something Michael would be willing to do?"

Bridget's eyes widen. "Really? They give those? I was joking."

"It's often a recommended treatment for sex addicts. I can give you the number of someone."

Bridget looks away, uncomfortable. Hannah understands. The idea of sitting in some room with your husband as they paste wires to him and ask embarrassing questions is not something she'd ever want to do either.

"I'd rate my marriage at an eight," Gail says.

"And what would make it a nine?" Kathryn asks, as Bridget stares at Gail in disbelief.

"Jonah and I have spent the last year going through so much therapy. We haven't been on a real vacation together in two years. I think we should plan a trip to Europe."

"Excellent," Kathryn says.

"An eight?" Bridget asks. "For real?"

"It's taken a lot of work to get there," Gail tells her.

Bridget looks unconvinced. Flavia nods as if she's listening, but she keeps turning to check on Lizzy, who seems detached, as if she's alone in the middle of a frozen cornfield.

"What about you?" Kathryn asks Hannah.

She's been paying attention to Lizzy as well. "A two." It's the first number that comes to her.

"And what would make it a three?"

Hannah doesn't want to play this game. But she doesn't want to be rude either. "I think it's just going to take a lot of time." It's a vague nonanswer.

"Time is a very important component," Kathryn says. "Recovery can be a long process."

"It's a lifetime commitment," Gail adds.

"Lizzy, is there anything you can think of that might help your relationship?" Kathryn asks.

"Maybe being twenty years younger."

"How would that help?" Kathryn asks.

"I could compete with what he likes to look at."

"Don't," Bridget says. "Don't compare yourself. Porn isn't real. Those girls are skanks. You wouldn't want to look like them."

"She's right," Hannah says. "Porn isn't real. It's a way to escape, to avoid dealing with an intimate relationship."

"That's what makes me so sad." Lizzy's deep brown eyes shimmer with tears. "That he doesn't want to have an intimate relationship with me."

"It's because he can't," Hannah says. "He probably has no idea how to do it."

"So does that mean our whole marriage has been a lie? If he's not capable now, he wasn't five years ago, or fifteen years ago. I thought we had something."

"It's not that black and white," Hannah says. "There were probably times he wasn't consumed with his addiction and you did connect."

She shrugs. "I don't know. I wanted to have children, and we couldn't. For years I've told myself that that was okay, that I've been fortunate to have a job I love and to be in a fulfilling marriage. And now I find out it's all a bunch of shit."

"Not all of it," Gail says sympathetically. "Even if it seems that way now."

"It's lonely." Lizzy's voice is barely audible.

Flavia hands over another tissue.

"When they're living in their addiction, you are alone. At least in your marriage," Hannah says. "I know it's not much, but you have us."

"Sometimes, don't you guys think we should just go out and sleep with anyone we want? Screw the rules." Bridget's knees bounce.

"I think that would only exacerbate our situations," Gail says. "Then we'd have our own secrets and guilt to deal with."

"I wasn't saying we should keep it a secret." Bridget grins.

"Revenge is never productive." Gail wags a finger.

"They broke their vows," Bridget says. "And when they do that, I say all bets are off."

"We all change throughout our lives." Gail looks directly at Bridget. "Should we always be reevaluating?"

"Yeah, maybe we should."

"What about if your spouse gets Alzheimer's?" Gail asks.

"That would be a different group," Bridget retorts.

Flavia toys with a few strands of hair as if she's looking for split ends. "Dema is a different man from that I thought I married, so I do not know what to do." Her face turns pink. "I thought to feel better, I should have sex with another man."

"Self-esteem is very important," Kathryn says. "It can get shattered and damaged in your situations. Are there other things you can think of that might help?"

Flavia pulls a makeup pouch out of her bag. "Sometimes I paint my lips and cheeks. Then I walk down the street with my big heels, my head high, and feel like I am worth the million bucks."

Hannah glances at Lizzy again. She's still withdrawn. "I think Flavia has a good point. It doesn't have to be makeup, but doing something to pamper yourself. Buying some clothes, or getting a manicure."

Flavia holds up her lipstick and nudges Lizzy's elbow. She perks up a little.

"Here." Flavia hands over the makeup.

Lizzy takes it, opens it, and smiles. "It's a pretty color."

"Try it," Flavia encourages, and takes out a mirror.

"No thanks." Lizzy gives it back. "But I think I will go out and get some new makeup this weekend."

"It's interesting how we use makeup as kind of a mask to hide behind,"

Gail proselytizes. "Almost like a Band-Aid, as if we're trying to hide the wound."

"I disagree," Hannah says. "Band-Aids get a bad rap. I get that they don't fix anything, but they do the job they're meant to do. They help the healing process, and if that sometimes means lipstick or high heels or a new dress, then I say go for it. Let's dress up next week. Wear whatever makes us feel good."

Flavia holds her shoulders high. "I will wear my red dress."

"I don't know what I'll wear," Bridget says. "But count me in."

"It will be black and pearls for me." Of course, now Hannah must come back, at least one more week. But if it helps Lizzy feel even a tiny bit better, then it's worth it.

"Mine will be a surprise." Lizzy smiles for the first time tonight.

Hannah looks at Gail, who says, "I'll think about it."

Kathryn glances at the clock, then begins to wind down the group. Lizzy has come out of her corner a little and isn't as slouched. Bridget's knees aren't bouncing, and Hannah is oddly relieved she won't be quitting after all.

Gail

Gail steps out of the shower and quickly dries herself, avoiding looking in the mirror. She can feel she's put on fifteen pounds. It's Friday morning, and she will start her diet today.

Jonah left early to meet with a colleague about the paper he's working on. She is so pleased he's started to write again. It's a healthy habit. From her walk-in closet, she picks a dark blue suit and a white blouse. She touches the outfit she bought for the dinner at the Harvard Club. She will also wear it to next Wednesday's group. Of course it's silly, this whole idea of getting dressed up, and it's certainly not the type of thing she goes in for, but in the spirit of camaraderie and solidarity, she's going to go along. She pictures Lizzy, how drawn and sad she looked. *There but for the grace of God go I.*

The zipper on her skirt doesn't close all the way, but the jacket covers the flaw. She will have an orange and some grapes for breakfast, a fat-free yogurt for lunch, and a salad for dinner. On the way out of the bedroom, she passes the large tapestry armchair. She picks up Jonah's light blue sweater, one she gave him. As she folds it, she gets a whiff of roses. She brings the sweater to her nose. Although the scent is faint, it's distinctly perfume, and not one she uses.

She feels sluggish as she walks down the hallway to the room they have deemed the library. Its wall-to-wall bookcases hold everything from law reviews to fairy tales. A long desk sits in front of the window. She opens her laptop and does a search for perfume smells on sweaters. Most of the sites explain how to get rid of the smells, but one site has what she's looking for. It suggests that you first familiarize yourself with the scent of your husband's regular clothes. Most important, you should not be able to smell someone else's perfume on his underwear.

In the laundry room, she finds a pair of his white underpants. She picks them up by the waistband and sniffs. There's a faint odor of detergent, mixed with some less pleasant smells, but definitely nothing like his sweater. Relieved, she's ready to smell all his dirty clothes just to be sure. When she's finished, she's convinced that she overreacted. He'd probably worn the sweater on a humid day, sat in an office with someone who had on far too much perfume, and the fibers absorbed the fragrance. Woolen fabric is known for its ability to attract scents, a fact she's heard in a number of trials.

She's half an hour late for work. Barbara has three briefs for her to sign before she's even had a chance to sit.

"You're due in court at ten o'clock," Barbara says as she places the papers on the desk.

"I have five minutes." Gail is terse, irritated with herself for being late. "I had some business at home to attend to."

"I'm sorry." Barbara fiddles with her light blue scarf, the same color as Jonah's sweater. "Would you like a cup of tea?"

"What kind of perfume do you wear?" Gail asks.

Barbara looks confused as she keeps fidgeting. "Perfume?" she asks.

"Yes," Gail answers.

"Uh . . . normally none. But if I do, White Linen."

"Does it linger on your clothes?"

"I haven't really noticed."

"What about if you're out somewhere, say a restaurant that uses a lot of garlic. Do you notice that on your clothes?" She looks into Barbara's blue eyes. They also seem like the color of Jonah's sweater, insipid and irksome. Why had she ever thought it would look good with his light skin?

"I'll try to be more mindful of it. Is there something that's bothering you?" Barbara asks.

Gail waves her hand. "No, nothing in particular. I've been wondering about some evidence." She pauses. "Court evidence."

"Yes, of course." Barbara backs toward the door. "Are you sure you wouldn't like a cup of tea?"

Gail stands and takes her robe from its hanger, then reaches for her purse. "What I'd like is for you to go to Macy's and buy a bottle of rose-scented perfume." She hands Barbara three twenties. "And don't worry about the cost. Get the one you think is best."

She takes the money. "Would you like me to do this now?"

"Is something the matter?" Gail asks. Barbara seems skittish. Granted Gail isn't in the most pleasant of moods, but she hasn't behaved in a way that would, on any normal day, unnerve the woman who's been her PA for seventeen years.

"It's nothing." Barbara picks a dying leaf from the plant.

"Meaning it is *something*. Out with it."

Barbara looks at her gold watch, a present from Gail. "Another letter," she says quietly.

"Why didn't you tell me when I first came in?"

"I was going to, but . . . you seemed preoccupied. I didn't want to bother you with anything more."

"From the same girl?"

"Yes."

Gail loosens her skirt a little, then zips her robe. "No return address, I assume?"

"None."

"I will speak to Jonah. I think a harassment order is the next step."

"Would you like me to shred it?"

"Yes." She sits. Her hip hurts. She should be walking into the court-room. But she feels light-headed, as if she's been under water too long. It could be low blood sugar. Or possibly high blood pressure, even though she did take Atenolol this morning. "No, don't shred it. Bring it to me."

Barbara scoots out, returns with the letter, and hands it to Gail, try-ing to keep her distance.

Gail reads the first paragraph.

I'm so sorry to have to write a letter like this. I always swore to myself I would never get involved with a married man. I wouldn't do that to another woman. But falling in love is a game changer.

What a silly young woman. Gail opens her bottom desk drawer and takes out a Kit Kat. The handwriting in the letter is neat, not indicative of any sort of mental illness, but it's hard to tell with only one sample. What Gail is sure of, though, is that she cannot keep receiving this sort of nonsense at work. It's too distracting. She will speak to Jonah tonight, ask him for the girl's full name. Then, even though he'll protest and tell her he'll take care of it, she will get a harassment order stating that this must cease. Gail licks the chocolate from her fingers and heads into court.

Bridget

It's nearly noon when Bridget wakes up on Friday. It took over two hours to fall asleep when she came home from work. She was dizzy and nauseated. Pregnancy and night shifts don't go well together. She gets up to pee and hears Michael playing guitar in the living room. With the band, part-time landscaping, part-time construction work, and random hours with UPS, he's not usually home during the day. It would probably be best to hide under the covers, but if she doesn't put something in her stomach, she's going to dry heave.

She walks downstairs, and he stops playing.

"You want me to make you breakfast?" he asks. He still has no idea she's pregnant. She's waiting for the right moment to tell him. Not a romantic, let's-build-a-family moment, more like a fuck-you moment.

"Nope," she answers. "Just having toast."

They both stand and watch the toaster. She tugs at her long T-shirt and looks at her belly. There's a tiny bulge, nothing noticeable.

"You should go back to bed," he says. "You look exhausted."

No shit. "I'm fine."

"You want to do something this afternoon?" He rinses his coffee cup.

"Not really."

"*The Avengers* is playing at the Premium cinema. They have great seats."

She's about to say no, go fuck yourself, but she thinks of movie theater popcorn and wants it more than she wants to knee Michael in the balls. This must be what they mean by a craving, because even as her toast pops up, she can only think of extra butter on popcorn.

"Sure. I'll go." She has no interest in the movie, but Premium tickets come with all the popcorn you can eat.

"It starts in like half an hour." He reaches over to touch her shoulder.

"I'll be ready in two seconds." She ducks under his arm and leaves her toast on the counter. Upstairs, she puts on an old pair of jeans and a black top.

On the drive there, he chatters about how much he's wanted to see this movie and how happy he is that they're doing something together. She just keeps saying, "Yep."

They pick two of the large center seats. About ten other people, three who are alone, are dotted throughout the theater. The previews take forever, and she's already finished with her first bag. She stands to get another.

"They serve here," Michael tells her.

It might be five minutes until someone comes by, and she needs more now. "I'd rather get my own."

After her second bag, there have already been at least ten fights on the screen. She likes Captain America and Robert Downey Jr., and now that her craving is gone for the moment, she can watch. But the plot doesn't interest her. She turns to look at Michael. He's transfixed and smiling.

She pokes his side.

He looks at her, grins, and turns back to the screen. Did he think that was a friendly nudge? She pokes him again.

"What?" he whispers, not turning this time.

"I want to go home." That will piss the shit out of him.

"Bridge," he whispers. "The movie just started."

"Yeah, well, I don't like it."

"Shush. I'm not leaving yet."

"Then I'm going to keep talking."

"Quiet," someone chides from a few rows back. Michael tenses, embarrassed. Good, she thinks.

"Take me home," she says.

"For God's sake, stop it. You're behaving like a child."

"I'm getting more popcorn," she announces.

When she returns, she puts the bag on Michael's tray, jiggles the straw in her drink, then finally sits.

"What is with you?" Michael whispers.

"You really want to know?" she asks.

"Come on, keep it down," the man from the back scolds again.

Michael shakes his head. At least he's not enjoying the movie anymore.

She finishes her third bag, feeling stuffed, uncomfortable, and queasy.

"I need to go home and puke," she says.

"No wonder." Michael punches the armrest. "Just use the bathroom here."

"I'm not throwing up in some gross movie theater bathroom. I want to go home."

"Come on, you two," the man says. "Show some respect."

Michael turns. "Sorry," he tells him.

"Yeah, apologize to him. Be nice to some stranger, but treat the woman you're supposed to love like dirt."

"Bridge, what is with you?"

"Maybe you should have worn a condom the last time you fucked me," she says, at the exact time there's a lull in the action.

"Okay, that's it," the man says, and stands.

"Don't bother," Michael says. "We're leaving." He yanks Bridget up and practically pushes her up the aisle.

In the lobby, he holds on to her arms and stares at her. "What the hell is your problem?"

She looks at the concession stand. She's dying of thirst. "I need a lemonade."

He follows her. "If this is your way of trying to make my life a living hell, good job. But it's not gonna work, because I'm just not gonna go out with you again."

She orders a large drink. "You've made my life a living hell."

"Ahhh, Bridge. I know. You tell me all the time. I get it already."

"You don't get shit." She heads to an empty table and sits.

"I'm not getting into this in public."

"You ashamed of me?"

He sits across from her and lets out a long, deep sigh. "No, I'm not ashamed of you. But I'm not airing my dirty laundry for the world to hear."

She glances around. There's a large woman who collects the tickets sitting at the entrance, and a pimply kid behind the counter. "Not exactly what I'd call the whole world."

"Enough." He stands. "I'm going back in." He strides toward the door. Regardless of how much she can't stand him, he still has the best ass.

"I'm pregnant," she shouts.

He turns.

"I'm pregnant," she says again.

He walks toward her and sits.

"When?"

"When did it happen, or how long have I known?"

"Both. Either."

"It happened when you didn't use a condom. I've known for a little over a week." She draws the straw from her drink and bites it.

"Wow," he says. "Didn't see this coming."

"That's what happens when you think with your dick."

She glances around again, this time looking for somewhere more comfortable to sit. The hard little café chair hurts her back. She'd like a couch. Actually, she'd love to lie down. She's suddenly so tired. Not sleepy-tired or stress-tired, more like bone-tired, a different kind of exhaustion than she's ever felt. She walks to a small vinyl-upholstered couch and plops down.

He joins her. She glares at him and scoots away.

"We always wanted kids," he says.

"I always wanted a faithful husband."

"Can we just keep the issues separate for a moment?"

"How? I can't just stick the fact that you broke my heart in one compartment and the fact that I'm pregnant in another. Maybe that's what you can do with all your shit. Maybe that's why you can watch a movie without thinking about what an asshole you are. I go around feeling like someone drilled a hole into my fucking chest, and you can sit in there and laugh at Ironman."

"Bridge, I do feel bad. I just don't show it the same way."

"You play the guitar, you walk around the house singing, you go off to work like nothing is different. I feel like there's a war raging inside of me. I can't concentrate. I'm exhausted, and I can't sleep. I'm so fucking angry one minute and sad the next. And you feel bad? Like how exactly do you feel bad?"

"Can we talk about this at home?"

"No. I want to see you actually feel bad about this."

He combs his hand through his hair. "I'm sorry. I truly am. I promise by the time the baby is here, things will have changed. They'll be better. I'll make it up to you."

"I'm getting an abortion."

"What?" He glares at her.

"You think I want you to be the father of my baby?"

"You always said you'd never get an abortion. You didn't care if other people did, but it wasn't for you."

"Yeah, well, you changed all that." She stands. "I need another bag of popcorn."

He follows. She takes her popcorn and walks out of the movie theater.

They get into his truck. The smell of popcorn fills the space and makes her nauseated. She puts the bag on the floor.

"Bridge, you can't do this. It's my baby too." He starts the engine but doesn't back up.

"Oh, believe me, I can do it."

"Please. Please don't."

"Can you drive already?" she asks.

His hands grip the wheel as he glances in the rearview mirror. His jaw is clenched, and she sees he's angry and frightened. For a moment, she feels good. She's gotten what she wanted, for him to feel like shit. Maybe he'll understand a little better how she feels. But then it occurs to her, it's not her he's frightened of losing, it's the baby, and that makes the hole feel like it's going to consume her.

Hannah

An untroubled spring breeze caresses Hannah's face. She's in the back-yard raking a small plot of land that Adam carved out last weekend. It will be nice for the kids to plant a garden, to watch things grow, to feel as if they've created something. Hannah has an assortment of seeds, and as soon as they come home this afternoon, they'll begin. It's a good family project. Without Adam, of course.

Her phone rings. She stops raking.

"Hi," Hannah says casually, expecting Bridget, expecting to hear the f-word in the next sentence.

"Is this Mrs. Jenkins?" a professional voice asks.

"Yes, may I ask who's calling?"

"This is Ms. Meriwether from Alicia's elementary school."

Hannah clenches the wooden rake handle. "Is she all right?"

"Yes, she's fine. But I think it would be wise if you and your husband came in." Her neutral voice gives nothing away.

"I already know all about what she said to Peter. She told me. Is that what you'd like to speak about?" Hannah wants to make it clear that she's not some delusional mother who thinks she has perfect children.

"I'm afraid I don't know about that incident."

Shit. "When would you like us to come in?"

"I was thinking this afternoon."

"Today? I'm afraid that won't be possible for my husband. He works in Boston. If you'd like, I can come on my own."

"I've already spoken to Mr. Jenkins, and he's on his way. He said he can be here at two-thirty."

Her hand slides down a little. "May I ask what it was Alicia did?"

"I think it's best if Alicia tells you that."

What could be worse than calling a boy gay? "Can you give me an idea?" Hannah asks.

"She defaced school property."

"Defaced? How?" Her breath feels sharp.

"I'd prefer we talk about the details when you get here. I'll see you in a little over half an hour. Good-bye, Mrs. Jenkins."

"Thank you for taking the time to speak with us," Hannah says, then realizes Ms. Meriwether has already hung up.

Hannah changes into a nice pair of slacks, a white blouse, and a long blue cardigan. It's a conservative *I'm a good mom* outfit.

She and Adam arrive at the same time.

"Do you know what this is about?" he asks as he holds open the front door. She notices his freckles are more pronounced. Did he have lunch outside? Meet someone behind a bush?

"The principal was vague," she says. "Something about defacing property. I don't understand. It's not like Alicia."

He straightens his tie. They are about to sit in the small waiting area when the secretary tells them to go ahead in.

Ms. Meriwether stands. She is Hannah's height and also has on a white blouse and blue sweater. After handshakes and introductions, she asks her secretary to call in Alicia.

Alicia walks in, shoulders hunched, her face pale, nearly translucent. Hannah's first instinct is to hug her, but she doesn't want to be smothering. Instead she points to the chair between Adam and her. Alicia sits.

She has her father's muted, gentle eyes, which at the moment are staring at her shoes.

"Would you like to explain to your parents what happened today?" Ms. Meriwether asks.

Alicia shakes her head. Wisps of hair that have escaped her messy braid frame her face.

"I think it would be better coming from you than me," Ms. Meriwether says.

Alicia shakes her head again and crosses her arms. Then she looks up at her father. She's begging for mercy, and he is certainly the most likely person in this room to provide that.

"Honey, it's okay," he tells her. "Whatever it is. We can talk about it. But first we have to know what it is."

Alicia hops out of her chair and throws herself at him. He takes her on his lap and kisses the top of her head. She's a twig in his arms.

"Perhaps," he says, looking at the principal, "it would be best if you told us."

Alicia burrows her head into Adam's chest. Hannah feels a jab of envy and reminds herself this isn't about her, and it's good her daughter can find comfort.

"There were actually two incidents. The first occurred on Wednesday at recess. One of the girls reported that Alicia called her a bad word."

Alicia covers her ears.

"Don't do that," Hannah says. "You need to listen." Her tone comes out much saltier than she wanted.

Adam gently pushes Alicia's hands down. "It's okay," he says. "Ms. Meriwether, can you tell us what the word was?"

"B-i-t-c-h," she spells out.

"Alicia, why would you call someone that?" Adam asks as he caresses her back.

She tries to burrow deeper.

"There must have been a reason. Were you angry at the girl?"

A nod.

"What happened?" he asks.

She whispers into her father's ear. Hannah keeps herself in check, not showing her irritation, as a closed-mouth, seemingly patient smile spreads across her lips.

"She says," he begins, "that this girl called her a rich brat."

Ms. Meriwether shakes her head. "From our investigation, we did not determine that to be the case. It looks as if Alicia said what she did un-provoked."

"Well, something must have upset her." Although Adam speaks slowly, Hannah hears his defensiveness.

"Yes, I believe something is upsetting Alicia. That is generally why children misbehave. I think it's up to us, and perhaps a counselor, to help us determine what that something is."

"And the other incident?" Hannah asks. Calling someone a bitch is not defacing property.

"It happened today, after lunch." Her lips pucker. "I would like Alicia to tell you."

She shakes her head and again puts her hands to her ears.

"Very well." She takes a deep breath. "After lunch, Alicia used the girls' room."

Graffiti on the bathroom wall, Hannah thinks. She glances at her daughter, whose eyes are shut.

"She urinated in the stall. On the floor, on purpose."

Hannah covers her mouth.

"Are you sure?" Adam asks.

"Yes." Her deep-set eyes watch Alicia.

"It could have been someone who was in there before her," Adam conjectures.

"She confessed."

"Perhaps she felt pressured." He keeps caressing Alicia's hair.

Hannah rubs her temples. Why on earth would Alicia do something like that? God, it would have been so much better if she punched someone. Even calling Peter gay was better. This isn't just bad, it's sick, and Hannah doesn't feel irritated or annoyed. She's wondering how to find the best therapist.

"Alicia," the principal says, "do you think you can look at your father and tell him what you told me?"

She shakes her head no, her eyes still closed, her ears still covered, although clearly she can hear.

Hannah gets up and moves to her daughter. She kneels and pulls Alicia away from the large hawklike wing of protection Adam has created. "We need to know if you did what the principal is saying you did. If it's true, we're not angry. We want to help."

Alicia's lips quiver as she gives a slight nod. Hannah wraps her arms around her daughter and feels the sobs before she hears them.

"It's okay, sweetie, we'll get help."

"Are there any problems at home that might have elicited this?" Ms. Meriwether asks.

"Nothing out of the ordinary," Adam tells her.

Hannah's not about to tell the principal the nature of the problems, but she's not going to lie outright like Adam. "There are a few issues."

"Nothing that would cause Alicia to do something like this," he says.

This is not the place to have an argument, but Hannah glances up at Adam and rolls her eyes, then turns back to Ms. Meriwether. "I'm not sure what caused this, if it's the tension at home or something else, but either way we will look into it."

"I have already scheduled Alicia to meet with the school adjustment counselor, but in this case, you might want to think of some further counseling as well."

"May I ask what consequences you intend to give Alicia?" Hannah asks.

"She already wrote an apology letter to the girl she taunted at recess. I will ask that she does the same to the maintenance people. Then at some point in the next few weeks, I would like her to write a private letter to me explaining what she believes was the cause behind her action."

"That is generous and fair. Thank you." Hannah stands and extends a hand.

"And you're sure it was Alicia?" Adam asks.

"Yes, I'm afraid so."

Alicia, who has hopped down from Adam's lap, waits at the door. She has traded the security of her father's arms for the hope of escape. Adam stays in the chair, as if he needs more time to digest the information.

"Why don't you pick up Sam?" Hannah says to him. "And we'll talk more at home."

Adam nods and glances around, then slowly gets up. He seems too large for this office.

In the car, Alicia sits in the front seat and stares out the window. Hannah waits a few minutes before talking.

"Can you tell me what you thought of before you did that in the girls' room?"

No response.

"Alicia, you're going to have to say something, and believe me, it's easier to say the truth."

"I don't know why I did it." She kicks the dashboard. "I don't know. And I don't want to talk about it. It's not true what you always say, that talking helps."

"It can help." Hannah turns onto their street.

"Yeah, really? You and Dad don't talk. You and him are such hypo—liars."

"Hypocrites," Hannah says.

"You pretend everything is all the same, but you never talk to each other. Just to me and Sam. You hate each other. I know you're going to get divorced."

"Alicia, where on earth did you get that idea?"

"I got up one night because I had a bad dream. I went to your room and Dad wasn't there. He was in the guest room."

Hannah feels herself breathe more easily. She can fix this. "Oh, sweetheart, that doesn't mean anything. He snores, and sometimes I can't sleep."

"Sometimes? And you want me to tell the truth? You're a liar. Because I've been checking every night, and you and Dad are never together, so I know you're getting divorced. That's what Heather's parents did before they got divorced."

Hannah pulls into the driveway. "We're not getting divorced, but you're right for feeling that things aren't perfect. We shouldn't hide that from you."

"I'm never going back to school either. Everyone knows. Eric said I wasn't toilet trained."

The car is in park. "Do you have any idea why you chose to do that and not something else, like punch a wall?"

She shakes her head. "I felt like it."

"Were you angry?"

"Not really."

"Frightened?"

"Not really."

"Not frightened we were going to get divorced?"

She opens the car door. "I told you already. I don't know."

"Please don't get out yet. Try to think of how you felt when you did it. Try to remember."

"I told you a million times, I don't know," she shouts.

Adam's car pulls in beside hers. The thought of seeing him, of having to talk this through with him, makes her woozy.

Alicia gets out and slams the door.

Hannah stays in the car as she watches the three of them climb the front steps. It could be a Norman Rockwell painting, the tall, hulking dad in the middle holding the hands of his children, leading them home.

SESSION FOUR

On Wednesday evening, Hannah takes her black cocktail dress off the hanger. There will be no babysitter tonight. Adam is coming home at six and taking the kids out for pizza and bowling. They have been making a concerted effort to do more as a family, although Hannah still doesn't speak much to Adam in front of the children. Wooden smiles and separate bedrooms remain intact.

Hannah explained to Alicia that mothers and fathers often go through periods when they aren't as close, like Alicia and her friend Tori. In the second grade they went for six months without speaking. It's no different from that.

She found a family therapist, and their first session is next Monday morning. There was some discussion over whether Sam should be there. In the end, they decided no. Don't fix what's not broken.

Hannah slips on red patent-leather pumps to add color, then drapes on a long strand of pearls.

In the kitchen, Alicia perches on a stool as she and Adam, who's just arrived, banter about the best toppings on pizza. Adam's eyebrows rise when he sees Hannah.

"It's group night," she says, which he knows. He doesn't know it's "dress-up night," and she's not about to explain.

Alicia's eyes squint, suspicious. A few months ago, she would have wanted to try on Hannah's shoes and pearls.

"What kind of group?" Alicia asks.

Since the episode at school, Hannah and Adam have decided to be as honest as possible with the children. "Just with a few of my girl-friends."

"Why the fancy outfit?"

Hannah forces a smile. "It's silly, but we decided we would get dressed up tonight to make ourselves feel better."

Alicia nods, contemplating the idea.

"We think you look beautiful," Adam says.

"Thanks." Hannah feels her cheeks turn pink.

"No we don't," Alicia gripes.

"Don't speak that way to your mother."

"It's fine," Hannah says, appreciating that Adam stood up for her. "She doesn't have to think I look good. I'm sure I won't always like all the clothes she chooses."

"No one goes to talk to their friends dressed like that." Alicia scrunches her face.

"Your mother is allowed to wear whatever she likes to see her friends."

"I think . . ." Alicia stops. Hannah watches as her daughter tries to figure out something mean to say.

"I'd be very proud to be seen with your mother looking like that," Adam says.

His compliment should feel good, but instead she is reminded that they don't go out, they don't have sex, they don't sleep in the same bed. She remembers an overnight flight to Europe, how they tried to fool around in the restroom. Adam hit his head. It was a hopeless, funny escapade. But now it's just another tainted memory.

"You look like a . . . someone who wants a boyfriend," Alicia grumbles.

"Oh, honey," Hannah says sarcastically as she looks at Adam. She knows she should restrain herself. "That would certainly not be me." The words slip out.

His face hardens. It was a low blow, even if Alicia has no idea of the underlying reference.

"You look old," Alicia sneers.

Hannah feels a sting. She tries to brush it off. "I am old, at least a lot older than you."

Adam stays silent, smoldering.

She should apologize. There was no call for such a searing comment, but when she looks at him and sees a tall, handsome man who likes to have sex with younger men, she wants to pound her fists on his chest. It would be so much easier if she felt nothing. She controls herself, walks to Alicia, and pats her head.

"Well, I'm off. Have a good night." Her smile is fake.

Alicia shrinks away. At least her distaste, the way her lip curls up a little, is real. Better that than the false mask Hannah has learned to wear so well.

She is the last to arrive at Kathryn's office. The extra time she took getting ready delayed her. She's not late, just not early for once. Everyone smiles and says hello. The room feels energized, excited—different. Hannah never imagined coming to this group would be something she'd look forward to, but right now it feels a lot lighter and easier than being at home. She could use the break.

She smiles at Bridget, who is wearing a silky peach dress with spaghetti straps, black-heeled sandals, and gold jewelry. Her hair, pulled back in a small bun, is beginning to show its natural dark roots. She looks pretty, subtle. Even Gail seems softer in an elegant teal suit with an off-white blouse. But most striking is her new haircut, slightly asymmetrical and sophisticated.

"It's nice to see everyone," Kathryn begins. "You all look beautiful."

Her compliment is sincere, and Hannah appreciates that she stepped out of her therapist box and voiced an opinion.

Instead of red, Flavia opted for a tight, black sleeveless turtleneck dress that clings to her graceful curves. "Dema, he look at me with the jealous eyes when I left." She twists the large silver cuff bracelet on her wrist.

"Yeah," Bridget says. "Michael was the same. All suspicious. He wanted to know why I would get dressed up to sit with a group of women."

"What did you tell him?" Gail asks.

"That it was none of his fucking business."

"I don't think Greg even noticed anything different," Lizzy says. Her long peasant skirt comes to her ankles. A colorful scarf is thrown loosely around her neck.

"Asshole," Bridget says.

"How could he not notice?" Flavia asks. "You look like a movie star."

Lizzy smiles. "Thanks. I don't seem to be on his radar screen lately."

"Do you find that difficult?" Kathryn's eyes are sympathetic.

"It all feels difficult," Lizzy replies. "I have to pinch myself in bed so that I don't start questioning him. Asking if he's watched porn, or why he doesn't want me."

Gail claps softly. "Bravo. Learning to accept that we can't fix them is the hardest thing to do."

"I can't promise I'll fare so well next week," Lizzy says.

"One day at a time," Gail tells her.

"No," Bridget says. "She's not in any stupid program. If she feels like asking, she should be able to. It's not like she's the addict."

"That's not what I meant." Gail adjusts her collar. "I meant that it's important to try and live in the moment and not worry about all the things that can go wrong in the future."

"So, Hannah." Bridget raises her eyebrows. "What did Adam say about your outfit?"

Hannah thinks of her remark to Adam and how Alicia looked at her. It feels as if her heart is being squeezed. "He thought I looked good."

"That's it?" Bridget asks.

"We're not really into giving each other compliments lately, that's all."

"One of the things Jonah and I decided to do was to give each other at least two compliments a day." Gail smiles. "At first it felt forced, but now I'm beginning to see how it's changed him. His face isn't so drawn."

"Does anything ever go wrong for you?" Bridget asks.

"Of course there are glitches. But I believe we've seen the worst of this, and I'm able to reflect back and see the things that have helped. Letting go of needing to fix his disease and complimenting each other were two of those things." She traces the edge of her new haircut.

"So, any glitches this week?" Bridget prods.

Gail rubs her hand along her skirt as if it needs smoothing out. "Funny you should ask." She takes a deep breath and sits up a little. "Yes, there was. I received another letter from the young woman who thinks Jonah is in love with her."

"That's a glitch?" Bridget's eyes are wide. "For me that would be a grenade."

"It may have been a trigger some time ago." Gail shifts. "But I was surprisingly calm about it."

Hannah wouldn't accuse her of being a liar, but she doesn't believe her either.

"What helped you to be able to remain calm?" Kathryn asks.

"Trusting Jonah."

"What did he say when you showed it to him?" Bridget asks.

Gail shifts again. "I haven't told him yet. I intend to, but there didn't seem to be any urgency. We are both very busy."

"I dunno," Bridget says. "It sort of seems like there's some denial going on there."

Gail nods as if she can take the criticism objectively. "We really have been busy, and I just simply didn't obsess about it."

"Weren't you just a little curious to see what he'd say?" Bridget asks.

"Until you brought it up, I suppose I wasn't." She looks at Kathryn, signaling that her part in this discussion is over.

"I want to get to that point," Lizzy says. "Where this stuff doesn't consume me. I would never have been able to stay calm."

Hannah shakes her head. "I want to stay calm too, but don't you wonder sometimes?" She sighs, thinking of how to phrase her next sentence. "I mean, they hope we won't react. And if we do, they make it seem as if we're crazy. About a year ago, when we were driving home from New York, we stopped at a Dunkin Donuts for coffee. I told Adam to go through the drive-through, but he insisted on going in because he wanted to stretch. I waited in the car, my thoughts reeling. Was he looking at porn on his phone, calling someone? He came back out a few minutes later, looking happy and . . . I don't know, content. I felt stupid and paranoid for thinking anything bad. But we're not paranoid, or over-reacting, or crazy. It's sane and normal to be suspicious in our positions." She hadn't expected to make a speech, but Hannah doesn't want Lizzy to think that where Gail is is necessarily the right place to be.

"It is important to listen to your feelings," Kathryn says.

"What I meant to say was that I have detached," Gail clarifies. "I know I have to take care of myself. I can't fix Jonah. I never could. If he is acting out, there is nothing I can do, so why make myself crazy over it?"

"I am not sure I understand this word *detach*," Flavia says. "I cannot see how it can be done if you are in a marriage."

"I think in this case, detaching is not obsessing about your partner's behavior, which can allow you to look at your own situation more objectively," Kathryn explains.

"The key is," Gail begins, "you have to put yourself first. You can't waste all your energy worrying about them."

"I too want to take care of myself, but can I do both?" Flavia asks, confused. "Can I be good to myself and also worry what Dema is doing? I would like to help him."

"I'm not saying I don't want to help Jonah. I want that more than anything. I just believe that the best help we can give is to let the person go. To trust that they will come to you when they need to. If Jonah is engaging in any addictive behavior, I believe he'll seek guidance. If he doesn't, he's just going to lie anyway, so what can I really do? Nag?"

"I do that," Lizzy says. "I badger. Greg tells me I do. I'm always harping on him about why he doesn't want to have sex with me. Sometimes I bring it up when it's not even what I want at that moment."

"I don't like that he tells you that you badger him," Bridget says. "And I don't like that you agree with him. Your husband is supposed to have sex with you, if that's what you want. And you should tell him that it isn't badgering, or nagging, or any other shit like that." She holds her head up.

"But," Gail says.

"You're not going to disagree with me on this one too?"

"Not exactly. But there is another side. Say someone is recovering from heart surgery. They may not be ready to have sex yet."

"Except he didn't have heart surgery. Last week it was Alzheimer's. I get that sex addiction is supposed to be a disease, but really it just doesn't compare to those."

"The point is, he may need time to recover," Gail says.

"Or he's still lying his ass off."

"That's not for you to surmise," Gail says.

"Someone has to say it," Bridget tells her, then turns to Lizzy. "Sorry, I didn't mean that to be mean to you."

"I shouldn't trust him," Lizzy says.

Kathryn turns toward the couch. "It's hard to find trust again when you've been betrayed. It can take a long time and a lot of very small steps."

Flavia raises a hand and looks at Lizzy. "I think you are brave. First to ask for what it is you want. And now to try to give him space. But you must not let him make you think you are the badger."

"Thanks," Lizzy says.

"I think I hate that the most." The sentence flies out of Hannah's mouth. She glances around, suddenly aware she began something she does not want to finish. It was one thing to talk about an inconsequential incident that happened over a year ago. It is an entirely different matter to have blurted out something that refers to her present life.

Everyone is quiet, waiting.

"What I meant was, I hate when I look like the bad one." She picks up her purse and places it on her lap.

"Why would you ever look like the bad one?" Bridget asks.

Hannah pretends to look for something. She pulls out a Chapstick and opens it, but doesn't put any on. "My daughter, Alicia, is acting out at school. I think it's because she feels the friction between Adam and me. I know she believes it's my fault and her father can do no wrong."

"Is there some way you can make her understand that you haven't done anything to cause the problems in your marriage?" Kathryn asks.

"She's only nine. Right now she trusts her father, and he's done nothing to hurt her. I can't take that away from her. She needs him." She puts the Chapstick back in her bag. Kathryn might have asked a good question, but parents should not dump their issues on their children.

"But he has hurt her," Bridget says. "By hurting you."

"Most addictions affect the whole family," Kathryn adds.

Hannah grips the wooden chair seat. Her neck feels hot. She's dizzy. The thought of Alicia urinating on the floor keeps intruding. Her beautiful little girl, doing something like that.

"May I ask what happened in school?" Gail asks.

Heat rises from Hannah's neck to her cheeks. "She's been calling other kids names."

"Misplaced anger," Gail suggests.

"Probably." Hannah fiddles with her pearls. She's said more than enough.

"It could be worse," Bridget comforts.

Hannah looks at her red shoes and regrets that she told everyone to dress up. She should have kept her distance last week. Now here they are being so nice, and all she wants is to be left alone.

"I guess it could be," Hannah says, although she's not sure how.

"Can I ask," Flavia says softly, "what did your husband do?"

Hannah feels a hitch in her throat. She circles her hand in the air. "The usual sex addict stuff, you know, secrets and lies."

"Oh," Flavia says, as if that explains everything. "I am so sorry."

"It's all right. I mean, I'm all right. Someone else should go." The clock ticks. Kathryn would be wise to invest in one that isn't so grating.

"We're here for you too," Lizzy says.

"Thanks," Hannah replies. She is surprised to feel a tear on her cheek. Flavia hands her a tissue.

"These things can be difficult to talk about," Kathryn says.

Hannah nods amenably. If she were Bridget, she might say, *No shit.*

"Perhaps if you could talk about why it's so difficult to talk," Kathryn suggests.

"Yes," Hannah agrees, with no intention of doing such a thing. Kathryn is being pushy. Her youth is showing.

Bridget scuffs a foot on the carpet.

Lizzy tugs at a thread on the couch.

Flavia twists her hair.

The seconds tick loudly, endlessly, annoyingly.

"So," Bridget begins, "I told Michael I was pregnant."

Kathryn glances at Hannah, who looks at Bridget, making it clear that it's okay to move on. In fact, better that way.

Kathryn hesitates, then turns to Bridget. "And how did he take it?" she asks.

Hannah can breathe again. As Bridget describes her outing to the movies, Hannah hears fragments. *Popcorn. Asshole.* She thinks that marriage is a tangled, complicated mess of a thing. And if you get too entwined and enmeshed, how can you just detach?

"I sort of did something bad," Bridget says.

Hannah nods as if she's been paying attention all along.

Bridget continues, "I told him I was getting an abortion. I did it to hurt him and I regret it, but I haven't been able to tell him the truth yet."

"Why do you think you can't tell him?" Kathryn asks.

She exhales dramatically. "Because he'll make me feel like a five-year-old for lying."

"But he's lied to you," Lizzy says.

"Two wrongs don't make a right," Bridget tells her.

"True," Gail says. "But with this disease, you slowly learn that you both need to be vigorously honest. Tell him why you lied. Explain that you wanted to hurt him because of how hurt you've been. You knew it was wrong, but it's human."

Somewhere beneath all the noise in Hannah's head, she is grateful and surprised Gail has such compassion.

"He's still gonna be pissed."

"Feelings aren't always nice, pretty things," Gail tells her.

Hannah tries to focus on Bridget, but she's dizzy. She pictures Adam going into that Dunkin Donuts a year ago. She repressed her suspicions, told herself when he came out with an extra bounce in his step he was just glad to be with his family. He'd kissed her and told her she was beautiful, made her feel warm and full, and now she would bet he went in to copy phone numbers off a bathroom wall. He was giddy, high with the anticipation of his next encounter. Hardly the kind husband or good father he shows to the world.

"I'm sorry," Hannah says, and stands. "I'm not feeling so well." She grabs her purse and hurries to the bathroom. The floor tiles are old and cracked. She kneels and vomits in the toilet. When she's finished, she sits with her back against the wall and cries.

Not even a minute later, there's a knock.

"Hannah," Lizzy calls.

"I'm okay," she replies.

"Can I get you anything?"

"No. I'll just be a minute."

"Okay. But come get one of us if you need to."

When it's quiet again, Hannah closes her eyes. Her stomach feels raw. Her head aches. She sees bright spots. Slowly her heart begins to beat regularly and she feels as if she can stand. From the old porcelain sink, she splashes cold water on her face, then glances at her heavily made-up eyes. Alicia was right, she looks silly, like she's dressed up for Halloween. As much as she'd just like to walk out to her car, she can't. Bridget and Lizzy, the others too, might worry, and they certainly don't need any added anxiety in their lives.

She walks back in as Flavia is telling the group about the court date.

"Please, keep going," Hannah tells her as she takes her seat.

"We were concerned," Flavia says.

"I feel better. Really. Don't stop."

"We did what you told us to do," Flavia tells Gail. "He got probation. If they catch him again, he will be in bad trouble. But for now, I feel relief."

Hannah looks at the clock. Five more minutes. She can make it. But then she has to go home and face her life, and the thought of that makes her nauseated again.

"I want to close today by telling you all how impressed I am with your courage," Kathryn says.

Hannah certainly doesn't feel courageous.

"So, drinks at the bar around the corner?" Bridget asks.

Flavia nods.

"I'm afraid I have to work in the morning," Gail says.

"You didn't get that spicy new hairdo and wear that suit to sit in here. Come on. We're all going. Right?" Bridget asks.

"I think I need to go home," Hannah says.

Bridget pouts. "You have to come. You were the one who told us to dress up."

Maybe it will help. At the very least it will ensure that her family will be in bed by the time she gets home.

"You are our glue." Flavia's eyes plead.

"One," Hannah agrees.

"I suppose one wouldn't hurt," Gail adds.

As they say good night to Kathryn, Hannah thinks about glue, how she's always been that for her family. But lately she's curling at the edges, like cheap linoleum.

Hannah plans to have one drink before driving home, washing off her makeup, and getting into bed. With luck she'll find some TV show that will distract her for an hour or so.

At the small bar around the corner from the Victorian house, they sit at a veneered table next to a large window framed with fairy lights. The room glows dim amber. Gail orders a glass of merlot. Lizzy, Hannah, and Flavia decide on appletinis. Bridget has water.

When their drinks arrive, Lizzy raises her glass. "To us," she says.

Their glasses clink.

"To saner lives," Bridget toasts.

The alcohol goes straight to Hannah's head. The fairy lights blur, and she feels content for a moment. It's a relief to be here, with women who know the truth about her life, or at least a piece of the truth.

"Think Kathryn has a boyfriend?" Bridget asks.

"I don't think it's really any of our business," Gail answers.

Bridget laughs. "It's a free country. I can ask."

"And I can answer." For once Gail's smile is unguarded.

It's funny how they thrive on disagreeing. Hannah was sure they'd be enemies—at best tolerate each other. But in an odd way, they make a happy pair.

"I am sure she has a nice man." Flavia wipes a lipstick smudge from her glass. "She wouldn't make the mistakes that we do."

"Just because someone is a good therapist doesn't necessarily mean they know how to run their own lives," Gail says.

With half a drink in her, Hannah feels bold. "What kind of work do you do?" she asks Gail.

"I can't really say."

"Why?" Bridget asks.

"It's just one of those things I'd rather keep private. When people find out, they tend to treat me differently." She finishes her wine.

"Oh, you're afraid I might be nice," Bridget says.

Gail chuckles. "No, not really." The waitress comes to check on their drinks. "Another round for the table," Gail says.

Hannah is ready to protest, but she decides one more will be better than some stupid TV show.

"Does anyone think of divorce?" Flavia asks.

"How can we not think about it?" Hannah replies.

"I don't," Gail says.

"For real?" Bridget asks.

"You see, I was married before. To a nice man, but we didn't love each other. There was no joy between us. So what I meant to say is that I know what it feels like to want to get divorced, and that's not how I feel now. I love Jonah, and I'm willing to take this journey with him."

"I say we talk about anything except our husbands," Hannah suggests.

"I have something," Lizzy says, her words a touch slurry. "After the second group, I was going to quit. I didn't think I needed you guys. Not that I thought I was better than all of you, just that my problems weren't as bad. But I don't know what I would have done without you last week." Her deep brown eyes shine.

"It's no secret I didn't want to come back," Bridget says. "If it weren't for Hannah, I wouldn't have."

Hannah feels embarrassed but smiles anyway. "I didn't really do anything."

"Give yourself more credit. You're like the real therapist of our group," Bridget says.

Hannah rubs at a spot on the table. Not only is she not a therapist, she's a hypocrite. She tells these women to talk, to share, to be open, and there is no way she could really tell them the truth about herself.

"Change of topic," Bridget announces. "How many men, not including our present nitwits—and yes, Gail, I know Jonah isn't a nitwit—but really, how many men have you slept with?"

"Are we just counting having intercourse?" Flavia asks.

"Yeah."

"And why are we talking about this?" Gail sips her wine.

"'Cause we're out having drinks, and it's fun."

"I'm not sure I'd term it fun."

"Can you just answer without any judgmental commentary?" Bridget replies, a playful grin spreading.

"Seven," Gail says.

"You didn't even have to think about that."

"Why would I?"

"I dunno. I guess if I really sat down and counted, guys in college and before Michael, it would take a few minutes."

"Then why ask?"

"Like I said. For fun. Anyway, my guess is that I'd be around fifteen." Bridget looks around expectantly.

"I'm afraid mine is much higher," Flavia admits.

"Four," Lizzy announces. "Boring."

"Well, you beat me," Hannah says. "Three. Adam and I met in college, the summer of our junior year. We just hit it off."

"I met Dema at the restaurant his brother used to own. But that went kaput."

"What are you doing for work now?" Hannah asks.

"I am a hostess." She traces her finger along the edge of her glass. "I even try to do the phone sex. I think it was easy money, but I only last two calls. The second man, he was telling me something so . . ." She shudders. "It was disgusting. He say he imagine me sitting in a bathtub, and him peeing on me."

Hannah thinks of Alicia and her mood plummets. She'd like one hour, just one, in which she doesn't think of Adam, or the effects of addiction, or bathroom stalls.

"You know what I think," Flavia says. "Those men by the bar are looking at us."

"At you, maybe," Hannah tells her.

"No. The tall, dark one, he has his eye on you."

Hannah looks up. The man smiles. She glances away.

"I'm just happy to be away from Greg," Lizzy says. "I know I shouldn't want to punish him, but I hope he's worried I'm out meeting someone else. I hope that makes him jealous."

"He should be jealous," Hannah says.

"Totally," Bridget seconds.

Hannah slips out to go to the ladies' room. She keeps her gaze lowered.

"Hey," the dark-haired man says as she passes.

On her way back, she looks at him. Once again he smiles. He has dimples and kind eyes.

"Can I buy you a drink?" he asks.

She stops. "I'm already over my limit."

"And what's that?"

"I've had two." She feels herself flirting, tilting her head, swishing back her hair.

"Three will do you good." He touches her shoulder. She doesn't back away.

"I'm with my friends."

"How do you know each other?" he asks.

She chuckles. "Can't really say." She likes his baggy jeans and work boots. Mostly, she likes how easily he smiles.

"One of them just gave me a thumbs-up," he says.

"Is she wearing a peach-colored dress?"

"Yep."

"I should get back."

"I think they want you here."

"And why would you think that?" she asks, moving a little closer.

"Male intuition." He places a hand on the bar and slides it, almost imperceptibly, toward her. She thinks of pawns inching their way forward on a chessboard.

"Like that exists," she says.

"A man-hater, are you?" There's no meanness in his question. His blue-green eyes watch her.

"A *some* men–hater," she replies.

"Trouble?" he asks.

"I think I will have that third drink." Hannah sits on a barstool.

"Jake," he says, and shakes her hand, holding it for a few extra seconds.

Drink number three arrives. "Hannah," she tells him.

She sips her drink and glances at the front table. The lights are dancing, her friends are laughing, and she feels better than she's felt in ages.

"You from around here?" he asks.

"Sort of."

"Woman of mystery?"

"Naturally."

Jake tells her that he makes cabinets, he has two yellow Labs, and he saves up his money so he can travel to historic battlefields. He's a closet history addict. She flinches at the word *addict*, but lets it go as he keeps talking. She isn't sure who looked at the back door first, him or her.

"If we smoked, I'd say let's go out for a cigarette," he tells her, brushing his hand along her forearm.

"Shame we're so healthy these days," she replies.

"We could pretend." He touches her hair and nods toward the door.

She finishes her drink. They stand at the same time. He takes her hand, and they walk to the back of the bar. She wonders if Adam meets men this way.

Outside, they find a little alcove behind the building. His kisses taste like the ocean. Somewhere at the edges of her consciousness, under the alcohol, she knows she should stop.

He holds her face and looks at her. "You really are beautiful."

She believes that he thinks that. She's known him for less than half an hour, and she trusts him more than her own husband. He kisses her again. A breeze tickles her neck. She doesn't want this to end.

A car door slams, and the noise jolts her out of the moment.

"What is it?" Jake asks, cupping her chin.

She rests her head on his chest, which smells faintly of sawdust. If she could just do this, feel another body next to hers, that would be enough.

"What?" he asks again, gathering her hair.

"I'm sorry. I can't."

"It's okay. I don't want you to think I'm trying to take advantage because I pumped that third drink into you."

"It's not the drink. Although that helped."

"What, then?"

"I'm married."

He kisses the top of her head. "I sort of guessed that from the wedding ring."

"You didn't ask," she says.

"I figured you have your reasons."

She nods, keeping her head on his chest, wanting to be held for a few more seconds. There's a faint smell of spring in the air. Everything feels oddly familiar and comforting.

"And you love him?" he asks.

"I do," she says.

"Lucky guy."

"He's a sex addict," she blurts.

"Oh." He strokes her hair.

"Sorry, I shouldn't have dumped that on you. I don't know why I did. The drinks, I guess."

"So he cheated on you?"

"Yes. But it's not just that. He's an addict." She pauses. "And his drug of choice is other men." The words seem to echo against the night sky.

He holds her tighter. She feels like crying, letting it all out, the way she should in group.

"We could have fun together," he tells her. "It might be good for you."

"I can't." She puts her hands on his chest and gently pushes herself away. It's just not in her to cheat.

She turns to go back inside and sees Bridget waiting at the door.

"I was just coming to check on you," Bridget says. "We were getting worried."

Jake's hand touches the small of Hannah's back. His way of saying it's okay.

"Just getting some fresh air," Hannah says.

"You picked a good night." Bridget gives a tight smile and leads the way in. They follow. Jake whispers, "Take care," as he stops at the bar.

Hannah continues to the table. Lizzy's cheeks are rosy; her eyes twinkle as she giggles. Gail has gone home.

"We're talking about the first time we learned what sex was," Lizzy says.

Flavia grins and pats the chair for Hannah to sit. Guilt bleeds from her chest outward as she thinks of Alicia propped on a stool, glaring at her, accusing her of dressing up to look for a boyfriend. An hour ago, going home to a sleeping family seemed tolerable. Not anymore. Now she feels as if she's just a false reflection of all she pretends to be.

Gail

Gail adjusts the wire in the skin-toned bra that she's wearing underneath her flowing ivory negligee. There had been a time she'd considered getting a breast reduction, but she didn't want to take the chance of losing sensation in her nipples. She stares at her open book, *The Four Loves*, a gift from Jonah. But the words are just black scrawls clustered in random formations. All she can think about is the letter and how she's going to tell Jonah.

He was supposed to be home by ten, before her, but he works late sometimes, much more infrequently than in the past. He's likely grading papers or getting lost in the latest research. At one time she would have worried; now she's just anxious to get this letter ordeal behind them.

The front door opens. She smooths out the cover and props herself up a little more. Looking down at her chest, she makes sure her nightgown hides any signs that she's wearing a bra. She would hardly consider herself vain, but she also doesn't want him to see the extent of gravity's influence. Modesty and decorum are very different from dishonesty, she tells herself.

"I'm awake," she calls.

He doesn't reply. Probably didn't hear her, although she can hear him. He's puttering around, opening the fridge, turning on the tap, running the garbage disposal. She's never understood his need to switch on the disposal. It's something to do with cleansing, similar to his habit of clipping his nails every morning.

The door is ajar. He pushes it open and stands at the foot of the bed. "Didn't think you'd be up," he says. It's ten past eleven. She normally reads until eleven-thirty.

She holds her book for him to see. "I'm really enjoying this." It's a white lie, not the kind that counts. She wants to show him she appreciates his thoughtful gestures.

"It's been a long day." He sits on the edge of the bed, bends to untie his shoes, and sighs slowly.

"Is everything okay?" she asks.

"Yes, just long," he replies.

"Are you coming to bed?"

He stands and unbuttons his light green shirt. "In a while." He glances into his closet. "I still have some reading to do." His hands knot behind his back as if he's silently debating some philosophical dilemma. Maybe one of Kierkegaard's.

She'd like him to lie next to her so she can hold his hand, inhale his scent. He always laughs when she says that there is something chocolaty about the way he smells. He's told her that's not exactly manly. She wouldn't have it any other way.

"I meant to tell you the other day," she says in the most cavalier tone she can muster. Her voice falters slightly, betraying her, although he doesn't seem to notice. He hangs up his shirt, then unbuckles his belt. "I got another letter from April," she says quietly.

He pulls the belt through the belt loops and puts it on a hook on the closet door. If there was anything to be worried about, he would never be acting so serene.

"What did it say?" He drops his pants and steps out of them.

"The same—how you are in love with her, but you are afraid to tell me." She has full control of her voice now.

"What did you do with it?" he asks.

"I was going to shred it, but I think at this point, I might need to take some action. A harassment order."

He gives his pants a good shake, then slides them on a hanger. She looks at his slender white legs and feels self-conscious about her thighs.

"You think that's necessary?" he asks coolly. Although her back is sweating, she likes that he's unfazed by this.

"I'm not sure. But I do think that she should be sent a message to stop." She pauses. "As usual, there was no address or last name."

"Hmmm." He takes off his underwear, tosses it in the laundry basket, and puts on his pajamas. He has no problem undressing in front of her. Something she still can't do.

"Do you know where she's living now?" she asks. The wire in her bra digs into her chest.

"Actually, I believe she's back at Harvard."

The muscles around her heart clench. "Really?"

"Yes. I believe Lilly said something."

She imagines Lilly, the department secretary, gossiping, trying to get a rise out of Jonah.

"How would Lilly know?" she asks as if the subject is mundane.

"She just seems to hear about those sorts of things." He buttons his pajama shirt all the way up.

She remains expressionless. "Were you surprised when you learned of it?"

His eyes are direct, honest. "I didn't feel much. Just hoped that she was doing well."

"And is she?"

He puts on his slippers. "I really have no idea. I didn't ask."

His responses settle her. "So you haven't seen her?"

"No." He shakes his head and shrugs as if he didn't have to think twice about it.

"Perhaps if you tell me her last name, I can find her address and have a letter sent. Something to let her know she should stop."

"You think that's really necessary?" He just asked that question. She knows he's hoping for a different response.

Her nightgown, which has slipped between her legs, clings to her thighs. "I think it would be wise."

"It's been a long time since she sent that last letter, hasn't it?"

Is he defending April's behavior? "A few months."

"Maybe we should just let it be. No response sometimes sends a more powerful message." He stands in the open doorway. Not as if he's trying to flee, but rather get back to his studies.

She nods. "Yes, sometimes. But in this case I think a letter, something that looks official, might be best."

"If that's what you want," he says.

"If you just tell me her last name, I'll have Barbara find her address. She's a wonder at things like that. You don't have to get that for me."

He nods. "That would be better."

More proof that he's sober. He knows to stay away. "Thank you for being so understanding," she tells him. She wishes the group could have witnessed this interchange and seen that there isn't always a need to respond with anger and fear. Bridget especially might be able to learn something, and although they have their moments of discord, Gail envisions herself as a sort of mentor for the younger woman.

Jonah gives a diminutive, appreciative smile and rotates his shoulder, ready to head out. He's been so agreeable, so easy to talk to about this.

"Are you going to read?" she asks.

"I was. Just for a bit, if you don't mind."

She does mind. She minds that he's not coming to bed, that he didn't kiss her good night, that he hasn't provided a name.

"So what is her last name?" she asks.

"It's Russian. Difficult to spell. I'll write it for you and leave it on the kitchen counter."

"Thank you."

He's about to leave.

"Why didn't you tell me she was back?" She should have just let him go, but she couldn't.

"I simply forgot," he tells her.

"Oh," she replies, trying to mirror his ease. It's the first time tonight she's felt as if he wasn't being genuine.

He walks toward her, his head bent, his eyes shy, young almost. For a moment she reads his demeanor as guilty, but when he looks into her eyes, she tells herself she's overanalyzing. He leans to kiss her on the lips, and she is soothed.

Hannah

Monday morning, Hannah gets Sam off to school, then wakes Alicia. At nine-thirty, they take Adam's car to the family therapist that Hannah found.

Beth Healy's office is in a small brick building next to Newton-Wellesley Hospital. The three of them sit in the waiting room. Hannah keeps smiling at Alicia, who keeps looking away.

Then she takes count. There's her therapist, Adam's therapist, their couples' therapist, his sponsor, her group therapist, and now a family therapist, a school counselor, and she's pretty sure Alicia will have her own therapist soon. That's eight. A family of four with eight therapists. Hannah picks up a *Better Homes and Gardens* magazine. Adam and Alicia are playing some game on his phone, and she wants to whip the magazine across the room. The eight therapists are because of him—the wonderful, thoughtful father who's taken time to download games on his phone that his daughter finds amusing.

Beth Healy comes out at exactly ten and invites them in. She's wearing a well-fitted red suit with black pumps.

Adam and Alicia sit on the couch. Hannah chooses one of two armchairs. Tall windows make the room light, and a dollhouse in the corner catches Alicia's eye.

After the introductions, Beth explains that she will split the sessions up. First she wants to talk to Alicia alone, then to Hannah and Adam, and at the end they'll all meet together.

Hannah and Adam return to the waiting area.

Fifteen minutes later, Alicia emerges smiling.

"There are some books over there you might like." Beth points to a table in the corner. "Will you be all right?"

Alicia stands very straight. "Yes, thank you."

Hannah feels proud of her daughter as she walks into the office.

"There isn't a lot I can tell you from our first meeting," Beth says. "But I do think it's wise that you've chosen to seek help."

"And why is that?" Hannah asks.

"Alicia is a very bright child, which I'm sure you're both aware of." She looks at them and smiles. "No particular disorder jumps out at me, but I do think she's very angry, and she could use some coping skills to learn how to deal with the turmoil of emotions she's feeling."

"But you think she'll be okay?" Hannah asks.

Beth gives a thoughtful therapist nod, a gesture that has become all too familiar. "I think we have some work ahead of us." She takes a legal pad from her desk. "I did get a report from the school psychologist, but I'd like to hear from the two of you as to what you think is causing the anger."

"My husband and I are going through a rough spell."

She waits.

"I've been struggling with some addiction issues, and it's been very difficult on Hannah," Adam explains.

"I see," she says. "Can you talk a little bit more about what the issues are?"

He looks at a painting on the wall as if he's actually studying the artwork. "It stems from my own childhood," he says to the picture.

"Oh, for God's sake," Hannah interrupts. "He's a sex addict, and I caught him cheating again. We're going to therapy. We're trying, but it's been very tense at home."

"Alicia did mention she was worried you were going to get divorced. Is that something that you see happening?"

"No," Adam says.

"Not immediately." Hannah glances at the green carpet. "I mean, we're trying to make it work. It would be better for the children."

"It's not always best for the children to stay together if you're unhappy."

"I know," Hannah says. "We're not only doing it for them."

"You're both in therapy?" Beth asks.

"Yes," Adam says.

"And you feel it's helping?"

"Yes," he says again.

She waits for Hannah.

"I suppose."

"May I make an observation?" Beth asks.

"Sure," Hannah replies.

"You seem angry. Understandably, of course, but I'm wondering if the tension I'm feeling here is what Alicia's picking up on at home."

"Probably." Hannah regrets she snapped so quickly at Adam. "I try not to act angry in front of the kids."

"Alicia's a very sensitive child. I think it might actually be more frightening for her to feel you're pretending. Have you ever thought about allowing her to see some of your pain? I'm not suggesting you explain any details, but sometimes it's surprising how relieved children feel when they actually see their parents fight."

"We don't speak to each other in the house," Adam tells her.

"Not at all?" Beth asks.

"Just the pass-the-salt type of thing," he replies.

"We have dinner conversations," Hannah says.

"Only with the children. We don't actually speak to each other except in couples' therapy."

Beth jots a few notes. "And how long has this been going on?"

"Since I caught him fucking another man in a public bathroom."

"Hannah," Adam chides.

"So basically, what Adam is trying to tell you is that I'm a rigid bitch with a thousand and one rules. He's always cheerful, like nothing is wrong, and I have to constantly restrain myself from screaming and yelling and telling him how he's ruined my life. Yes, Alicia picks it up. She sees me get tense, and of course it looks like it's my fault, and he doesn't have the balls to explain to her that he's hurt me. That people can do that to each other, even mothers and fathers."

"You never told me you wanted me to say anything." He tilts his head, bewildered.

She throws up her hands. "Can you think for yourself? Perhaps you could do the right thing without being told."

"I'm not sure how to tell her," he says.

"I think that's something we can discuss in here," Beth interjects. "You might be able to start with something like Hannah suggested. Something to the effect that things are difficult between the two of you because you acted in ways that were hurtful."

"And what do I say when she asks what I did?"

Beth scribbles a few words on her legal pad. "You might explain it in terms she can relate to. Perhaps a friend of hers once lied to her or betrayed her in some way."

"And if she wants to know more?" he asks.

"You're the parent. You set the boundaries. You can say that she doesn't need to know all the details. That's not her business. What is her business is that she understands that she's not the cause of the problem, nor is she wrong for feeling things aren't okay."

"He doesn't understand boundaries," Hannah says.

"Damn it, Hannah. I know I'm not perfect, but I'm trying to do the right thing here."

She can't stand him. The way Alicia favors him. The way everyone thinks he's such a nice guy.

"I think it's been very helpful for me to see the dynamic between you.

You're in a very difficult situation, and we need to find the right words to help Alicia understand." Beth glances at her watch. "Would it be all right if I brought her in now?"

"Yes," they say in unison.

For the last ten minutes, Beth explains to Alicia that many, many parents fight, that it's very hard to understand, that it's not necessarily anyone's fault, least of all hers. Alicia soaks in her words, nodding at a rapid pace.

On the way home, Adam suggests they stop at Friendly's for ice cream. There he goes again, always the nice guy, the good dad. But when she glances over her shoulder and sees Alicia smile, she knows that she's going to have to bend a little more, not for his sake, or hers, but for her children.

SESSION FIVE

After last dress-up night, Hannah now finds herself contemplating what to wear to group. She doesn't kid herself though. She's dressing for Jake, not herself or the other women. Tonight she decides on a navy tank dress, a fitted jean jacket, and pearl stud earrings—a mix of sexy and traditional.

During group she listens as Flavia tells of having sex with other men, as Bridget talks about Michael and her preparations for a polygraph. She listens as Lizzy explains that school is her safe haven and Gail relays that Jonah was so unruffled about the letter from April, it's clear their marriage has overcome the biggest hurdles. Hannah feels obligated to say something about herself, so she tells them about the new family therapist and how she hopes it will help Alicia.

As the hour ticks away, she feels occasionally connected, but there are moments when the signal breaks, as if a synapse is missed, and panic floods in. To calm herself she thinks about how comforting an appletini will be.

The session comes to a close, and Kathryn thanks them all for coming.

At the bar, they sit around the same table as last week, and as soon as Hannah takes her first sip, she feels as if her nerve endings aren't quite so raw, as if she can finally think. Hannah notices that Lizzy closes her eyes for a second after she takes a drink and guesses she feels the same way.

"You look like you're in postcoital bliss," Bridget tells Lizzy.

She smiles. "The bliss part feels right."

"He still does not make love to you?" Flavia asks.

Lizzy shakes her head. "Not yet."

Gail sips her merlot. "What about trying to go away to a hotel?"

"I suggested that, but he sort of winced. I think that puts more pressure on him. It has to happen naturally, and until it does, I'm just going to enjoy other things in my life, like spending time with you all." She lifts her glass. Hannah joins in the toast and finishes her drink.

Bridget takes out a small notepad and a pen. "I've been thinking," she says.

Gail grins. "This should be good."

Bridget smiles wryly. "We're making a pact."

Hannah laughs. "I haven't done that since I was a Girl Scout." She glances around for their server.

Bridget rolls her eyes.

"Sorry," Hannah says. "I didn't mean to sound derogatory."

"Here's the deal." Bridget ignores Hannah. "No one is allowed to do anything rash, anything out of the ordinary, unless they call at least two other members of the group."

"And what does this *rash* mean?" Flavia asks.

"Well, it can mean different things for different people. But obviously something like jumping off a bridge applies to everyone. If you think you want to do that, you have to call two people."

"Okay, I will sign," Flavia says.

Gail places her hand in front of Bridget. "Have you been considering anything dangerous?" she asks.

"Suicide? Hell, no. Homicide? Hell, yes."

Gail lets out a breath. "You're sure?"

"Do I seem like the type to hurt myself?"

"I just needed to check," Gail tells her.

"So aside from killing oneself or one's spouse, what else?" Hannah asks. She signals the waitress to bring her another drink and looks for Jake.

"Doing something way out of the ordinary. Say Gail wants to hire a male hooker. That kind of thing," Bridget explains.

Gail laughs.

"Okay, like running away, or binge drinking, or shaving your head, or getting a tattoo on your neck. Things like that. Maybe slashing your husband's tires." Bridget pauses. "Actually, scratch that one. That's sane, not rash. But you get the idea."

"I think it's good." Gail rests her chin in her palm.

The waitress brings Hannah her drink.

"Other comments?" Bridget asks.

"I like it," Lizzy says.

Bridget rips off a few sheets from her notepad. "I'll pass around five pieces of paper. We each get everyone else's number. I know some of us already have them, but this makes it official."

Hannah writes down her cell and home numbers on one of the sheets, then sees Jake at the bar. She drinks her appletini as if it's water, hands the paper to Bridget, and slides out of her chair.

"Hey, you." He smiles as she approaches.

"How are you?" she asks.

"Can't complain. And you?"

She laughs. "I could complain, but I'm not going to."

"A drink?" He looks at her empty hands.

"Sure."

"You here with your friends again?"

"Yep," she says.

"You look like such an interesting group."

"How so?"

"In that none of you look the same. I mean, it's like you don't really go together. I don't mean it in a bad way. Just that lots of times when you see a group of women, they all kind of have on the same clothes, or they're around the same age, or . . ."

"Yeah, I get what you mean." The drink tastes fruity, as if it barely has any alcohol.

"You never did tell me how you all met," he says.

She watches his lips. God, she'd love to kiss him. Right here. Right now, in front of everyone. His cheeks are ruddy, and she brushes a finger along one of them.

The third drink goes down more quickly than the second. She orders another.

"Come meet them," she tells Jake.

On the way to the table, she sways a little and decides it's because the old wooden slats of the floor are uneven. She's not drunk. In fact, she feels refreshed and alive.

"Hey, everyone, I want you to meet my friend Jake." She grabs a chair from the neighboring table.

Flavia gives a sexy wave, Lizzy says a demure hello, Gail turns toward the wall, and Bridget glares at Hannah.

"Nice to meet you all," Jake says quietly, and drinks his beer.

"That's Gail." Hannah points. "Flavia." She moves her finger. "Lizzy and Bridget."

"Hi," Lizzy says again, more meekly.

Hannah slaps the table. "So what are we talking about?"

"Private stuff." Bridget narrows her eyes.

Jake pushes his chair back and picks up his beer. "Well, I have to go. I'll catch up with you later." He stands. "Take care of yourself."

Hannah waits until he's out of hearing range. "What's with the icy reception?"

"What the hell is with bringing someone over here?" Bridget asks.

"He's a friend." She finishes her drink. "Might be good to get a sane male perspective on things."

"He's not a friend. You met him at this bar last week, and we don't know the first thing about him."

Hannah shrugs and takes off her jacket. The fourth drink is working wonders. "He's nice."

"Does he know anything about us?" Gail asks.

"Of course not. You think I'm going to go blabbing that our husbands are a bunch of perverts?"

"Shush, not so loud," Bridget tells her.

"And please don't refer to our husbands that way." Gail uses a coaster to fan herself.

"Yeah, that was really uncool," Bridget says.

"You want a ride home?" Lizzy asks Hannah.

"Me?" Hannah shakes her head and grins. "I'm not ready to leave. And they are a bunch of perverts."

"Stop," Bridget warns.

"Or what?"

Lizzy stands. "Come on, let me give you a ride."

"No. I want to know what she's going to do to me if I keep talking." She stares at Bridget.

"I'm not here to fight. I just don't think it was cool that you brought someone to our table. What if he knew one of us?" Bridget asks.

"He doesn't." Hannah is ready for drink number five.

"He might start asking," Gail tells her. "He might start putting the pieces together."

"And then what? He'll call the newspapers? Don't you think you're all being a little overdramatic?" Hannah looks around for the waitress and notices Jake facing away from them. She embarrassed him. A wave of self-hatred grips her gut.

"You need to respect us." Bridget points emphatically to herself.

"Oh my God, like I don't? Are you kidding? And where is the waitress?" She turns her empty glass upside down.

"No more drinks." Lizzy touches Hannah's arm. "I'm going to take you home."

"I'm not leaving." She shakes her head again.

"Come on." Lizzy picks up Hannah's jacket.

"Go home with her," Bridget says.

"I think that's a wise idea," Gail adds.

Hannah stands. She likes how she feels, as if she's walking across one of those fake rickety bridges. When she gets to the door, she turns to catch a glimpse of Jake. He doesn't see her. Lizzy keeps hold of Hannah's arm. She doesn't need the support, but she doesn't mind it either.

In Lizzy's car, Hannah reclines the seat but immediately gets the spins.

"Shit." She sits up. "I think it was that fourth one." Hannah covers her mouth as she hiccups.

"I couldn't handle four."

"I used to be able to. But it's been a while. I've been so busy playing the good fucking mommy and wife that I forgot what fun it was to go out and get smashed."

"What's your address?" Lizzy asks, holding a GPS.

"Twenty-four Garden Gate Road, Wayland, Mass. 01778."

"You need a bottle of water or anything?"

"You know what?" Hannah begins. "You're too good for what's-his-face."

Lizzy smiles. "Greg."

"I bet Jake would be thrilled to have sex with you."

The GPS gives directions to get onto the highway. "I'm not really interested. But thanks, I guess."

Hannah's stomach feels like it's tumbling in a dryer. She takes a few deep breaths and tries to focus on the moon, which is a sliver short of full. "I don't feel too great," she finally says. "Think you could stop?"

"Do you want to wait for a McDonald's or something?"

Hannah covers her mouth and shakes her head. Lizzy pulls over.

Hannah opens the door and dives out. At least she manages to vomit in the grass and not on the pavement.

Lizzy rubs Hannah's back. "You going to be all right?"

"Unfortunately, yes." She stands straight, hating the aftertaste of alcohol, throw-up, and apple. "I can't believe I . . . fuck . . ."

"It's okay."

"God, I'm an ass." She looks up at the slate gray sky.

"Don't say that." Lizzy holds open the car door.

Hannah gets in and leans her head on the window. They drive for a while. Her throat doesn't burn as much, and she starts to feel much more sober than she ever intended.

"I'm sorry," she says. "I thought a few drinks could give me a reprieve."

"Please, it's fine. We all understand."

"Think they love us?" Hannah asks.

"Bridget and Gail?"

"No." She chuckles. "Our husbands."

"Someone once told me that love is an action verb." Lizzy takes the exit.

"What kind of action is Greg taking?" Hannah asks.

"Um . . ." Lizzy turns onto Hannah's street. "I guess he's been going to the twelve-step groups and therapy."

"Right. But has he done anything for you?"

"I suppose. He's trying to get better."

"That's for him."

"And for us." Lizzy slows the car to a stop in front of Hannah's house. The front porch light is on. "What about you?" she asks.

"Adam tries, but I won't let him do much. If he brought home flowers, I'd throw them away, and I'm not ready to actually do anything fun with him. It wouldn't be fun. I'm still too angry." Hannah opens the door and puts one foot on the street, then turns back to Lizzy. "Don't settle," she says.

The house is quiet. Hannah grabs two water bottles from the fridge and goes to her room. She sits on the edge of the bed and feels as if someone is pounding a hammer on her temples. Her eyes are dry, her throat is still sore, her stomach acidic. What an idiot, to go out drinking like she's seventeen, as if that would ever help her or her family. One addict is enough. It occurs to her that if she had to come up with a word that was the antonym of *love*, it would be *addiction*.

Lizzy

Lizzy gets back on the highway. She's not settling. She doesn't have to stay with Greg. She makes enough money—just—to live on her own. Her life would be full without him. It's not as if she needs a man. She happens to like Greg. Love him, actually. Really, she does. She wouldn't stay if she didn't. Right? Of course not. The question is, does he love her?

By the time she pulls into her driveway and gets out of the car, she fully intends to wake Greg and get an answer.

In the bedroom, she switches on the overhead light. Greg groans, pulls the comforter over his head, and turns toward the wall.

Lizzy sits on her side of the bed. "Can we talk?" she asks.

He rolls on his back and covers his eyes with his forearm. "What's up?" He sounds resigned, as if he's doing her some huge favor.

"Why do you stay with me?"

"Aw, Liz. Not now."

"It's important to me," she says.

He exhales. "You always come back from your group like this. Get some sleep; we can talk tomorrow."

Blue veins streak the underside of his arm. "I always come back like what?"

"Like . . . wound sort of tight."

"You're right, I do. Isn't that the point of the groups? To listen to others? To learn? Isn't that why you go to yours?"

He yawns. "Yeah. I learn. I like to listen. But I don't leave with questions."

"Why not? I mean, I would think when you listen to other people and what's going on in their relationships, it would bring up questions about ours."

"Well, it doesn't," he tells her, irritated.

"I don't get that."

"Look, Liz, we're different. That's all. I get different things from my groups." He rubs his eyes. "Can we talk about this some other time?"

"I just have one question," she says.

"Fine. One."

"Why do you stay with me?" She tosses her earrings from one hand to the other. He's right, she's tense, very tense, and he could make it better. All he'd have to do is reach over, touch her, tell her he stays because he loves her.

"We work well together." His voice is weary.

"What does that mean exactly?" she asks.

He moves his arm away from his face and slaps the mattress. "Liz, come on. It's past midnight. I answered your one question."

"Just tell me what it means. That we work well together."

"We enjoy each other's company."

"Like you're enjoying mine now?"

He sighs. "Look, we go out to dinner and have fun sometimes. That's all I'm saying. Now can I please go to sleep?"

The hook snaps off her earring and little black beads race along the floor. It's a cheap piece of jewelry, easily replaceable, yet she begins to cry. Greg doesn't seem to notice that she's broken her earring, that she's in tears, that his answer was woefully inadequate. She can't have lived eighteen years with this man and settled for a few fun dinners.

"Are the women you watch prettier than me?" It's a childish question, but she doesn't retract it. Instead she bends down, grinding a bead with her thumb into the floor.

"Not all," he mumbles.

"Not all?" she asks.

"What do you want me to say? Just tell me, because whatever I answer isn't going to be right for you."

It's true, it seems as if his answers are never what she wants to hear. She leaves the broken earring and curls on top of the comforter. "You know how when you love someone, you think they're beautiful because you love them?"

"Jesus, Lizzy, please, can we go to sleep?"

"Do you think I'm beautiful?"

He slaps the mattress again. "Yes, I've felt that."

"But you've never told me."

"Correct," he states.

"And you can't tell me now?"

"Correct."

"But you have felt it?" she asks.

"Yes." Another exasperated sigh.

"And you say that you're becoming more open and honest from your groups?"

He shoves down the covers and swings his legs out of bed. His feet smack the floor.

"So you're just going to leave?" she asks.

"I need to use the bathroom. Is that all right with you?" He sounds nasal and defensive.

As she watches him stomp away, she looks at his slender hips and imagines him jerking off. She shudders, then stands to unwrap her scarf and is hanging it on her closet door when he comes back in.

"So why aren't you interested in me?" she asks.

"It's not about you," he yells.

"Of course not. It's about you, and you . . ." She pokes a finger at his chest. "You, you, you."

He slaps her hand away.

She swats at him.

He grabs her wrist. "Stop it," he tells her.

She shoves him with her free hand. He shoves back. She stumbles, almost falls, but regains her footing. She pushes him again. He thrusts the heel of his hand into her chest. Her head jerks back and hits the framed painting on the wall. She hears a crack.

The picture tumbles, and the glass shatters. Her hands flap idiotically, frantically. There's a pinch at the back of her head. She reaches to massage it and feels something sharp. She tugs it out, then stares at the red stains, the color of strawberries.

"Lizzy, are you all right?" He glances at her hand, at the piece of glass. She doesn't know. She feels okay, just a little off-center. Her hand grazes the back of her head. It's wet and sticky.

"Let me see," Greg says. But he doesn't look because the sight of blood makes him nauseated. She wonders if she's going to have to watch another person vomit tonight.

"I'll just get a washcloth," she tells him. But when she takes a step she gets dizzy, and the door looks as if it's turning. She steadies herself by putting a hand on the dresser; then she sits, slowly. Between a few pieces of glass are two black beads from her earrings. She thinks of collages and ice chips, of how her floor looks like a piece of art, and how in her pocket are the numbers of the women in her group. Is this the kind of situation in which she should call two other people?

Lizzy squints, narrowing her vision, focusing only on the glass and beads.

"I'm taking you to the hospital," Greg says.

She puts her head between her knees and breathes. He sits next to her and caresses her back. She closes her eyes, comforted by his touch, happy he is taking action.

Bridget

She's read that pregnancy can increase body temperature. Hers feels like it's gone up ten degrees. Bridget fans herself with one hand as she scans her closet and decides on a pink summer dress, something innocent and light.

She checks her profile and rubs her stretching belly. She used to think that pregnant women who caressed their stomachs were just seeking attention, but now she believes it's one of those instinctual things, sort of like monogamy, that's good for the baby and the family. Although Michael sure as hell didn't get the fidelity gene.

Most of the red dye in her hair has washed out. She's back to black. Her combat boots clash with the pink dress, but she likes the look.

Today is their second meeting with Joe Ramirez, the man who will be conducting the polygraph, an ex–FBI agent. He looks like he's around her father's age, and the first time she met him, she had a fantasy about him beating the shit out of Michael. Lately, she finds herself constantly daydreaming. Sometimes it's about the baby, about how the three of them will be a happy family. Sometimes it's about her kicking Michael out, and him begging her to let him stay. She imagines moving to New Hampshire, buying a small piece of land where she'll keep goats and chickens. Five minutes later, she's picturing herself in Hawaii, living on a beach. One second she sees herself engulfed in Michael's arms, the next second she's dumping his stuff on the street.

"You ready?" Michael calls from downstairs.

She glances at herself again, crunches her wavy hair, and thinks she'll never be ready. Not for this. But she's not about to back out either.

They take his truck, which has been baking in the sun. As she puts her feet on the dashboard, her dress slips down so that her legs are almost entirely exposed. He tries not to stare, but he can't help it. Although she'd never admit it to him, she'd wouldn't mind if he found some deserted street where they could have sex.

She takes a few papers out of her purse, leans her head back in a provocative pose, and fans herself. He takes the bait and slips a hand down the front of her dress.

She closes her eyes and moans softly.

"You are one sweet thing," he says, keeping one hand on the wheel, and one on her.

Her feet, still resting on the dashboard, move apart slightly, just enough to show him what she wants.

"I know someplace we can stop," he says.

"On the way home," she replies. It will be a reward for getting through their appointment. Yes, she said she would never have sex with him again, but what the hell? He's willing to take a lie detector test. That should say something good about their marriage.

She opens her eyes, unfolds the paper in her hands, and tries to act like he's not making her hot. Then she reads the questions that she's written for their session today. She's no longer in the mood. She pushes his hand away and drops her legs.

Before the actual polygraph, they have to meet with Mr. Ramirez three times to talk about the procedure. It's nothing like what they show on TV. There isn't a list of fifty questions. No surprise attacks. You get one topic to focus on, and the questions need to be worded in a way that the answers all converge and address the major issue. At first Bridget thought it was crap that Michael got to review the questions. That way he could prepare—practice keeping his heart rate down and his breathing calm—but Mr. Ramirez assured her that's not the way it worked.

"So, want to know what my first question is?" she asks.

"Joe said we're supposed to wait until we're with him." Now he has both hands on the steering wheel and is watching the road, as if he can't be distracted when he's driving, which is such bullshit. He's just avoiding the subject.

She reads from her paper. "Since our marriage date, August 12, 2007, have you had sexual intercourse with more women than the two you've told me about?"

"Bridge, I'm not answering until we get there."

"What the fuck difference will it make if you tell me now or when we're in his office?"

He slows for a light. "How the hell do I know? But what if it does? What if I answer now and somehow that affects the results and makes me look like a liar when I'm not?"

She sticks her hand out the window, hoping for a breeze. There is none.

"But you are a liar."

"Look, say what you want to me now, if it makes you feel better. But I'm not answering any of the questions until we get to the office."

The light turns green. The tires screech, and she stuffs the papers back in her purse.

Ramirez's office is a bland beige. She smiles, trying to show him that she's ready for this, and she can deal with whatever she might learn. Once again, he spends fifteen minutes explaining how to word questions, how long the test will take, and how important it is that they both have contingency plans if the results don't come out as they expect. Finally he asks her for the list of questions she's prepared for today. He puts on a pair of wire-framed glasses and nods as he reads. His hair is glossy black, probably from some gel people used to use in the eighties. It's his eyes that convinced her to return. They're reliable.

"Okay," he says. "We still need to narrow this down. It seems unclear to me, Bridget, if you want to know if Michael has had intercourse with other women during your marriage, or if he has feelings for any of those women."

"I guess I want to know if he has feelings for them," she says.

Michael shakes his head. "I've told you I don't. Plus, Joe has explained you can't have such open-ended questions. I mean, of course I have feelings."

"You make no sense." She leans forward, wanting to get in his face. "You just said you don't, and then you said you do. Which is it?"

He sits back. "I don't have loving feelings. But I'm not a robot. So I have some feelings."

Ramirez coughs. If he didn't have black hair, he might blend in with the decor. His pants and shirt are also beige. "Michael, you bring up a good point. Asking about feelings can be vague." He looks at Bridget. "You may want to think about wording the question something like, Has Michael ever told any of the women that he loved them during the period in which you two were married?"

"That's too specific," she says. He may have told them lots of other things that imply love, or lust or like. "Does he still think about having sex with them?"

"That's also a little tricky. It's better to stick with concrete actions."

She looks at Michael. "Do you still think about having sex with Vivian?"

"No."

"Never?" she asks.

"No, never."

"I don't believe you."

"That's why we're here," Michael says.

"Right," she tells Ramirez. "So I guess I'm just going to stick with the questions about whether he had sex with more women than he told me."

"All right." He jots a few notes. "So, Michael, are you comfortable with my asking you if you have had intercourse with more women than the two you have told Bridget about?"

He scratches his head.

"It's not a difficult question," Bridget says.

He crosses his legs, then uncrosses them. "It's just that I can't remember all the time, and I'm worried if I say I can't remember, it will come out like I'm lying."

"If you really can't remember and that's the truth, the test will validate that," Ramirez says.

Bridget grips the arms of the chair. "How can you not remember?"

"Maybe I was drinking."

She looks at Ramirez, who's watching her like she's some sort of porcelain doll. She's not going to fucking break. She just wants the truth. "So if he can't remember because he was drinking, then how do you ask?"

"It's something we have to consider. I don't know how much Michael drinks, but do you want your focus to be on that?"

"No," she answers without hesitation.

"All right, so I think we should stick to asking if he's had intercourse more times than he's told you. Remember, this is only the first polygraph. We can focus on other issues in later sessions."

"No fucking way," Michael says. "I said I'd do one. What's this about more?"

"The literature I gave you strongly suggests sex addicts have a polygraph once every three months. I have clients who do it for themselves, not for their partners. It actually helps them stay sober. You can think of it like someone who has a weight problem needing to stand on the scale to remind themselves of their goal."

"He didn't read any of the pamphlets you gave us," Bridget tells Ramirez.

"I didn't have time," Michael says, glancing away.

"But you have time to play the guitar and watch baseball."

"Maybe you both need more time to think about this," Ramirez suggests.

"He's just trying to get out of it. I knew he would," Bridget says.

"I wouldn't be here if I was just trying to get out of it. I'm doing it for you." He's about to comb his fingers through his hair but stops himself. She's told him it makes him look nervous. "For us," he says.

She crosses her arms. "Fine. Then we'll just stick to the question about whether you had sex with more people than you've told me."

His work boot taps the floor. "Um . . ." He runs his hand through his hair.

She feels like her heart is a pebble thrashing around in a tin can.

"There have been, haven't there?" she asks.

"I swear I didn't remember it until we got here. I guess I sort of put it out of my head. Is that something people do?" he asks Ramirez.

"It happens, yes. There are people who compartmentalize, and until they are forced to confront certain events, they are capable of forgetting. We normally see this sort of thing with post-traumatic stress disorder." He brings his pencil to his mouth. "With dissociative disorders too."

She wants out of this beige nightmare. Her heart hurts. She really thought this whole polygraph thing was going to help, to prove to her there weren't more lies. She's been so fucking delusional.

"Bridget," Ramirez says, "you look pale. Are you sure you're all right?"

He sounds so far away. The pebble is thrashing. She wants to go back to that hotel on Huntington Ave and turn the air conditioner on high until the only thing she can feel is cold.

"I want to know if he ever brought any of the women flowers," she finally says.

Ramirez writes that down. "That's certainly something we can find out. May I ask why that might be important?"

"It would tell me if he cares about them. If he brings them flowers, then he does have feelings."

But she knows, as soon as she's spoken, that it's stupid what she's asking. Stupid and pointless. She told herself she'd leave him if there were more lies, and now she's sitting here in her pink summer dress knowing full well there were more, and she's still contemplating a way to rationalize staying with him. If he didn't bring them flowers, if it was really all about the chase, and the conquest, and not about love or caring, then maybe . . . But—no.

She can't. She can't take it anymore. She gets up and walks out, right to the parking lot. Heat radiates from the blacktop. The afternoon light is unforgiving.

Neither of them says a word on the ride home. Michael parks the truck in front of the house. Bridget hops out and hurries to her car in the driveway. No way can she be with him. He holds up his hand for her to stop and talk. *Now? Now, fuckhead, you want to talk?* She gives him the finger, backs out, and drives to the hotel on Huntington Ave.

At reception, she asks for a room on the first floor.

"I have two-thirty-four," the woman says.

"Is that the first floor?" Bridget asks.

"Yes, it is, ma'am."

That someone just called her ma'am and that a first-floor room is in the two hundreds is just the cherry on top of this day.

Bridget crashes onto the bed, yanks a pillow from under the cover, puts it over her face, and screams at the top of her lungs. When she's done, her stomach feels like it has butterflies, but she's not nervous and she doesn't feel sick, even if she should after all the crap that happened today. She places a hand on her belly. It's there again, the gentle flutter— the baby moving.

SESSION SIX

❦

Hannah's bed is strewn with clothes. In the end, she decides on a plain white sleeveless linen blouse, jeans, and gold hoop earrings, a simple, nonthreatening, blend-in-with-the-wallpaper outfit. She has to apologize to the group for her behavior at the bar last week. As soon as she's done that, she plans to sit quietly for the rest of the session. She recalls her first week of group, how she didn't want to get out of the car, how her instincts told her, *don't go*. She should have listened.

Adam and the kids are watching TV in the den. She pokes her head in. "See you later," she tells them.

"You haven't left yet?" Adam asks.

She refrains from saying anything snide in front of Alicia. "Leaving now." She waves good-bye.

She wants to be late. She wants them to be immersed in someone else's problem and not even notice her. Surprisingly, she's not the last to arrive. Flavia isn't here.

Hannah sits on the wooden chair and folds her hands in her lap. Bridget avoids eye contact. No surprise there. Gail has the beginnings of a scowl. No surprise there either.

"Gail," Kathryn says, "is there anything else you'd like to tell us?"

She turns to Hannah. "I was talking about a trip to Ireland that Jonah and I have decided to take. It wasn't that important. What I'd really like to talk about is boundaries."

Hannah's face heats. "I'm sorry about last week. I shouldn't have brought Jake over."

"Maybe you shouldn't have had so much to drink," Gail tells her.

She's right, of course. Still the scolding stings. "I'm sorry."

"Are you worried about how much you've been drinking?" Kathryn asks.

"No. It's only when we went out after group that I drank, and I'm not doing that again," Hannah explains.

"You have the right to tell him anything you want about your life," Gail says. "But I don't want him connecting the dots and figuring out anything about my situation."

"Really," Hannah says, "I get it. I know I was wrong."

Gail takes a deep breath. The buttons on her blouse strain. "We understand why you did it. We only need to make sure it doesn't happen again."

"As I said, I won't be going again."

"No harm done," Lizzy says. "Please come out with us, though."

"Thanks. But I just don't think it's a good idea. Not for a little while at least."

"Probably," Bridget mumbles. "Not like you really liked us anyway."

Hannah looks straight ahead at the cream-colored wall. She's done what she came to do. There's nothing left to say. She had too much to drink. She acted like a jerk. If Bridget needs to interpret that as dislike, Hannah isn't going to argue.

"Are you okay?" Kathryn asks.

Hannah feels irritated. Her hands, still in her lap, clench more tightly. "Yes. I'm sorry I made a mistake and violated boundaries."

"What I'm trying to get at"—Kathryn leans forward—"is why you would have too many drinks in the first place. That is often a sign that you're trying to avoid something."

"You think?" Hannah says. Kathryn seems unflustered by the sarcastic remark.

"Yes, I do think that."

"I'm always trying to avoid my life. As in right now. I only came to say I'm sorry. I really have nothing else to talk about."

"Really? Nothing?" Bridget asks.

"Not that I can think of," Hannah replies with a nonchalance she doesn't feel.

Bridget kicks off her flip-flops. One of them bounces on the carpet. "I don't think she trusts us. It's like she can't talk to us. About the real stuff," she tells Kathryn.

Hannah shakes her head. "I talk to you."

"You don't. Not really. The rest of us, we open up in here. We put our pain on the line."

Bridget's right. Hannah is a coward. But she isn't about to let them see that. She sits taller. "I'm sorry if it's not enough for you. It's the best I can do." She glances around the room. The only one who meets her gaze is Kathryn.

"I have wondered," Gail says, looking at a painting, "why you haven't told us about your situation."

"It's private." Hannah crosses her arms in front of her, then realizes that makes her look more defensive. She drops them to her sides.

"I think we're touching on some very important issues here," Kathryn says. "These addictions involve all sorts of secrets and lies, and they have a ripple effect, impacting many different relationships."

"You know the old saying," Gail comments. "You're as sick as your secrets."

If she is trying to tell Hannah she's sick for not talking about her husband's transgressions, then so be it. Hannah nods politely in Gail's direction, then faces Kathryn.

"The thing is," Bridget says, "you can tell that douche bag Jake about your life, but you can't tell us. How do you think that makes us feel?"

"I have no idea what you're talking about." But then she remembers something—how that night she kissed Jake behind the bar she smelled something soft, like spring, but it wasn't that at all, it was Bridget's perfume. She'd been standing outside longer than Hannah had realized.

"You told him your husband was a sex addict," Bridget says.

Kathryn adjusts herself in her chair so that she's facing the exact midpoint of the circle, favoring no one. "I think it's important to understand that everyone is going to share their stories in different ways to different people."

"It's about trust." Bridget picks up one of her flip-flops and bends it. "It's like she doesn't trust us."

"I'm sorry you feel that way." Hannah knows she sounds aloof, protective, but it's only because she feels as if she's going to burst into tears, and she doesn't want to do that.

"We understand how hard it is," Gail says. "We all grapple with the shame and humiliation."

"I get it." Hannah holds up a hand. "I know you're all here to listen. I just don't have much to say right now."

"I think it's important that you know we aren't going to judge you or your husband." Gail speaks softly.

Hannah's skin blisters. "I get it. Can we move on? Please."

"We know about Adam." Gail extends her arm as if she's reaching out to Hannah. "It's okay," she says.

Hannah feels ill. She glares at Bridget. "I understand that you might have overheard something you shouldn't have. But how dare you tell anyone."

"I didn't know what to do with the information. I wasn't gossiping, if that's what you think. Plus, Gail can be trusted. She'll take our secrets to the fucking grave," Bridget says.

Gail places a hand on her chest. "She's right. I wouldn't tell a soul."

"That's not the point." It feels as if hot lava is roiling under Hannah's skin.

"Can you talk about what you feel the point is?" Kathryn asks.

"My situation isn't up for public discussion."

"Perhaps you can talk about why it's so hard for you to talk about your situation," Kathryn suggests.

Hannah can feel all eyes on her. Kathryn is only being a good therapist, yet Hannah feels exposed and enraged.

"It just feels private."

Bridget picks up her other flip-flop. "Then why come to this group in the first place? I mean, the point is that we're supposed to talk about our lives, not keep everything all bottled up. Maybe someone else would make use of your spot."

"I've thought about that. And I agree. When I began this group, my intentions were to share. But in the past few weeks, I've learned that I'm not comfortable doing that. I'd gladly give my place to someone who might make better use of it."

"I think it might be very helpful for you to work through this." Kathryn's voice is gentle.

For Kathryn's sake, Hannah would like to oblige, but for her own sake, she can't. "I don't agree."

"It's hard," Kathryn says, "that people might know more than you wanted them to know. It can feel as if you have lost control."

Hannah nods. "All I know right now is that I'm not ready to disclose everything. I'm sorry if I upset anyone. That was never my intention."

"You push people away." Bridget stretches out her arm and makes a halting gesture. "I know you can be warm and caring, but just so you know, you push people away."

Hannah's eyes fill. Bridget is right. She is doing that, and she can't stop herself, and she doesn't know why. What she does know is that if they keep going, if they keep picking at her, she's either going to start screaming for them to shut up or she's going to throw up.

"Can someone else please talk?" Hannah asks. The words come out squeaky.

"I'll go," Lizzy volunteers. "Last week, after group, Greg and I had a huge fight. I ended up kind of hitting him, and he shoved back. I banged my head and had to get a couple of stitches."

"If he laid a hand on you, that's abuse," Bridget says.

"I started it."

"That doesn't matter," Gail interjects.

"I know, but it ended up being sort of good. We actually held hands and laughed at the hospital."

"It doesn't seem as if it's something to laugh about," Kathryn says, alternating her gaze between Lizzy and Hannah.

"I know it doesn't sound that way. But you know the kind of laughing that you do to release tension? It was like that. We enjoyed each other's company. And it wasn't a bad cut."

"You might be minimizing," Gail says. "What was the fight about?"

Lizzy waves a hand. "It was stupid. About him not making me feel loved."

"How is that stupid?" Bridget asks.

"It was late. I was haranguing him with questions."

"And you don't feel like he abused you?" Kathryn asks.

"Definitely not. If anything, it was me. I was the one who wanted to get into it, physically. It was pent-up rage."

"That's how I felt at the polygraph place. Michael didn't even pass the fucking pre-test. He admitted to more lies. More women. And I wanted to kick the shit out of him. I couldn't be with him. I went back to that hotel on Huntington. I stayed there for three days until I couldn't afford it anymore."

"And now?" Gail asks.

"We're in the same house. Hardly together, though."

Hannah squeezes her hands. She feels the rage too, only not at her husband. "I can't take this," she says. "I can't sit here and listen to what they do to you." She looks at Lizzy. "Maybe you had a happy moment with Greg, but he treats you like shit. Over and over, and you let him. He gives you nothing. You're a beautiful, talented woman. You deserve more."

"Hold on," Bridget says.

"No, you hold on. Michael is just going to keep lying. He'll find a way out of the next polygraph too, and even if he takes one and fails, he'll figure out how to make you stay with him." She faces Gail. "I don't know about your husband. I hope to God it's what you think. But the fact that you just got another letter from his girlfriend doesn't exactly promote confidence."

Gail points her chin forward. "She was never a girlfriend. I think you're projecting right now, and this isn't about us, but about you."

"Here's what I do know. Five percent." Hannah holds up her hand. "Five. That's it. Five percent actually get rehabilitated. That leaves ninety-five percent who don't. There are five of us in this group and if one of our husbands actually does get better, that's twenty percent. That's—"

"We're not imbeciles," Bridget says. "We get the math."

"It's just that we can't keep fooling ourselves. No offense to you, Kathryn, but it's not like this group is going to cure our husbands."

"I don't think that's why we're here," Lizzy says. "I think we know the statistics. But we still have hope."

"Yeah, we have hope," Bridget chimes in.

"Really, hope? You know who else had hope? Concentration camp victims. The Nazis used to drive them to mud fields. They'd dump them off and tell them whoever found a four-leaf clover would be saved. They dug until their fingers bled. That's where hope gets you."

"Maybe we have reasons to believe there is something in the mud," Bridget says. "Maybe you're the one fooling yourself. Maybe you don't talk about any of this shit because you don't want to face the fact that your husband is gay."

The air withers. Everything stops. Time, movement, voices.

"I'm sorry," Bridget mumbles. "I didn't mean for that to come out."

Hannah stands and walks to the door. "I don't think my being here is helping anyone." But just as she's about to leave, Flavia bursts in.

She holds the hand of a man with olive-colored skin, thick, wavy black hair, and a five-o'clock shadow. "I am so sorry to interrupt," she says. "I knock, but no one seems to hear."

Hannah takes a step back. Flavia is radiant in a white sundress with her hair French-braided so that it looks like a crown.

"Flavia." Kathryn stands. "Perhaps your friend could just sit in the waiting area for a few minutes."

"Of course. This is my husband, Dema." Flavia kisses his cheek. He beams. She says something in Greek, then rubs the small of his back. It's clear he doesn't want to be separated from her, even for a minute, but he does what she asks of him and leaves the room.

The moment the door is closed, Hannah turns to Flavia. "You look amazing, and it's nice to see you, but I can't stay."

"I would like it if you could bear with us for a few more minutes," Kathryn tells Hannah.

"If Flavia wants to tell us something, I'll listen," Hannah says.

"I have come to thank all of you. And to tell you that we have made a decision." Flavia smiles. "Dema and I, we have talked for many hours and in conclusion have decided to move back to Greece."

"Whoa." Bridget is halfway out of her seat.

Flavia tugs at her gold chain. "His friend, he has a restaurant on a small island. It will not be much. The economy is terrible, but for us it is enough."

"But what will you do?" Lizzy asks.

"I will find something. It is a small place. There are no subways, and for Dema it will be safer. We can be happy again. We leave in three days."

"Three days," Lizzy says. "You don't want to think about it more?"

"I did much thinking on my own, then with all of you, and finally I made up my mind. I know myself. It is a good decision."

Hannah approaches and gives her a hug. "Good luck."

"And the same to you. I have learned so much from your kindness and wisdom."

"Thank you," Hannah says, and slips out of the room.

She gets in her car, looks at the second-floor window of the Victorian house, and feels defeated. She didn't lose the battle exactly. She just can't keep up the fight. She needs a break from all of this—from the group, from couples' therapy, from all things sex addiction. Home might not always be comfortable, but it sure beats the hornet's nest she was just in.

Gail

It will be good to go out tonight, to sit with an intelligent group of people, to have substantive dialogues. Most of all, it will be wonderful to be with her husband, to be a team, an intellectual force.

The long table is beautifully dressed with white linen and sparkling crystal. Gail has on her teal suit, which Jonah had told her looked like a lovely summer breeze.

They are seated near the far end. She reaches for his hand under the table, and he gives her fingers a quick squeeze. As the guests arrive, many of whom are professors from Jonah's department, she feels his tension and again reaches for his hand. She would like to assure him that he does in fact belong here, that he should never underestimate himself. But he pulls his hand away this time, and she feels a moment of sadness at not being able to give him the comfort he deserves.

Gail chooses the rosemary-braised lamb shanks for her main course. The chatter is animated and vibrant. There is talk about the political climate, the economy, and gay marriage. This is the sort of environment she belongs in. She can't help but contrast it to last night's group.

For dessert they eat truffles, and Gail talks to the man seated across from her, Paul Bennett. He is a philosophy professor at Boston University and genuinely interested in the judicial system.

"The human element can never be discounted," Gail tells him.

"Yes, it is fascinating how the course of a narrative can alter with only the slightest shift in emotion."

"We try so hard to be objective, to separate facts from feelings. There are times we must try to do that." She stirs the dainty spoon in her coffee. "But of course it is never truly possible."

"May I be very bold and ask if I could sit one day in your courtroom and observe a trial?"

"It is always open to the public. And naturally I would be honored." She feels proud.

"I'm sorry, but I didn't catch your last name earlier."

"I'm Jonah's wife. Gail Larson." She gazes directly, confidently into his light brown eyes.

He grins and tosses his napkin on his plate. "It is a small world. Just yesterday Dr. O'Reilly was speaking of you."

For a moment, the clatter in the room feels strangely far away, as if some sort of bucket was thrown over her head. Then the noise returns— the tinkling of silverware, the refined laughter, fragments of sentences.

"Are you ill?" Paul asks.

"No." Gail pushes back her chair. "I'm terribly sorry, but will you excuse me for a moment?" She leaves the table as quickly and unobtrusively as she can.

In the restroom, she walks into the last stall. Her heart thuds. She worries about her blood pressure. The only time she met Dr. O'Reilly was for her initial interview. How could a woman who wanted to be president of a university lack such basic judgment? What else did Dr. O'Reilly say? Not that Gail is about to ask Paul. A perfectly delightful evening is now ruined. Another woman, Gail thinks, might blame her husband; after all, it is because of him she went to see Dr. O'Reilly in the first place. But Gail doesn't feel angry at Jonah.

. . .

The following morning, Gail calls Dr. O'Reilly, who says she will "clear the decks" and be available immediately. Gail gets off the phone quickly, not wanting to divulge the reason for the meeting.

In Dr. O'Reilly's office, Gail chooses the chair closest to her adversary. Her years of experience in court will allow her to conduct this deftly.

Dr. O'Reilly wears a confident smile. "It sounded important," she says. "I'm pleased you felt comfortable enough to call and reach out. How may I assist you?"

"I was at an event last night with some distinguished professors in the Boston community. I sat across from a man named Paul Bennett." She pauses, watching Dr. O'Reilly's eyes lower.

"I know Paul," Dr. O'Reilly says.

"I viewed us as having much in common. We are both women who have risen in our fields. We are expected to be trustworthy, to hold confidences." Gail sits squarely in her chair as O'Reilly shrinks in hers.

"I did mention to him that I knew you. But I didn't, and would never, say anything about the circumstances under which we met," Dr. O'Reilly defends.

Gail shakes her head. "I'm afraid that isn't the point. You violated boundaries. You have broken my trust, and I don't think I need to explain to you how devastating that is."

Dr. O'Reilly tugs at her skirt. "I am so terribly sorry. I never meant to hurt you. And I truly don't believe anything will come of this. Again, I merely mentioned that I had met you."

"Do you know what happens when a juror speaks to a friend, when they break confidentiality? A mistrial is declared. We have to begin the entire process again. So many people are hurt by what the juror always claims to be an innocent mistake. I normally understand that the person didn't have the foresight to see the consequences of their behavior. But I cannot give you that benefit of the doubt. You are in a position to know better." Gail works at maintaining her courtroom presence.

"Again, I can only express my deepest apologies." O'Reilly glances up, then shifts her gaze to the desk.

"I am disappointed. You have put a whole group at risk."

O'Reilly holds up a hand. "I know it was completely unforgivable of me, but I don't think this needs to affect the group."

"When I began this process, I did so because you came highly recommended. I wasn't convinced having a graduate student run a group of this nature would be wise. But I must say that Kathryn has been excellent. Her compassion, her ability to handle conflicts, and her maturity have impressed me. I cannot say the same about you."

Dr. O'Reilly rubs her hands together. "My only excuse is that I felt proud to know you."

"But you do not know me. Not really. I do, on the other hand, have a more realistic explanation of why you did what you did. You are too eager to make all the right connections."

"No. I have nothing to gain from name-dropping."

"Of course you do." Gail waves dismissively. "I assume you will be telling Kathryn."

Dr. O'Reilly nods.

"If this does leak out," Gail says, "I would like her to know she had nothing to do with it. I am not unwise when it comes to understanding human nature. Kathryn will question herself, wonder if she wasn't clear about confidentiality. Ultimately, she may blame herself, and I do not believe that would be fair."

"I understand. But I just don't see that there is any possible chance of a leak."

"You already opened the faucet."

O'Reilly paws at her necklace. "I have an appointment with Kathryn this afternoon. I can assure you I will get all of this cleared up." She leans forward, her concerned expression bordering on disingenuous. "And allow me to say, one last time, that I did not tell Paul anything of consequence. I would never do that."

Gail places her hands on the armrests and stands. "I believe I have made myself clear. The stakes are high. We both have the ability to damage each other's career."

"Thank you for coming. For being honest. Again, you have my word that you have nothing to concern yourself with."

"I hope that is the case."

Once outside, Gail's legs feel unsteady. She kept her composure, even though there were moments that she wanted to lash out, to yell, *How dare you? How fucking dare you?* She stops and smiles. A few months ago, before she met Bridget, a phrase like that would never have grazed her thoughts.

At her office there is a mountain of work waiting. But Gail can't concentrate on it. She thinks of the power Dr. O'Reilly has. All she needs to do is pick up the phone, call Paul Bennett, and somehow let it slip that Jonah is a sex addict. It would devastate both Gail's and Jonah's careers. For the next five minutes Gail does a deep-breathing meditation exercise. When she is finished, she takes her phone from her purse.

Kathryn picks up after the first ring. As Gail explains the events, she is surprised to find herself crying.

"Would you like to come and see me?" Kathryn asks.

Gail takes a tissue from her pocket. "No. But thank you for offering."

"I am so sorry this happened," Kathryn says.

Gail is struck at the sorrow in Kathryn's voice, how different it is from the fear of repercussion that leached through Dr. O'Reilly's apologies.

Kathryn

Kathryn cannot stop replaying the conversation with Gail in her mind. On some level, considering O'Reilly is motivated by prestige, it shouldn't have been such a shock to hear what she did. Yet every time Kathryn thinks about it, she feels breathless.

The question now is, how will O'Reilly handle this? After going through a variety of iterations, Kathryn expects O'Reilly will minimize the breach, apologize, and expect to continue as if nothing has changed. If she had been less critical in the past months, more helpful, Kathryn would likely be willing to move forward. But at this point, it's time to find a new supervisor.

Considering the situation, O'Reilly can do little but be understanding and give Kathryn a strong reference. The conversation will be difficult, embarrassing even. No student wants to see her mentor in a compromising position. But Kathryn will keep it professional and short.

O'Reilly's door is open. A first. Still Kathryn knocks.

"Come in," O'Reilly calls from her desk. She is scavenging through a heap of papers.

Kathryn closes the door and sits, as she always does, on the chair farthest from her supervisor. She takes out her notebook, a security blanket of sorts, and places it on her lap.

O'Reilly finally settles in her desk chair and faces Kathryn. Her hair, usually pumped up with a few wayward tufts, is flat, as if she's wearing a black bathing cap.

"So," O'Reilly says, "how was the last group?"

Kathryn opens her notebook, needing a moment. She certainly didn't expect O'Reilly to begin with such a normal question. But perhaps a gentle lead is best.

She sits taller. "I think there's been a breakthrough. Bridget confronted Hannah, who I think is getting close to talking about her situation."

"I must be very up-front with you." O'Reilly takes a deep breath. "All of the women replied to the survey I sent out a couple of days ago. I have read and reread them, and I am very concerned that you do not have a good handle on the group."

"*I* don't have a good handle?" Kathryn asks, surprised.

"For one, Flavia is leaving."

"Yes, I know. She's decided to move to a small island in Greece with her husband. They think it will be safer for him there where there are no subways."

"You don't think there will be young women on this island?" O'Reilly pretends to be baffled, as if Kathryn hadn't thought of this.

"Of course there will be. But the opportunities will be reduced. It's like an alcoholic who . . ."

The wattle of skin under O'Reilly's chin flaps slightly as she shakes her head. "I understand the analogy. But you are aware we advise at the minimum three sessions for someone to transition out of the group."

It was stupid, Kathryn thinks, not to expect O'Reilly to take a strong offensive position. "I'm aware of that. But it's what we advise. It's not mandatory."

"But Hannah leaving?" O'Reilly says. "We can certainly agree that might not be so good."

"Hannah's not leaving." Kathryn's palms sweat, although she maintains a front of calm.

"That's not what she wrote." O'Reilly rummages through some papers on her lap. "Ah, here it is. I printed it out this morning. She writes that you've done a good job, but the group is not for her at the moment. It seems as if what you're considering a breakthrough was more of a breakup."

"She's upset. She feels vulnerable. But she is a very smart woman, and she'll see that it will benefit her to return." Kathryn hopes this will be the case.

"I have the sense you aren't listening to me." O'Reilly waves the paper. It creates a slight breeze. "I don't think you're facing the reality of this. I also don't think three members are really enough to carry on a group of this sort. I'm advising that you take a few weeks to terminate and rethink your thesis. Perhaps you should go back to working with drug addicts."

Kathryn holds the arms of the chair. "Absolutely not. I will continue the group, even with two members. The last thing these women need is another untrustworthy person in their lives." She lets go of the chair. "To be honest, I thought we would be having a very different conversation. Gail called me a few hours ago. She told me everything."

O'Reilly stands and walks to the window. "I think Gail is making much more out of this than it warrants."

"You mentioned that you knew Gail to another professor. You have only met Gail once. During our intake interview."

"I mentioned that I had heard of her. Yes." She turns. "Gail misunderstood, and frankly, when she came to see me I was so taken aback, I didn't know what to say. After I'd given it more thought, I realized that what I had said to this professor, who shall go unnamed, was that I had read about one of Gail's cases in the paper."

Kathryn stares at the stalwart, thickset woman, briefly admiring her determination. "You only remembered this after meeting with Gail?"

"Are you accusing me of lying?" O'Reilly asks, appalled.

"I'm not sure what I think at the moment. I suppose I'm confused. I am wondering if the real reason you want me to terminate the group has to do with Gail, and not with how many members will be left."

"As I said, I did nothing wrong." She walks back to her desk and fumbles through some papers. "I think the group isn't working, and I will stick to my belief that it is time to terminate."

"And I will adhere to my belief that that is not the case." Kathryn closes her notebook. She doesn't need a prop.

O'Reilly places a hand on the large silver shell hanging from her necklace. "I think you might be too attached to the women."

Kathryn understands the manipulative tactic, yet she still wonders, is she too attached? She has felt furious at their husbands. She has spent many hours researching the specifics of each man's addiction. And even more time learning about trauma.

"I am attached to them," Kathryn says. "But that's my job. To care."

"Yes, it is your job. But I think you have lost your objective perspective. And with two members not returning, I will once again strongly advise you to terminate."

"No. I will not do that, but I think it would be wise if you and I terminated. I don't think anything useful can come out of this relationship."

"There is no one I don't know here at the university. Who do you think people will listen to, me or you?"

"I would hope they would have an open mind."

"I could ruin your career," O'Reilly says.

Kathryn stares in disbelief. O'Reilly is cold and critical, but she has never thought of her as mean. "Why would you do something like that?"

"I'm sorry. Perhaps that was uncalled for. Spoken in the heat of the moment. I think it's also a reflection of how difficult the issues in the group are. It puts us all on edge."

Kathryn takes a moment. "I don't believe I'm on edge because of the group or the issues in it. I am on edge because I no longer trust you."

"Kathryn, please. Let's not take this to the level of absurdity."

"My feelings are not absurd." She thinks about the women, how they talk about their husbands trying to make them feel as if they're crazy. She has never understood them as well as she does in this moment.

O'Reilly sits and sighs. "Look, there have been a few miscommunications. Let's both try to regain some perspective on this. Perhaps I spoke too rashly in suggesting you end the group." She nods as if she's being self-reflective. "I'm willing to give it a few more weeks together."

"I'm sorry, but that's not possible for me." She thinks of how the husbands bargain, of how the women, who love them, keep trying. But Kathryn is not in their position. She has no ties to O'Reilly.

"I really don't know who will take you on," O'Reilly says.

"I'm sure I'll find someone." She puts her notebook in her briefcase.

"I am the chair of this department. Think carefully before you make your next move."

Kathryn looks at O'Reilly, then slowly stands. The woman Kathryn was so nervous to meet months ago is a wounded narcissist who will do anything to protect her image. But Kathryn holds the trump card. She knows what O'Reilly did.

She picks up her briefcase and walks to the door. "I have worked hard, and I believe I am a good therapist."

O'Reilly glances up. There is a fleeting panic in her eyes, as if she's being discarded. But the moment doesn't last, and her gaze turns sharp. "I'll call in a couple of days. Give you some time to think this over."

"That's considerate of you, but it won't be necessary." She zips her partially open bag and smiles, politely and professionally, the way she imagines Gail might smile at an annoying attorney.

Lizzy

It's been almost a week since the last group, since Hannah said that Greg didn't treat Lizzy well enough. For the past six days, Lizzy has made mental checklists of all the ways Greg shows her that he's invested in her and their marriage. He does the yard work; he's made dinner a couple of times; he's been telling her he loves her before they go to sleep. That counts for something. So does the fact that he's texted her a few times during the day, just to say hi. A new and improved behavior.

His small steps to let her know that he does in fact think about her have made her realize that what she actually wants is closeness and friendship. Those things don't require sex. And the five percent bracket that Hannah mentioned—Lizzy did some research of her own. Most sources stated a higher recovery rate. Granted, no one claimed anything near fifty percent, but fifteen was about average. So there's no reason not to have hope, especially since Greg's addiction isn't like the others. Never having sex with another person puts him in a whole different category.

Every day that Greg has been sober gives them something to build on. It reminds Lizzy of growing crystals. The seed crystal is the most delicate. It needs perfect conditions. Once the seed has formed, a few bumps won't stop the progress. The environment doesn't need to be so closely monitored. Greg is past the seeding stage and on his way.

School is winding down for the year. It's nearly lunch period on Tuesday. She hands out study guides for the final, two and a half weeks early. Preparation and practice: she's tried to drill those lessons home.

Her cell phone vibrates at exactly the same time that the classroom phone rings. She assumes Greg is sending her a message, and that gives her a burst of happiness. She'll look at it during lunch. She picks up the classroom phone.

"Lizzy?" It's the secretary, Geraldine, from the front office.

"How can I help?" Lizzy asks.

"Joe would like to talk to you," Geraldine says quietly.

"Sure," Lizzy says. Joe has been the principal for ten years, and he's never been anything but complimentary and supportive.

"Can you come during your lunch break?" There's an urgency in her voice.

"Sure," Lizzy says, this time tempering any buoyancy in her voice. "Do you know what this is about?"

"No. He just told me to call you."

"There hasn't been some sort of accident?" That's always a fear—a car crash, the death of a student.

"No."

"Good." Lizzy breathes an audible sigh and hangs up the phone. Students are packing up.

"There are still three minutes left," she says.

"Two minutes and twenty-five seconds," Bryan calls out.

"Okay, two minutes. You could have done a problem in two minutes." But she's smiling, and they all know that class is essentially over.

She touches her pocket, feeling her cell phone, and has an urge to take it out now to read Greg's message. But she'll save it.

The bell rings, and the students are gone in under twenty seconds.

Lizzy sits at the table in Joe's office as he closes the door. Why would they need a closed-door meeting? In all her years of teaching, she's never been reprimanded for anything.

Joe sits with her. She feels a snag. He usually stays behind his desk and multitasks, checking e-mails as he talks. He glances at her, but because he has a wandering eye, she's never quite sure where he's actually looking.

"How are you?" His thick eyebrows form a single black line.

"Fine." She tilts her head, expecting to hear what's really going on. Lunch period is only twenty-two minutes, and she needs to get ready for her next class.

He stands, walks to his desk and picks up a pencil. "This is difficult," he says, and joins her at the table again.

She feels herself sink. Something terrible has happened to a student. Geraldine just didn't know of it yet, even if she is the hub of gossip.

"What is it?"

He taps the eraser of the pencil on the table, then seems to note his own nervousness and puts the pencil aside. "It actually started last week."

Her face gets hot. She nods for him to continue.

"I received an e-mail from a parent."

Someone complained about her? Maybe Brianna's parents. Their daughter is flunking, but it's hardly Lizzy's fault. She nods for Joe to continue.

"They were concerned about their daughter, Kristie. She's in—"

"My AP class," Lizzy tells him. "She's getting a solid A."

"I don't think anyone is questioning your teaching or her grade."

Well, that's a relief. She looks at Joe. "What is it?" she asks again.

"It's probably nothing. A misunderstanding. But I did receive a few more e-mails from concerned parents this week."

Now her face must be as red as a lobster. "About what?" She doesn't hide her dismay.

"Your husband, he works . . ." He taps the pencil again. ". . . worked for a small business in town."

"Yes. For TKL, the computer software company. What does he have to do with . . . ?"

"Well, from what I understand, and this might be entirely incorrect, he was let go at the beginning of last week."

She shakes her head. "No."

Joe looks in her direction, although his eyes seem to be focusing to the side of her. "That's good to hear."

"Sorry, Joe, but I'm confused. What does this have to do with Kristie or any of my other students?"

"It seems that they believe your husband was let go because of something to do with . . ." He lays his thick hands flat on the table.

For a few seconds she feels as if she's not breathing. She meant to ask Greg if he ever watched porn at work, but she was never able to get the question out. He wouldn't do something that stupid. It would be analogous to her keeping a bottle of vodka in her file cabinet. There are things you just don't do. Addict or not.

"He's been going to work every day," she tells Joe.

He reaches to pat her shoulder. "Look, you're a fabulous teacher, one of the best I've ever seen in my career. And I'm sure this will all get cleared up. But . . ."

"I don't see what there is to clear up. He hasn't lost his job. I would certainly know about that." She pauses. "What did Kristie's parents say?"

"They believe your husband was let go because of some sort of sexual misconduct. I think they're worried that, well, guilt by association."

She takes her cell phone out of her pocket. Toys with it. Guilt by association? That kind of thing happens in North Korea, not a nice, liberal suburb of Boston. "What do they think, I'm some kind of pervert?"

"Not you. Of course. You know how parents are these days. Hovering. Overprotective."

"What exactly are they saying?" Her voice is louder.

"That he might have been inappropriate. That their children might not be safe."

She can't be hearing this correctly. "Greg has never been inappropriate with children." As soon as she says that, she has a moment of doubt. It's not as if he can really be trusted.

"I'm sure that's the case. But as I said, you know how parents can be." He makes a face, as if he's fed up with them, as if they're all absurd, yet that's what he has to deal with.

"Yes. But . . ."

"They're concerned. I think all this recent stuff with Sandusky hasn't helped. You know how people blame his wife."

"This is crazy. My husband's hardly a Sandusky. Besides, it's not as if the students are ever even in contact with him."

"But you did have the AP students at your house for a barbecue after their exam."

"Yes."

"And your husband was there?"

"God, I feel like I'm on the witness stand. Yes, he was there. But we were outside the whole time. I mean, what are you proposing, that he took one of them into the bathroom or something?" She feels removed from herself, as if this is happening to someone else.

"No. I'm sure nothing happened, and as I said, I think the whole ordeal with Penn State has made parents even more paranoid."

Her head feels like thick mud. The bell rings. "I have a class." She stands.

"I have someone covering. Don't worry. We'll take care of it."

She sits down.

"I've put a lot of thought into this," Joe says. "I want you to know that. I want to do what's best for you. To protect you."

"But I don't need protection."

"I'm afraid—" The pencil breaks. He gets up to throw it away. "I'm afraid you might. You can use the school's lawyer."

"Lawyer? What am I being accused of?"

"Nothing." He holds up a hand. "Nothing, of course. But as I said, guilt by association."

"What's my husband being accused of?"

"I shouldn't have brought up lawyers. I'm sure you won't need one. I just wanted you to know, should it come to that, we will be happy to provide legal support."

"I don't understand. Why would I need legal support?"

"I've seen these sorts of things before. They can get out of control. I would hate to have parents e-mail you and suggest things about your husband."

She finally decides to look at the message on her phone. It's not from Greg, it's from the dentist, reminding her she has an appointment tomorrow.

"Lizzy?" Joe says.

She can't imagine sitting in the dentist's chair.

"Yes. Sorry," she tells Joe. "I don't know why I looked at this now."

"Everything all right?"

"Yes. Fine." She clicks off the message. "Fine," she says again. If she keeps telling herself that, perhaps it will be.

"Your husband?" Joe asks.

"No." She puts her phone back in her pocket. "No, he's fine."

"I was thinking, since we're so close to the end of the year, it might just be best . . ." He pauses. "It might be best if you took the time off. We'll get it all settled and start fresh next year."

She stares at him as if he's speaking a language she doesn't understand. But then the words nudge into her brain. They swim toward her slowly, underwater.

She can't give up her classes. This time of year is key. It's when she ties all the material together, makes her students see the big picture. It's the pinnacle, the big bang, the finale in the fireworks show.

"I can't. I have to review for finals. And you won't be able to just find a chemistry teacher to fill in."

"No, we can't find anyone with your expertise, but we'll manage. The students will be okay."

She shakes her head. "No, you don't understand. We haven't finished the unit on acids and bases yet, and that chapter always confuses them."

"Lizzy, it's all right. They'll be fine."

Of course they'll be fine. But she won't be. She can't sit at home and do . . . what? Stare out the kitchen window when everyone else is getting ready for finals? "I can't," she says firmly. "I'm sorry."

"The thing is"—he stands and walks to his desk—"I'm really doing this because I want to protect you. It's just a couple of weeks. I already have someone to cover your classes."

"But . . ." she says.

"I know, it's hard." He opens his laptop and glances at it. "It's not fair. And I'll be available to talk to you whenever you want."

The computer beeps as he turns it on. He looks at the screen, and she thinks of an e-mail she received from a man named Valerian, about helping to build a school in the Peruvian jungle. For twenty minutes she contemplated going, and then she looked into airfares, which were too expensive. She replied, thanked Valerian, and said perhaps the following year, if they still needed help on the project. It's a fantasy, of course, taking off to the jungle.

"Lizzy," Joe says. "Joan is available to talk to you now if that will help."

She certainly doesn't need the twenty-eight-year-old school psychologist, who looks as if she spends four hours a day sculpting her muscles.

"No, I wouldn't like that. Thank you." She stays sitting as Joe settles behind his desk, looking as if he wants to get back to work. "I'll finish out the week at least."

"Why don't you go home? Rest. Let me worry about this."

"I'll leave at the end of the day."

He shakes his head solemnly.

"Now? I should just get up and leave now?"

"We think that's best."

"We?"

"The superintendent and myself. I'll be sending home an e-mail, explaining that you will be taking the remainder of the year off."

"What would you say my reason is?"

"We can talk about that. If you'd prefer, I can say it's for medical reasons."

"I'd prefer that you tell them I haven't done anything wrong, and neither has my husband." Her voice splinters. She puts a hand to her throat.

"I know how hard this must be."

She walks out without saying another word. Joan jumps up from chatting with Geraldine. Lizzy passes them as if they aren't even there. In her classroom, she smiles at the students and tells them she has to help a friend. Then she grabs her pocketbook, her keys, and the plant on her desk. She puts the plant down. It would look silly to walk out with a plant. She'll be back tomorrow. This mess will get cleared up. They can't do this. She'll get the union involved. This is like a witch hunt, cruel and archaic. It must be against the law. And Greg hasn't even been fired, let alone for what they're saying. This is America. They can't ask her to leave based on some unfounded rumors.

She takes out her phone, intending to reply to the dentist, but she calls Greg instead. She doesn't get into details, just that she's upset, very upset, and asks if he can meet her at home. He tells her he'll be there in fifteen minutes.

She waits twenty minutes, then thirty. She calls him again. No answer. She texts. No reply. She thinks of calling Hannah, but then remembers what she said, that Greg couldn't be trusted.

She vacuums, needing something to do, but the noise feels as if it's mimicking her nerves. In the kitchen, she chops vegetables for soup and throws them in the slow cooker. Ten more minutes, then she'll call the local hospitals and see if he was in an accident.

It just can't be true what Joe told her. Obviously, if Greg had been fired, even if he didn't tell her, she would have known. She's not that obtuse. There would have been clues that he wasn't going to work.

She sets up her laptop on the kitchen table. Maybe Joe e-mailed her to tell her he made a mistake, that he found out it was just a malicious rumor after all. There are four new e-mails, all junk. She scrolls down, finds the e-mail from Valerian, and reads it again. She remembers the phrase *relocation cure.* She can't recall where she heard it, but whoever used it also said it never works, that it's just a form of escape. But if she decided to go to the jungle for the summer, she wouldn't be running, she would be doing something productive.

The front door opens. Greg whistles as he looks through the mail. How can he be so laid-back? Doesn't he remember how distressed she was on the phone? After a couple of minutes, he strolls into the kitchen. She thinks he looks thinner and wonders why this is the first time she has noticed.

"What's up?" he asks.

"Something terrible happened." She's about to cry. "I was asked to leave school."

"What?" He pulls out a chair and sits. He looks shocked, and although she feels herself shaking, his surprise just confirms that this was all some huge cosmic mistake.

"I . . . Joe called me into his office. It was so humiliating." She covers her face for a second. "He told me he's been getting e-mails from parents saying they don't want me to teach their children because you got fired from work for some sort of sexual misconduct." Tears flow. "They don't want me to teach there anymore. At least for the rest of the year."

Greg pounds his fist on the table. "What the hell. You haven't done anything wrong."

"I guess I'm like that wife of Sandusky. Somehow I'll allow you to molest their children."

"How dare they?" His mouth twitches. His eyes remind her of small glass beads.

She puts her head on the table and weeps. "I don't know what to do."

"Tell them to take a flying fuck."

She lifts her head. "Will you call Joe? Tell him you didn't get fired. Tell him . . ." She stops to catch her breath. "Just tell him how ridiculous this all is."

He pushes himself away from the table. She watches him open a cabinet and stare at a box of ziti.

"Will you?" she asks.

He takes out the box, studies the side of it. "If you want me to."

"I do. You have to. I can't live like this." She pulls up a file from her computer, ready to give him Joe's number.

Greg sits at the table again, now looking at the front of the box. "The thing is . . ."

She stares at him. His shoulders hunch. His slight underbite seems more pronounced. He should be taking out his phone to make the call.

"What?" she asks.

He flips the box over. "I was let go from work."

She feels the way she did in Joe's office. As if the words are thick molasses, and they don't make sense. "When?" she asks.

"At the beginning of last week."

"But you've been getting up every day and . . ." In fact he's dressed in work clothes now.

He opens the box of ziti, then closes it. "I haven't actually been going in."

"Where do you go, then?" She stares at him. Who is this man?

"I drive around. Go to the library. Come home for a few hours." His mouth keeps twitching.

"When were you going to tell me this?" she asks.

"I wanted to wait until you finished school. I thought that would be better for you."

"Better for me?" She's not angry, not sad, not anything but totally and completely confused.

"You know how hectic things are at the end of the year. I just thought, better wait until then, and we can, you know, sit and talk about it." His head is bowed. She notices his hair is thinning.

"I thought they liked you there," she says.

He opens the box again, this time taking out an uncooked noodle. "They do. They did."

"So what happened?"

"Cutbacks."

She pulls the box away from him. "Really?" She hates the thoughts that are formulating. "You didn't get caught watching porn?"

He doesn't answer, which tells her he did. Goddamn him. And someone in town found out, told someone else, and . . . She stands. Her heart pounds.

"I'm sorry," he whispers.

She walks to the slow cooker, puts her hand on the lid, and waits. She doesn't know what she's waiting for. The world to end, the phone to ring, the nightmare to stop. She can feel the beginnings of a migraine above her right eye, like a dull thud from a hammer.

"Lizzy," he says. "I'm sorry that I didn't tell you. I didn't want to hurt you more. But it's wrong what they're saying about me being some sort of child molester. That's just fucking wrong. They can't do that. It's libel."

"Slander," she says, and looks out of the kitchen window. The bushes in the back are full and leafy. "I'll never work there again." She talks more to herself than to him.

"They can't do this to you. We'll fight them." He sounds righteous.

She massages the ache above her eye. "It will never leave me. People will whisper behind my back. Parents will get their children switched out of my classes."

"They can't do this to you. I'll fucking take them to court."

Slowly she turns to face him. "No one is taking anyone to court."

"I might have watched a little porn, but I certainly am not going to sit around and let people say that I'm some sort of child molester."

His mouth is strained. The skin around his jaw folds. He's too old to just go out and get another job. "Did they give you a severance package?"

"I didn't want one."

She nods. "Just for the record, have you ever actually stopped watching it?"

He hangs his head. "I've tried."

"Can you just answer the question?" Her heart isn't pounding as hard, and her head feels clearer, in an odd sort of numb way.

"No. I haven't been able to."

"And what about your groups and your therapy? Have you been going to those?"

"Some."

"Some? As in two groups a week, one a month? Can you be a little more specific?"

He slaps the ziti box on the table. "It's not as if I write them all down."

"Okay, so make an educated guess."

"I don't know. A few. Okay? A few," he shouts.

"And therapy?"

"My schedule was tight, so I missed a couple of appointments."

"But you haven't been going to work. How is your schedule tight?"

"I'm not talking about this week or last. Before that. It wasn't easy sneaking out and lying about different things I had to do."

"Was it easy to watch porn at work?"

He stands. "I don't have to take this shit."

It's three-thirty. School has been out for over an hour. She wonders what her students are saying, if they even noticed she's gone. She runs into them at the grocery store, the mall, the gas station, even at the Cape.

Greg stomps to the door.

"Are we finished talking then?" she asks.

He swivels around. "Look." He juts his hand forward, pointing a finger at her. "I wanted to help you, but if this is just going to turn into a bitchfest about how this is all my fault, then I don't need to hear it."

There isn't any point, she thinks, in trying to explain that, actually, it is his fault. Not so much for watching porn or even lying, but for not taking responsibility for his addiction.

"Well, then, I won't say it." She should just let him walk out, keep her mouth shut. "So go ahead, go to your study and do what you do best."

He lunges forward and grabs a chair. He is about to throw it, but instead slams it back on the floor. "Making those sorts of comments doesn't help anyone."

She grabs the box of ziti from the table and whips it at him. It nicks his temple. He stares at her, indignant.

"You're out of control." He shields his face with his hand as if he needs to protect himself.

She grabs a frying pan off the stove, then crashes it down. Metal bangs on metal. "I am not out of control," she screams.

"It's not safe in here," he tells her, and hurries out.

She picks up the slow cooker, carefully, methodically, and smashes it on the ground. Greg doesn't come back to see what happened. Lizzy sits at the table and watches the tiny rivulets of soup snake along the floor.

She doesn't know what time it is when she hears the front door close and Greg's car start. He didn't even have the decency to tell her he was leaving.

At eleven, he still isn't home. She goes to bed but can't sleep. Calling him, asking him if he's okay, begging him to come home so they can talk would be pathetic. Instead, she goes to the dining room, pours herself a large glass of merlot, and takes it to the bedroom. Eventually she passes out.

SESSION SEVEN

Shame fuses Lizzy to her bed. The only phone call she receives is from the dentist, wondering why she missed her appointment. The flu, she lies.

Thoughts come in fragmented bursts. She wonders how to kill herself, only to realize she's not brave enough, nor does she have the means. Then come moments of panic. Will she have to stay in hiding with the shades closed forever? She imagines walking calmly into her classroom, telling the sub to leave. What would they do, escort her out in handcuffs? She's hardly a criminal. She thinks of all the things she's going to say to Greg, all the things he's going to promise.

There hasn't been any word from him, and it's now Wednesday, time to get ready for group. Time to shower and change out of the clothes she's been wearing since yesterday morning.

Drained, she fights inertia and chooses a pair of black jeans and a clean, pressed white blouse. Fake it till you make it. She will convey the impression of resilience. This may be a setback, a shock even, but she will get through. After all, people survive wars and concentration camps.

The light outside is piercing. She considers running back in the house, but she can't let the others down. Driving feels surreal as she glances at trees showing off their first hints of green. People walk as if they have somewhere to go. Lizzy wants to throw up. Or have a truck barrel into her. She glances at her phone that doesn't ring.

In the second-story office, she takes her seat on the couch, nods to Kathryn, and smiles at Bridget and Gail. Hannah is absent.

Kathryn looks at the open door. Lizzy feels a chill. She touches the vacant spot next to her, missing Flavia.

"Before we begin," Kathryn says. "I need to share a small change I'm making. I will be getting a new supervisor, who may want to touch base with you, just to make sure things are okay. If you're not comfortable with that, please let me know."

"I'm fine with it," Bridget says. "I kinda thought that woman you were working for before was a bitch."

"A supervisor isn't exactly someone you work for," Gail explains to Bridget. They look at Kathryn. "Was this your choice?" Gail asks.

"Yes."

Gail nods. "Because of what we discussed?"

"I feel it's best."

"Okay, what the hell is going on?" Bridget asks.

Gail smiles at Kathryn before turning to Bridget. "There was a small breach in confidentiality. Nothing that concerns you, but I think Kathryn did the wise thing. And I am grateful for it."

Kathryn nods. "Thank you. If you're ready, I think we should move on."

"Agreed," Gail says.

"Has anyone heard from Hannah?" Kathryn asks.

"Like *that's* about to happen," Bridget scoffs.

Kathryn looks at Lizzy, who shakes her head and folds her hands in her lap. She feels confused. The timing is wrong somehow. It's as if last week was decades ago. Another lifetime.

"You okay?" Bridget asks Lizzy.

"Yes, thank you. Fine." She nods. Smiles. Touches the empty seat again, and then refolds her hands.

"You sure?" Bridget presses.

"Yes. Of course."

"You seem a little, I don't know, spaced out." Bridget leans forward, trying to make eye contact. Lizzy glances at the floor.

"A lot came up last week," Kathryn says. "It would be understandable if it was difficult to return here tonight."

Lizzy tries to remember last week. Flavia looked like a princess. She recalls that, and Hannah seeming angry at the world.

"Gail, how are you feeling about everything?" Kathryn asks.

"I think Hannah needs a cool-down period."

"She had no right to say the things she did," Bridget says. "It didn't have anything to do with us."

"Why do you think that?" Kathryn asks.

Bridget shrugs. "It's obvious. She doesn't talk about her husband, which is what she's worried about. So instead of having the guts to say what's bothering her, she vomits her shit all over us." Bridget sweeps her hand through the air. "She tells us our husbands are liars and cheats, when what's going on is that she's keeping her own fears all locked up."

Gail nods emphatically. "I agree. I know Jonah is being honest. And I do think that Hannah is projecting. You know, Kathryn, you said in our first meeting that the relationships we make in the group can be a reflection of what's going on outside, and I think that's true with Hannah. She's erupting, and instead of working it out with her husband, she's testing out her feelings on us. I think it would have been really good if she could have come tonight. To plow through it." She punches her fist forward. "That's what you have to do."

Bridget turns to Gail. "You're right. Her anger is like some sort of cancer. Like, when she heard that we knew about Adam, that really triggered her. We got a glimpse of what was really going on. I think she's probably more ashamed than all of us put together." Bridget pours herself a glass of water.

"Shame is powerful." Kathryn stands and closes the door.

"She was right about Greg," Lizzy whispers.

The others look at her. Her mouth tastes like sulfur. One second the room feels freezing, the next it's a hundred degrees. She not sure if she's shivering or trembling.

"I knew you didn't seem right," Bridget declares. "You caught him again?"

Lizzy clamps her hands together. Maybe if there was a window open in here, that would help. Or if Kathryn had left the door open.

"Not exactly," she says, and glances at the horses in one of the paintings on the wall.

"Would you like to talk about what happened?" Kathryn's voice is gentle. It makes Lizzy want to cry.

"Uh . . ." Lizzy begins. She wishes she hadn't worn her white blouse. It's sticking to her and she can feel wet spots under her arms. If Flavia were here, she would be rubbing her back, coaxing out the words.

"Take all the time you need," Gail says.

"Thanks," Lizzy replies. Although saying that was difficult.

"Did you find out he was with other women . . . people?" Bridget asks.

"No. I wish . . . I mean . . . no. I don't know what I mean. I can't imagine how hard that must be for you two," Lizzy says. "This was something different. It was like my life just went up in smoke."

"Did he move out?" Gail asks.

"Maybe. I guess." Lizzy pauses. "I was asked to leave my job."

No one speaks. Lizzy hates the silence more than she hates Greg. She rubs her hand on the couch. "Greg was fired," she whispers as her hand moves back and forth. "Somehow some parents found out, and they think he's some sort of child molester."

"Both of you lost your jobs?" Bridget asks.

"I didn't actually lose mine. I'm still getting paid." She stops moving her hand. "The principal thought it would be better for me. You know, not to have to be targeted for something my husband did. He thought it would be better if I took the rest of the year off."

"What did your husband do?" Gail reaches into her pocketbook and takes out a small notepad.

"He got caught watching porn."

"But not for anything to do with children?" Gail clarifies.

"No."

"Thank God." Gail sighs. "So he was watching porn at work?"

"Yes."

"They have no right to let you go. That's discrimination." Gail jots something on her notepad.

"Yeah, you didn't do anything wrong." Bridget gets up and moves to sit with Lizzy.

She would rather have the couch to herself, but she knows Bridget means well, and she would never hurt someone else's feelings.

"I can help you get a lawyer," Gail tells her.

Lawyers aren't going to fix anything. "No. I really think that my principal wanted to do what was best for me and the students. It's not like I'm fired."

"But what are you supposed to do now?" Bridget hands Lizzy a tissue. "Just sit around and watch the fucking grass grow?"

"I like to garden," Lizzy says, pulling at the tissue.

"How are you managing with all of this?" Kathryn asks.

Lizzy shrugs. "Okay. Not great. It was hard to even get here."

"It's important you came. You shouldn't deal with this alone," Kathryn says.

Bridget strokes Lizzy's shoulder.

"I had these weird dreams," Lizzy says. "I'm with Greg, we're having a picnic in a field of daisies, and we're so happy. Then I wake up, and my life is a mess. Like, I'm not sure which part is a dream anymore."

"You've been through a major trauma, and you're experiencing the side effects of that." Kathryn scoots her chair a few inches toward Lizzy.

"Have you eaten?" Gail asks, putting her notepad in her purse and taking out a bag of peanut M&M's. She brings them to Lizzy. "The nuts have protein. Your blood sugar might be low. That can make you feel weak."

"Thanks." Lizzy fiddles with the yellow packaging. She's not hungry.

"You mentioned Greg left," Kathryn begins. "Is that permanent?"

"I don't know. I didn't ask him to leave. I'm afraid he might hurt himself."

"That would serve him right," Bridget utters. Then she covers her mouth. "I didn't mean that."

"I know what you meant." Lizzy pats Bridget's knee.

"Do you have anything planned for the next few days?" Kathryn asks. "Sometimes it's helpful to have a schedule."

Lizzy shakes her head.

"You can come hang out with me before I go to work," Bridget suggests.

"If you feel up to some light part-time work, I can look for something," Gail chimes in.

"Thanks. You guys are so nice. But I think I just need some time to get it all sorted in my head."

"You shouldn't make any big decisions," Gail tells her. "After a traumatic event, like a divorce or a death, you should take it really slow. Pamper yourself. Don't do anything rash."

"Yeah, she's right," Bridget says.

"I won't." She looks at the door. "I'm sorry. I've taken up so much time."

"Hey, that's why we're here. Maybe next week it will be one of us." Bridget chortles.

"Knock on wood." Gail taps the armrest.

Before they leave, promises are made to keep in touch, to reach out. Lizzy is grateful, but she wants to be left alone, to get back to her bed. This was so much more exhausting than she ever imagined.

Lizzy

Lizzy sees Greg's car in the driveway. Her heart pauses, then hammers wildly. She parks and takes careful steps toward the house. Her brain, though, is not behaving carefully. Demands, pleas, accusations, and threats intersect in a maze of confusion.

All the lights are on.

"Greg," she calls, afraid of her anger, her despair. Afraid of why he's here.

She looks for him in the kitchen. He's not there. Slowly she climbs the stairs. He's in their bedroom, taking things out of his closet and putting them in a white trash bag. She watches for a few moments, her heart leaking.

"Greg," she says softly.

He turns. "You don't normally come home this early."

Doesn't she? Does it matter? "What are you doing?" she asks.

He motions from the closet to the bag, as if it's obvious. Which of course it is.

"You haven't answered any of my calls," she tells him, taking a step into the room, then retreating back to the threshold.

"I didn't think it would be good to talk right now. Everything ends in a conflagration."

It's an odd word, she thinks. "But we have to talk."

"Agreed. But not when we're both so irrational." He throws in a shirt and his golf shoes.

"I don't think I'm irrational," she tells him. She takes the tissue Bridget gave her from her pocket and twists it. It reminds her of the pastries her mother used to buy.

He holds up a sweater, debates whether or not to put it in the bag, decides against it. She got it for him for Christmas. It's a Ralph Lauren.

"Where were you?" she asks.

"Just some hotel."

"Did you watch porn?"

"This is why we can't talk." He picks up the bag, then lets it thump back on the floor when he realizes she's blocking him.

"Were you?" she asks again.

"Yes. I was." He's defiant.

"Did you masturbate?"

"Liz, I'm not going to dignify that with an answer."

"Why not?"

"Look, this is why I need to leave for a while. Questions like that just aren't constructive."

She twists her pastry tissue until it rips. "I hate that you make me feel so unwanted. I hate that you lied to me. That you make me feel like a pest for asking perfectly good questions."

"Listen, we can't do this. I talked to my therapist. She thinks it was good that I left the other night. She thinks it would be better if we met under her supervision."

"Because, what, I'm going to hurt you? I'm dangerous?"

"No." He picks up his bag again. "But it was volatile, and she thinks it would be wise to have a cooling-off period."

"I can't believe this. You act all calm, like you're the sane, rational one. Can't you see what you did to my life?" She digs her nails into the door frame.

"Look, I'm dealing with a lot right now. I feel like a bomb just went off at my feet."

She digs harder. "You feel like a bomb went off? How does that make sense?" she asks.

"It's how I feel," he says, as if using the word *feel* means she can't disagree.

"But you knew a bomb was there. I mean, a bomb really did go off in my life, because you threw it at me," she tells him.

"You're not making sense. I need to get going. I have a call scheduled with my sponsor." He approaches the doorway.

She glares at him. She's not about to move. He'll have to push her out of the way.

"Please," he says.

She grips the door frame with both hands. He retreats to the master bathroom. When she hears a few drawers open, she follows.

He's taking the toothpaste. She lunges, rips the bag. White plastic clings to her fingers. She peels it away and grabs the half-filled tube.

"You can't have this," she yells, holding it close to her chest.

"Fine." He bends, picking up the lumpy, torn bag from the bottom. In her rashness, she's given him an opening. He scurries out.

She faces the mirror and looks at the aqua-colored swirls on the toothpaste tube.

Bridget

Bridget sprawls on the bed in her underwear. It's Monday afternoon, and the May heat wave is unbearable. Her room is a hot box, and if she wasn't so damned stubborn, she would have agreed to let Michael get her an air conditioner.

The damp washcloth on her forehead is no longer cool. She had hoped she'd be able to sleep an hour or so before going in to work, but since that's not happening she sits up, deciding to head to the air-conditioned mall and eat orange sorbet.

She glances at her lacy yellow bra. Aside from her stomach, which pouches out, her boobs have grown the most. They're barely contained, but she's never going to get some huge contraption with underwire.

Standing in front of her closet, she looks for an unconstricting piece of clothing as the fan blows on her legs. She's just about to take a cotton dress from the hanger when there's a knock on the door.

"What," she says, irritated, knowing it's Michael.

"I have a surprise for you."

"I've told you. I've had enough surprises from you in the past year. And you know what? Telling me everything doesn't actually help me.

Ever think of that?" She drops her hand from the dress and walks back to the bed. No way will she open the door. It's like willingly allowing in pain. She's done with that. The whole boundary thing is beginning to make some sense.

"Bridge, please. It's not that sort of surprise. It's a good one. You'll like this, I promise."

"If it's that good, just leave it right there, and I'll get it later." Her stomach flutters.

"It's really heavy. You can't lift it."

At least now it isn't a surprise anymore. She knows it's an air conditioner, and for that she is willing to break her no-Michael-in-the-bedroom rule.

"Just a sec." She unlocks the bolt, opens the door, and smiles. Not at him, at the box.

"Bridge," he says, standing in the doorway. "You look amazing."

She glances at her small potbelly and bulging breasts. He hasn't seen her in her underwear since the last time they had sex, which of course was the time she got knocked up.

"That window." She points.

He walks in, places the box on the bed, and wipes his forehead. "No, really, you look amazing."

It sucks that he looks amazing too—hot and sweaty, his eyes all lit up, ready to take her. Damn him. The worst thing she could do right now would be to cave. She turns away.

"Can you just put in the fucking air conditioner and stop gawking at me," she tells him.

"Sorry," he mutters, and rips open the box.

Just looking at the packaging makes her feel cooler. "How long will it take?" she asks.

"Fifteen minutes, give or take a few."

She waits in the computer room, which will soon be a nursery.

"It's ready," he shouts after about ten minutes.

She can feel the cool air from outside the room. It's heaven. No need to go to the mall now. She's going to lie down, spread her arms and legs, and enjoy.

Michael cleans up the packing. She waits for him to leave, but he stands in front of the box, tapping it with a screwdriver. Maybe he needs to cool off for a few minutes, and although she wants him out, she's not a complete bitch.

She hovers at her dresser, moving a jewelry case from one corner to another. Still he stands there. "There something you need?" she finally asks.

"I just wanted to talk for a little."

She guesses he wants to do more than just talk. He plops down on the foot of the bed, which gives a tired sigh.

"I need to rest." She sits on her side with her back to the air conditioner.

"I love you. I love our baby. I know I totally, completely fucked everything up, and I'm not asking for your forgiveness. But I just can't keep sleeping on the couch anymore."

Cool air blows on her back. She shakes her head. He has the balls to ask if he can sleep in their bed again? No way. "So you got an air conditioner because you want to sleep somewhere comfortable? Well, it sure as hell isn't going to be in here." She pauses. "Ever. Not even if you take one of those fucking polygraphs every week."

"I know."

He sounds defeated. He should be making promises, telling her that he'll go twice a week if that would help.

"So if you know, why the hell would you ask if you can sleep with me again?"

"I didn't ask that," he says, too calmly.

She turns and looks at his wide shoulders, feeling as if she's getting zapped with some sort of cattle prodder. Still, she's going to keep playing it tough. "Then what are you saying? We should move? I'm not about to pack up and leave now just because you need a bed."

"I didn't say that."

She doesn't like that he's so unruffled, that he's not getting angry or begging to sleep with her. Her heart feels as if it's that pebble again, pinging in its tin can.

"That would just take the cake," she tells him. "With everything else we're dealing with, let's just throw in a move."

"Bridge, stop," he says. "You're not listening. I'm not asking you to do anything."

"Yeah, right." She points to the air conditioner. "I know what you're trying to do. You think you've been punished long enough, and it's time to come back to your bed."

"I don't think you're punishing me. I know you're only trying to take care of yourself."

"And the baby," she adds. She wants to fight, to yell and cry, to show him that what he did still hurts, but she can't seem to get a hook in.

"Yes, and the baby. You're going to be a great mother."

Cool air streams in, yet she sweats. "So get to the point."

"I think it would be best if I moved out."

Her heart pings in its metal canister. Move out? After everything he's done, she doesn't even get to kick him out?

"You . . ." She gets up and moves to stand in front of her dresser again. Brushing her fingers through a small dish of jewelry, she asks, "Who will you live with?"

"I'm going to stay at my brother's for a while."

"That's an hour away." She turns and faces him. His forehead is so furrowed that his eyebrows nearly touch.

"I'll be here whenever you need me." He looks sappy and honest. And more than that, resolved.

"What about when I go into labor? You want me to call a cab?" She's grasping.

"That's not for a long time." He looks as if he's about to stand, to walk to her, comfort her. But he doesn't get up. "We really don't need to worry about that yet."

"Right, once again, push off responsibility."

"That's not what I'm doing. I'm trying to be responsible. Give you time and space to heal. When it gets closer to the baby's due date, I can stay on the couch."

"And if the baby comes early? Then what?" She puts her hands on her hips.

"Bridge, if it happens that fast, which it probably won't, you can call an ambulance."

"Easy for you to fucking say. Just call an ambulance. Nice. Real nice." She flings out her arm.

"I understand you're afraid, but right now I think you're just coming up with disaster scenarios, and those aren't going to happen."

Finally, something to grab. "And why do you think I come up with the worst-case scenarios? Think it might have something to do with what you've put me through?"

"I get it, already." His back arches. "Really, I do. I did irrevocable damage to our marriage. I know that. I can't take it back. I can't fix it. I can't fix you, and I can't fix us. I'm just working on fixing myself. That's the best I can do."

Her hands lock back on her hips. "Typical. So typical. Just worry about fixing yourself. You learn that in your twelve-step group?"

He stands, and although he has his head lowered, she's struck by his height. "This is why I have to move," he says. "I just can't keep doing this. I'll get polygraphs, I'll still be your husband, but every time we're together, it just can't be this contentious."

"What's with the big words?"

"Look, I know it's easier to be angry. I know that helps you, and if you want to call and yell at me during the day, I'll listen. But I need to be able to sleep on a regular bed at night."

"When?" Her eyes fill.

He walks to her and holds her. She lets him. He smells like deodorant and soap and a hint of sweat.

"It's going to be all right," he assures her.

"What if we try? You sleep in here with me . . . We . . ."

"You know we can't do that right now. You need to take care of you. And I have to be out of the way for that to happen."

She steps away. "Stop being so fucking understanding. It sounds condescending."

"Can you see what you're doing?" he asks.

Of course she can. She can see all the messed-up things she's doing. Trying to get in a fight. Trying to win. Trying to get him to stay, so she can kick him out and tell him to come back. Trying, most of all, to get control.

"Just go. Take your stuff and get out." She knows she sounds like a total bitch, but it's all she has, a tiny bit of power.

The second he's gone, she slams the door as hard as she can. She hates him. Hates him because she loves him. Hates him because he understands that she needed to slam the door on him, needed to feel like she was getting rid of him.

She slides to the floor, keeping an ear close to the door, listening to see if he's really going to go. He wouldn't leave her when she's so upset, but the house shudders when the front door shuts. She curls into a ball.

Maybe if she would have knocked on wood the way Gail did last week, this wouldn't be happening. She was the idiot who said that it was possible one of them would be next. It wasn't supposed to be true. It was just the nice thing to say at the time. To help Lizzy. What really sucks, though, is that Hannah might be right about her percentiles. What sucks even more is that Hannah is the one person Bridget wants to call.

Hannah

Tuesday morning, Hannah is up at six. The day promises to be hot and humid. She pulls on a pair of jeans and a sleeveless navy blue blouse. The morning routine has changed. They now eat breakfast as a family. She brushes her hair and puts on a dab of lipstick and some cover-up under her eyes. Granted, they are miles from being whole again, but she's determined to show Alicia no one is giving up.

In the kitchen she squeezes oranges for fresh juice. Sam and Adam like to eat scrambled eggs and bacon. Alicia still has Cheerios, trying to keep up the act that eating breakfast with her family is a new sort of torture. Every once in a while, her posture isn't so hostile. Progress, as expected, is slow.

Sam's feet swing happily under the table. The eggs are just about done. Hannah puts three strips of bacon on Adam's and Sam's plates. She gives the eggs a final swirl.

"Thank you," Adam says as Hannah serves him.

Sam breaks his bacon into small pieces. He likes to make a design before he eats. Alicia pours milk in her cereal and rolls her eyes at her brother.

"Let's be grateful that Mom got up and made us this nice breakfast," Adam says.

"Like she made the box of Cheerios," Alicia snaps.

Hannah looks at Adam and shrugs.

"Rome wasn't built in a day," he says.

She nods and sips her orange juice.

"Guess what?" Sam asks, legs still kicking under the table.

"What?" Hannah replies, just as Adam's phone, sitting on the kitchen counter, starts screaming the "Chicken Dance." She hasn't heard that ring since the day in the mall.

"Bawk, bawk," Sam shouts.

Adam makes a move to stand, but Hannah is already at the counter. She recognizes his sponsor's name and shuts off the phone.

"Who was it?" Alicia asks.

One of the stipulations at meals is that there are no electronic devices.

"Someone from Dad's work," Hannah tells her. "He can return the call after breakfast." Then she looks at Adam quickly, nastily, just enough to show him it wasn't work. She knows she has no right to be angry that his sponsor is calling, yet she is. Is it too much to ask that she get through one meal, one day, without having to think about her husband sneaking around with other men?

"So, slugger." Adam nudges Sam's elbow. "What were you going to tell us?"

He sticks a piece of bacon in his mouth. "I get to take home Izzy for the summer."

"Who's Izzy?" Alicia tries to sound as if she's not interested.

"Our class iguana."

"Gross. I'm not living in the same house with one of those."

"He's not gross. You are."

"Sam," Hannah says, still feeling annoyed about Adam's phone, "we need to talk about this before you make a commitment to watching him."

"I already told my teacher I would," he whines.

"You're an idiot," Alicia tells him. "You can't tell your teacher until you get a note from your parents. That's the rule."

"No it's not." He holds his fork as if it's a weapon. "And you're a dumb face."

"Stop with the names," Adam says. "We'll work it out."

Hannah picks up her glass and takes it to the sink. She's irritated with herself for not being more patient, for not being able to sit and enjoy breakfast with her children. Adam hasn't done anything wrong, yet she wants to throw something at him. She hates his platitudes—*We'll work it out*. She used to have faith in his *It'll be fine* and *Everything's okay*. But he was lying to himself as much as he was lying to her. And she was a moron for believing him. The glass slips from her hand and breaks in the sink.

"You okay?" Adam asks.

"Fine. Everything's just perfectly fine." She gives him another dirty look, then glances at Alicia, whose eyes are squinted. She hasn't missed the nasty undertones.

Hannah throws out the broken glass. Alicia finishes her cereal. Sam has a bite of scrambled eggs.

"Time for school," Hannah tells them.

She clears the table. Adam grabs his cell phone, then helps them gather their things.

When he returns from taking them to the bus stop, he comes toward Hannah.

"Sorry about my phone going off," he says.

She turns on the dishwasher. The whooshing noise is comforting. "Not exactly the best way to role-model no electronic devices."

"I thought it was off." He pours himself another cup of coffee and stands next to the counter, his head tucked down.

She detests her irritability, his submissiveness, their worn, tired rhythms, the steps that don't seem to change.

She sits at the table. Her shoulders slump. Her brain feels like it's slumping too. "I just don't know what to do anymore. I thought the group would help, but it turned into a freak show."

"I'm sorry," he tells her.

"Bridget said that I push people away. I don't talk about the specifics of your addiction or the fact that my daughter is a mess and urinated on the floor. The truth is I haven't been able to talk about much of anything. I just can't, and I know it makes me seem cold and withholding." It's the most open she's been with Adam in ages.

"You're warm and understanding." He joins her. "You don't push people away."

"You don't think I push Alicia away?"

"Of course not. You're doing everything you can to help her."

She spins a lone fork that was left on the table. "What if I'm not, though?"

"What do you mean?"

"I mean, what if being a good mother really meant that I should have left you years ago?"

He sighs and moves his hand closer to her. "If you want me to leave, I understand."

"I don't know what I want." She's back to feeling slumped. It's hard work, this protecting, defending—pretending. "I blame myself," she says.

"Hannah, don't. None of this is your fault."

"But it is. In part. I didn't go into this blind. I knew I was marrying someone who was sick, and I chose to believe you were better. It's what I wanted to believe. It was selfish on my part. I wanted to have children. I wanted to have a normal, happy family."

He reaches to touch her shoulder, then retracts his hand, knowing it's against her rules. "There is nothing selfish about you," he tells her.

"Of course there is. I'm no better than all the rest of the parents who tell themselves they're staying together because it's best for the children. If I really wanted what was best for them, I would have left you when they were toddlers, when I found out you'd been screwing around again. When you gave me an STD. But no. I decided to believe you'd work it out. As much as you lied to me, I lied to myself. I told myself you were really going to get better. Because I couldn't imagine living on my own with two babies."

"You've done everything for them. And you can't go backward."

She hangs her head, looks at her blue flats. "True. I can't know how my life would have been different if I didn't marry a sex addict, or if I didn't have children. I think about that. I think about how it was selfish to have kids."

"Don't spiral like this. You're a great mom. We'll work it out."

"I hate when you say that. Like it's all going to be fixed; like it's just a broken spoke on a bike. What if we can't work it out? What if I get a call from the principal and she tells me Alicia defecated on the bathroom floor today?" She flicks the fork and watches it career off the table.

Adam bends to pick it up. "Alicia's getting better."

Hannah pushes back her chair and walks to the counter. "Last night at the dinner table, when you were making the mashed potatoes, Alicia called Sam *cunt breath*. Cunt breath. I mean, where the hell did she ever even hear that? She's nine, for God's sake."

"Why didn't you tell me?"

"I was going to. But honestly, I couldn't repeat the words last night. I don't know what's wrong with her. What if she's just a bad seed?"

"Hannah, stop it. You know that's not true. She's—"

"What was that?" Hannah whips around. "Is someone here?" she calls.

Adam walks to the front door, opens it, and glances outside. "Nothing," he says.

A shiver whispers through her, a warning. Or maybe it was just a cloud passing over the skylight, but when she looks up, all she sees is a relentless blue. She walks upstairs. Alicia's door is closed. Nothing out of the ordinary. Adam usually closes doors, but she should check anyway.

The moment she looks into Alicia's room, she sees the movement under the covers.

"Alicia," Hannah says.

"Get out."

That's the last thing Hannah is going to do. "Honey, can we talk?"

"You hate me. You think I'm a bad seed."

"I love you. I would never, never hate you. And I don't think there's anything bad about you. You're my beautiful, precious girl."

"You're a liar. I heard you." The words are muffled by the blanket.

Hannah tugs the comforter down. Alicia pulls furiously at her hair.

"I'm not lying when I say I love you." She sits on the bed and pushes Alicia's hands down. "Both your father and I love you more than anything."

"But you think the principal is going to call you. You think I'm bad," she shouts.

"I don't think you're bad at all. Maybe you're going through a rough time. But you're a wonderful, good person."

Alicia's blue eyes glisten with tears.

"Why didn't you get on the bus?" Hannah asks.

"I forgot my homework."

Hannah glances at the door. Adam is standing there, a mountain of shock. "Alicia heard some of our discussion," she says. He walks in, stone-faced, and sits on the desk chair.

"Mommy and I were just talking things out," he explains. "We love you and your brother. Nothing will change that." His mouth barely opens when he speaks, although his face softens.

"Mom didn't even want to have us."

"No." Hannah pulls Alicia toward her, holds her. "No, I always wanted you."

"I'm never going back to school."

"Of course you are," Adam says.

She pushes Hannah away. "Leave me alone."

"We're not going to leave you alone," Adam says. "We're going to do everything we can to help you."

"I don't need help. And I hate that lady Beth. And I hate you." She kicks her legs. "And Sam."

"I thought you liked Beth," Hannah says.

"Well, I don't." She pouts.

Adam scoots his chair closer to the bed. "Alicia, life isn't always easy, and right now you're going through a tough time. When you get through it, you'll be stronger. But you know how you have to take medicine if you're sick? Well, now the medicine doesn't come in a bottle. You have to see Beth. And you have to go to school. It might be hard today, and tomorrow. But if you don't go, it will only get worse."

"What kind of medicine do you take?" Alicia asks Adam.

"I don't take medicine," he tells her.

"What's a sex addict?" she asks.

Hannah sighs. "Where did you hear that?"

"You said it. You said Dad was one."

"It's something that . . ." She doesn't have the slightest idea what to say.

"It's something you'll learn when you're a grown-up," Adam says.

"You think I'm stupid. I know what sex is," she yells.

"And how do you know that?" Hannah asks, staring at one of the purple polka dots on the comforter.

"It's on the computer."

"What do you mean?" She keeps staring at the dot until it's charred into her brain.

"Sometimes Sam turns it on when he's playing his stupid games. He thinks it's funny."

Hannah glances from the dot to Adam. He knows computers and porn.

"What kind of things does he watch?" Adam asks.

"Gross stuff. It's disgusting. People who do that are disgusting."

"Does he watch it every day?" Hannah asks.

"I don't know. Ask him. He thinks it's funny. Like he thinks farting is funny. So now do you believe me? That I know what sex is?"

"I think you might know the wrong things about it," Adam tells her. "After school we'll sit together and have a talk."

Hannah shakes her head. "I just don't understand how he got onto those sorts of sites."

"What's important now is that Alicia goes to school." Adam sounds measured. Hannah wonders if this is what people like Adam can do. Take all the stuff they don't want to think about, zip it up, tuck it away, and act like life is fine. She can do it to a degree, but not as cleanly and efficiently as Adam.

"I'm not going back to school," Alicia says. "Ever."

"Of course you are," Adam tells her.

"You just want to get rid of me so you can do what those people on the computer do."

"No, we don't want to get rid of you," Hannah tells her.

Adam walks to the bed and picks Alicia up. "It will be good to think of schoolwork and see your friends." He's firm, yet soothing.

"I don't have any friends."

"You have loads of them," he tells her as he carries her out. "We're going to have something yummy to eat, then Mommy and I are going to take you to school."

Adam sits with Alicia in the kitchen, gives her a bowl of ice cream, and tells her a few knock-knock jokes. It takes about twenty minutes, but eventually she smiles and agrees to go to school.

On the ride there, Hannah keeps glancing back at Alicia. Her knees bounce, and her skin is pale. When they get to the building, Hannah instructs Adam to wait. She'll walk Alicia in. No child wants a two-parent escort.

In the office, Hannah tells the secretary that Alicia wasn't feeling well this morning, but she is much better now. Then she squats and hugs her.

"I love you." She kisses her cheek.

Alicia shuffles away, defeated, head down.

Hannah wants to run after her, but she tells herself that taking Alicia back home right now wouldn't help. Under that rationalization there's another feeling, a feeling that terrifies Hannah—relief that she'll have a few hours' break from her daughter.

She gets in the car with Adam. As soon as they're out of the parking lot, she screams, "Fuck."

"No shit," he says.

"And how do they see that kind of filth on the computer? I thought it was hard for kids to access."

Adam shakes his head. "It should be. I really thought I had everything blocked."

"What are we going to do?" she asks.

"We need to set up an emergency appointment with Beth."

"Agreed."

"We need to come up with a plan of exactly how we're going to explain all of this," he says.

"Goddammit. Why didn't you ask her if she had her homework?" she asks.

"I did."

"I can't believe we didn't see her."

"I know," he says, and grips the wheel.

They glance at each other. For the first time in forever, she feels like they're actually on the same side.

Lizzy

Lizzy had some good moments in the last week, even some good hours. Hope comes, like photons, in small, discrete packets of light.

She makes manageable goals. Getting rid of clothes. Doing a fifteen-minute workout—she uses an old video. Washing all the sheets and towels. Poking around in her little garden, pulling up weeds. Researching Peru.

Then there are the things she tries to avoid but can't. Like checking e-mail. Joe forwarded her the message he relayed to parents. It was vague and damning, stating she was on leave for personal reasons. She would rather he had said she had a tooth infection.

Greg has been out of touch. She's texted, called, e-mailed. He hasn't replied to anything, not even her suggestion they meet with his therapist. If she manages to go ten minutes without having a conversation with Greg in her head or checking her phone and e-mail, that's a good run.

It's ten A.M., Tuesday. Gail and Kathryn have checked in. She expects Bridget to call in the next hour.

Number one on her list today is to clean out the cabinets. In the kitchen, she pulls out cans of soup, spices, and old boxes of spaghetti. The doorbell rings, and she freezes with a jar of Ragu in her hand. She doesn't have on any makeup, and she's wearing cotton pajama bottoms and a tank top. She grabs a jacket from the front hallway closet, imagining greeting the police who are coming to tell her they have bad news about Greg.

After one deep breath, she opens the door. Standing in front of her is a middle-aged woman in a pink Lilly Pulitzer dress.

"Hi, my name is Anne Wadely. I represent the Breast Cancer Society."

Lizzy smiles dumbly, relieved it's not some do-gooder from school handing her a basket of "cheer," herbal teas and chocolate chip cookies.

"We're going door-to-door seeing if we can get people to join in the fight—"

"Of course. Let me get my purse." Lizzy hurries inside, grabs her bag, and rejoins Anne on the steps.

"We always take donations, but the main reason for my visit is to see if you'd be willing to send out cards to your neighbors, asking them to donate."

"No, I'd rather just give some money." She rifles through her wallet. She only has a few dollars. Her life has been so fractured, she can't remember the last time she went to an ATM.

"I'm sorry," Lizzy says. "Let me write you a check. Who do I make it out to?"

"Breast Cancer Society. Are you sure you wouldn't like to send out some cards to your neighbors?"

"No. Not right now." She hands Anne a check.

"We have just found—"

"No, thank you." Pink dress or not, this woman needs to stop. Lizzy closes the door and checks her wallet again. It's time to live with some semblance of normality. She will go to the bank, get some cash, stop at the grocery store, and not hide behind the shades of her home.

It's important to plow forward. Gail said that about Hannah. Granted it was in a different context, but the message still applies.

Her first stop is the bank. As she waits at the ATM, her nerves are skittish. She doesn't want to run into anyone she knows.

When it's her turn, she enters her PIN, then touches the screen to withdraw one hundred dollars. The machine declines her request. She tries again, feeling embarrassed that someone might think she doesn't have any money. Again, she is denied. Flustered, she grabs her card and walks into the bank.

Over the past few years, she and Greg have saved nearly forty thousand dollars. So it can't be that there's no money. In fact, they have an appointment to consult with a financial analyst, someone who will help them invest.

A tall, young Indian man wearing a dark green turban approaches. "Hello, my name is Amrit, may I help you?" He has an American accent, but not East Coast, maybe Californian.

Lizzy shakes his hand. "I don't know why my card isn't working."

He gestures to a desk that is partially partitioned from the main floor. She takes a seat across from him and gives him her card. The keys click and soon he's studying her account on his computer.

"Ah," he says. "It is because you have only a maximum cash withdrawal of five hundred dollars a day."

"But . . ." She stops, not wanting to discuss her marital problems. "Can I make the limit higher?"

"Of course you may. We only do it to protect you." He clicks a few more keys. "What would you like your maximum to be?"

"Can I make it anything?"

"Yes, of course." His words are less languid, less California. A trace of impatience.

She feels ignorant. Her head has been firmly planted in the sand when it comes to money and finances.

"Uh . . . would it be all right if I took a look?" She is about to stand and walk around so she can see the screen.

Amrit motions for her to stay seated and turns the computer. It takes a moment to understand, but she sees that for the past week Greg has withdrawn five hundred dollars a day.

There's a few hundred left in the checking account. "Can I see our savings account?"

"If you'd like." Amrit inputs more information.

There's only sixteen thousand. "This isn't the entire balance, is it?" she asks.

He glances at the screen. "Yes, that is the correct amount. Do you have another account with us?"

"No." At least none that she knows of. "Is there any way to see the deposits and withdrawals?"

"Ma'am, they are all on the screen."

"Sorry. I'm not used to looking at these." She can see that all her paychecks are direct-deposited. She can also see that significant sums have been moved to their checking account. She studies the transactions, feeling as if she's a large, wet snowflake disintegrating as it hits the pavement.

"Ma'am, would you like to increase your withdrawal amount?" Amrit glances to the waiting area.

Lizzy sees there are a few people, but now isn't the time to be submissive or polite and hurry away like a good girl.

"Can I open a new account?" she asks.

"Of course. You may do anything you like." He bows his head. "We are here to serve the customer."

"And can I transfer this money here into the new account?" she asks.

He clicks away, then nods. "Yes, you have the capability to do that. Either account holder can move the money."

"Okay, then, I'd like to do that."

"Checking or savings?"

"Can I make it just in my name?"

"Yes, if that is what you would prefer." He pauses. "Checking or savings?" He doesn't sound as if he's trying to serve.

"Checking, please."

She fills out the paperwork, enters a new PIN number, and leaves the bank wondering how long it will be now before Greg gets in touch.

Hannah

Hannah spent most of the day calming herself down. It helped that Adam called Beth and the three of them had an hour-long conference call. Beth assured them that they could work through this. She's dealt with children who have seen all sorts of things, including porn. She's also managed cases where the children have heard much worse than what Alicia heard this morning. The bottom line, Beth said, is that Alicia is loved, and if children are loved and cared for, and they know that, the other things can be worked through.

At five to three, Sam drops his backpack a few feet from the front door and barrels into the kitchen.

"Mom," he yells. "I got a hundred on my spelling test."

"Well, that deserves a treat. How about a brownie?" She made them for Alicia, to reward her for going to school after such a tough morning. But Sam could use one as well.

"Yay," he shouts, and hops on a stool. She gives him a brownie and a glass of milk.

Adam is leaving work early. They're going to sit with the children and have a talk before dinner. It won't be a long, detailed lecture; rather they will explain that sex should be a beautiful, intimate act, not something you should watch other people doing. The hypocrisy of some of the things they plan to say isn't lost on Hannah. But she will do everything in her power to ensure Sam doesn't become a sex addict. With the explosion of accessible, anonymous Internet porn, she can't afford to shy away from these difficult conversations.

She watches Sam practically stuff the whole brownie in his mouth, then looks beyond him, expecting to see Alicia. She's not there. More than likely, she went to hide in her room. After everything that happened this morning, it's understandable.

"Looks like you need another one," Hannah tells Sam. He gulps down some milk and grins.

"I'm going to get your sister, and we're going to water the garden. No TV or video games on the computer when I'm gone."

"Why?"

"It's a beautiful day outside."

She heads to Alicia's room. Surprisingly, the door is open.

"Alicia," she calls, "I made brownies."

Hannah walks in. The bed is ruffled from the morning, and although there are lumps, none seem big enough to be Alicia. Still, Hannah runs her hand along the comforter as she looks around the room.

"Alicia," she calls. Her heart beats a little harder as she walks to the closet. The idea that Alicia may be curled up in some fetal ball is disturbing. But she's not in the closet either. She checks the bathroom, the den, her bedroom, Sam's, the guest room, the other bathrooms, and finally the laundry room. She must be outside.

"Come on," Hannah tells Sam. "Let's go to the garden."

Alicia isn't there either.

"Sam?" Hannah asks. "Do you know where your sister might be?"

He has already turned on the hose and is pointing it at her.

"Turn that off," she shouts.

He blasts her face with cold water.

"Damn it, Sam." She marches over to turn off the tap, then grabs his arm, giving him a good shake.

"I thought we were watering," he whines.

"Do I look like a garden?"

He lowers his head. "No."

"Have you seen your sister?" she asks.

"Nope."

"Where did she go when you came home?"

"Dunno."

"Think. Did she go to her room? The living room? Which way?"

"She wasn't on the bus." He's distracted by a fly buzzing around his head.

"She wasn't on the bus?" Hannah asks.

He pulls up his shoulders so they're close to his ears. "I don't think so."

"Why didn't you tell me?"

"She wasn't on the bus this morning either." He looks like he's about to cry.

"You're right, she wasn't. And it's not your job to watch her. But are you sure she wasn't on the bus this afternoon?"

He nods timidly, and she feels guilty for being so snappy.

She checks her pockets for her cell phone. It's not there. She left it in her room. Alicia has probably been trying to call. Hannah runs inside. There are two new text messages. The first one is from Adam.

Just checking in. How are you?

The next one is from Bridget.

Can we talk?

Hannah calls the school.

"Pine Hill Elementary, may I help you?"

"Yes, hi. This is Hannah Jenkins. My daughter, Alicia, missed the bus. Is she in the office?"

"No. I don't see her here."

"Well, could she be around there? Maybe waiting at the front of the building?"

"I can't see the front of the building from here, but if you'd like, I'll check around and call you back."

"Yes, thank you. That would be wonderful. My number is—"

"I have it here. It came up on caller ID."

"Right. Thanks." Hannah hangs up, not wanting to waste an extra second when the secretary could be out checking. Poor Alicia. She must be panicked. After a couple minutes, Hannah can't stand the wait.

"Sam, we're going to drive to the school and find Alicia." She hustles him to her SUV.

Slowing down is the most she can manage at the stop signs. She peels into the school parking lot and pulls in front of the entrance. As she hops out of the car, she thinks of Bridget. She'll call her as soon as she has Alicia.

"Out you go," she tells Sam, and races into the building with him.

The secretary, she assumes the one she just spoke with, is staring at her computer.

"Hi, I'm here to pick up Alicia."

"Oh." She turns. "I was just going to call you. I couldn't find her."

"Did you check the bathrooms?"

"Uh . . . no, actually. I thought she probably went home with a friend."

There's no time for a discussion of what Alicia may or may not have done. Hannah grabs Sam's hand and tears into the girls' room.

"Mom," Sam screams. "I can't come in here."

"Jesus, Sam. You scared me. It's fine. We're just looking for Alicia."

She pushes open every stall door. No one is in the girls' room. She races down the hall to the next bathroom. When she's checked them all, she looks in the boys' rooms, then goes back to the office. The secretary is packing up to leave.

"I can't find her," Hannah says.

"Did you try her friends?"

"I'd know if she was going to a friend's house."

"Maybe she forgot to tell you. It happens all the time."

Possibly. But peeing on the bathroom floor doesn't happen all the time, nor does hearing your mother say maybe you shouldn't have been born. She yanks Sam's hand and runs back to the entrance. No Alicia. She checks the playground. There are a couple of children with their parents. No Alicia.

She drags Sam back to the car.

"When was the last time you saw her?" she asks him.

"Um . . ." He pulls the seatbelt strap across his chest. "This morning, I guess."

"Can you just take a deep breath, close your eyes, and think really hard?"

He does what she tells him.

"What do you see?"

"My castle Legos."

"Just focus on Alicia. Then tell me what you see."

He shrugs. "Nothing."

Hannah feels like bursting into tears. She calls Adam.

"What's up?" he answers.

"Alicia didn't come home from school."

"Slow down. I'm sure she's fine. She probably just missed the bus."

"No. She's not fine. She didn't miss the bus. I'm at the school, and she's not here, and no one has seen her. I'm calling the police."

"Hang on. Let's just think for a second. Did you call her friends?"

"I would know if she went to a friend's," she shouts.

"Let's just try a few before we call the police. Do you have their numbers?"

"Of course," she snaps.

"I'm leaving the office right now. Call as many people as you have numbers for. I'm sure we'll find her."

"I don't know if I should stay at the school or go home."

"Go home. She might have tried to walk there. I'm on my way out.

Drive the route you think she might take, and I'll meet you in about half an hour."

She hangs up and calls all the friends' numbers in her phone. No one has seen Alicia. She drives two miles an hour down the side streets. There are no young girls with blond hair. At home, she pulls out Alicia's class list. She calls all the numbers that she hasn't already tried. Mostly she gets voice mail. The few people who answer haven't seen Alicia. Two of them don't even know who she is.

Hannah runs to her bedroom and grabs a recent photograph of Alicia and Sam at the beach. She doesn't know what the rules or laws are, but she can't wait at home. The police have to help her.

Just as she's about to bolt, Adam walks in.

Lizzy

At this time in the afternoon, most of Lizzy's students are participating in sports or working at part-time jobs. She doubts many, if any, are studying for their chemistry final. Not that she should be worried about it, but she does wish she could have finished teaching the last unit. She sits in the living room, with the shades open, reading a book she found on the shelf the other day, *The Language of Letting Go*. If only it was as simple as learning a language, perhaps she could get somewhere. It just feels, at the moment, that there's far too much to let go of. Basically, her whole life as she knew it. The book is open to the chapter on grudges, but as she reads the words, her thoughts are elsewhere—on Greg's whereabouts, the missing money, finals, the group, pornography, the trafficking of underage girls . . . One of the tenets of the book is to let go of all the thoughts and worries that plague you, to live in the now—the present. She totally sucks at that.

The front door flies open. Startled, Lizzy drops the book. A few moments later, Greg stands in front of her, his forehead furrowed, his eyes particularly beady.

"What the fuck," he says.

She hadn't expected him until tomorrow. After all, he'd already withdrawn his five hundred for the day. She holds on to the arm of the couch and scoots back as far as she can.

"How the hell am I supposed to live on nothing?" he asks.

"I couldn't take out any money when I went to the bank," she replies. "How am *I* supposed to live on nothing?"

"You could have written a check to yourself and cashed it." He walks to the other side of the room and kicks the leg of an armchair.

"We were supposed to have forty thousand saved. What happened to that?"

"What happened to that is bills and the mortgage and taxes. Who do you think takes care of all that?"

"I know. But I thought after those bills, we were going to have a good chunk to invest."

"Well, I didn't account for some of the increases."

"Over twenty thousand worth?" She stands.

"There's cable and phone bills. Car insurance. Health insurance . . ."

"Wait. I pay for health. And how much can phone and cable be?"

"That's not the point. You transferred all of the money." His eyes look swallowed by rage.

"My money went into that savings." She backs up so that she's close to the stairs.

"I paid bills," he yells.

"Bullshit." She stomps her foot. "Stop with the lies. I don't know what you spent it on, but you're not spending my money anymore."

"How am I supposed to eat?"

"Get a job."

"Fuck you." He marches toward her.

She walks backward up a stair. "I have to look after myself too."

"Then we're going to have to live in this house together," he tells her.

"Is that a threat?" she asks.

"It sure won't be pretty with the two of us here."

She holds the banister and continues stepping backward, feeling her way up to the landing. When she looks down at him, he is thin and hunched, no longer her handsome husband who looks fifteen years younger than his age. How can the man she always thought was perennially good-looking, blond with a boyish grin, suddenly be red-faced and gnarly?

"You can have your study and the guest room," she tells him. "The bedroom is mine."

"Trust me, I don't want to be in there with you."

Considering the fight they've just had, his comment shouldn't faze her, yet it stings, and as soon as she closes the door to the bedroom, she cries. Quietly, of course, so he can't hear her.

Hannah

Hannah and Adam take separate cars to the station. Sam goes with Adam. They arrive at the same time and wait at the front desk. Two women officers nod but don't get up. No one comes to help.

Hannah raps her fingers on the counter. She can't stay in here for long. She has to keep moving, keep looking, get back home, try all the neighbors' houses. God, Gabby. How could she not have thought of Gabby? Of course that's where Alicia would go. Hannah takes her phone out of her pocket and finds Gabby's number.

She picks up after two rings. "Hi," she says cheerfully.

"This is Mrs. Jenkins. Is Alicia with you?" Hannah holds her breath.

"No. I haven't seen her since the other night when I babysat. Is something wrong?"

"She didn't come home after school." A policeman who looks about eighteen approaches. Adam makes a motion for Hannah to get off the phone.

They sit on the orange vinyl chairs in the lobby of the new station.

"My name is Officer Kadlik. I'll be taking the report."

"Our daughter didn't get on the bus this afternoon," Adam says. "We've checked everywhere, and we can't find her."

Officer Kadlik has light green eyes, and his smooth skin looks like it has no pores. He would be easy to photograph.

"You checked with all of her friends?" he asks.

"Of course," Hannah says. "We tried everyone."

"And you're sure she's not asleep at home somewhere?"

"Yes, I'm sure she's not asleep at home." Hannah knows she sounds snarky, but this guy doesn't seem to be getting the urgency of the situation.

"Ma'am, I need to ask. It's funny how many times the child is sleeping at home."

Nothing is funny about this. "She's not home. I'm sure."

"And has this happened before?"

Hannah glances around. They need someone older and wiser.

"No," Adam says. "It hasn't happened before."

"Is that a real gun?" Sam asks.

Officer Kadlik smiles. "It is, but it's locked."

"I want to be a cop when I grow up."

"Sam, not now," Adam says.

"Cute kid," Kadlik comments.

"This is a picture of Alicia." Hannah displays the photograph.

"I just have a few more questions before we get to that," Kadlik tells them.

She's ready to scream. "Maybe someone else should be here to listen as well."

"If you want, Officer Green is supposed to be back in like"—he looks at his watch—"twenty minutes or so."

"No, we don't want to wait," Adam says. "We want you looking for our daughter as soon as possible."

He nods and glances at his clipboard. "She's not at home?"

"No," Hannah and Adam say at the same time.

"And is someone at the house right now in case she comes home?"

"I called my mother," Hannah says. "She should be there by now."

The walls are an asparagus color, the wrong shade for a police station. In fact, everything about this place feels wrong.

"Good. Because you want to make sure someone is there. In case—"

"Yes, we understand that," Hannah says. "We need you to start looking."

"As soon as I get the report," he says. "Um . . . It's just that we have to tell you, when you file a missing child report in Massachusetts, DCF will automatically have to investigate," he whispers, not wanting Sam to hear.

"DCF?" Adam asks.

"Department of Children and Families."

"Why?" Hannah can't sit much longer.

"Possible neglect."

"That's ridiculous," Adam says.

Officer Kadlik shrugs. "Sorry, it's the law. That's why I asked you those other questions. Just wanted to make sure we had all the bases covered before making an official report."

"She's not at home. We want to make a report," Hannah tells him.

Kadlik nods. "Okay. What did you say her name was?"

"Alicia. Alicia Jenkins. She's nine, almost ten. She has blond hair. She's a little over four feet. Blue eyes. And she's thin."

"How do you spell Jenkins?" he asks.

"J-E-N-K-I-N-S," Adam overenunciates.

"Have you ever been in charge of a case like this?" Hannah asks.

"No, ma'am. This is my first . . . missing child," he says carefully.

She flinches.

"I think we need someone with more experience," Adam says.

"If you don't mind waiting." Kadlik is about to stand.

"We do mind. Can we just get on with it?" she asks.

"Any reason you think your daughter might not have wanted to come home?"

"She was upset this morning. She overheard my wife and me having an argument."

"About?"

Adam glances at Sam, then back at Kadlik. "Personal matters."

"It might be better if just one of you gave the answers," Kadlik explains. "There's a lot of, you know, private stuff. I have to know about all of her relationships. If there's anyone in the family who might want to cause a problem. Who doesn't like her, that sort of thing."

Hannah turns to Adam. "Why don't you take Sam home? Check the houses on Forest Ave. I'll do this part."

She answers all of Kadlik's questions quickly and efficiently. When her phone rings she jumps, sure it's Alicia. But then she looks at the caller ID. It's Bridget. Hannah can't talk. Not now. She'll explain to Bridget later that she wasn't trying to avoid her, that she's not angry anymore about what happened in group. Hannah ends the call and turns her attention back to the young police officer.

It's been hours. Not a word from anyone. Hannah paces from one end of the living room to the other as Adam sits on the couch next to the lamp, which projects a round glow onto the ceiling.

"I feel like we should be doing something," Hannah says as she begins to bargain with God. *Take my life, just let my daughter be okay.*

"I know. But they told us the best thing we could do is wait here. She could come home any second."

"I just keep thinking of all the things I should have done differently."

"Don't torture yourself like that."

"I can't help it." She stops in front of him. The dim lighting shades his eyes. "I've been grouchy and tense with the kids. Alicia's sensitive. I should have been more aware, not so wrapped up in my own pain. I should have—"

"Stop." He stands to hold her, but she takes a step backward, as if he's about to strike. "Please don't blame yourself. If it's anyone's fault, it's mine. I put you in that pain."

"What if I would have talked more about myself in group? What if I would have told them what was really going on? I'm so caught up in appearances." *Please God, do anything you want to me, just don't let Alicia be hurt.*

"We can what-if ourselves to death. It's not going to change anything." He sits.

She begins to pace again. "I blame you. But I have a part in this too. I've been so ashamed of you, of us. So frightened of everything, of people finding out you might be gay, of the children learning." She shakes her head. *I'll be okay with anything if she's okay.*

"Hannah, I'm not gay."

She doesn't reply. She keeps pacing, from the portrait of the children back to the light switch on the other wall.

"Hannah, did you hear me? I'm not gay."

She stops and looks at him. "How do you know?" *He can be gay if Alicia is all right.*

"I love you. I love making love to you. What I've done with other men isn't about you. It's a compulsion. Something I have to keep working out."

"But will you? Work it out?"

"Yes," he says without a beat or pause.

"And then?" She would give up her husband for her daughter.

"I don't know. Maybe we can move past this. Maybe we can't."

"I hate the maybes." She's moving again. "Maybe they will find Alicia. Maybe they won't. I need something more solid."

"I love you. You're a wonderful, kind mother."

"I'm going to call the station again." She veers off her path, eyeing her phone on the glass coffee table.

"They'll call us the minute they know anything."

"I have to do something."

Adam stands. He puts an arm around her. "Let's go for a walk around the block."

"What if she comes home?"

"Your mother is here."

"I can't leave the house." She wants to scream, kick the wall, smash the lamp.

"Okay, then we'll stay here. We'll pace together."

"If they find Alicia, I'm going to call Bridget and Lizzy and Gail and tell them I'm sorry. Tell them I want to keep meeting with them. That I'll talk to them, work through all this mess inside of me. I'll volunteer more at Sam and Alicia's school. I'll spend more time with my mother. I'll—"

Adam wraps his arms around her. "Shush," he says. "They'll find her."

"You don't know that."

He holds her tighter. "They'll find her," he says again.

Her weight shifts into his. She believes him. She has to.

Lizzy

izzy and Greg have stayed in their respective rooms for the past few hours. She's cried, tried to rest, checked e-mails, thought about calling Kathryn, and even made a feeble attempt at meditation. But the knots in her stomach and her heart and lungs remain.

She feels like a prisoner, and then she thinks about a speaker who came to the high school a few months ago. He was wrongly incarcerated for seventeen years, until DNA proved his innocence. To Lizzy it seemed the worst of all fates, but he wasn't bitter. With his long white hair, he stood in front of an auditorium filled with teenagers, who were mesmerized as he told them that he decided that this was his journey, and he would use what he learned to help others. He didn't allow resentment and bitterness to win.

Neither will Lizzy.

She e-mails Valerian. *If you are still looking for volunteers, I would love to spend time helping. I am available immediately.*

Next she e-mails Joe. *Now that I understand my situation, I will take your advice and stay out for the remainder of the year. I will return in August.*

She signs onto the banking site where they have their mortgage and pays the next three months.

Valerian replies. *We would love to have you. Although we cannot pay anything, we are happy to provide room and board.* She wasn't expecting to get paid.

She cancels the phone, Internet, and cable. As her students would say, she gets unplugged.

Finally, she packs a bag with light clothes and a few toiletries.

Without Internet, Greg's central line has been shut off. He will go into a rage when he realizes it. It's not him. It's his addiction. She understands this. She also understands that it's time to leave.

The alarm clock next to her bed reads 8:43.

She should feel sad, maybe scared, but she doesn't. Instead she feels as if she knows exactly what to do, as if this was meant to be all along, and finally the turmoil inside of her is gone. She imagines a rock garden with a serene pool of water. Strange after all of this, after the nights of hoping Greg would make love to her, after the humiliation of sitting in Joe's office, after this morning's financial blow, she is neither ashamed nor disappointed.

She pauses at Greg's study door and holds up a hand, about to knock, but then lets it fall. His addiction owns him. There's no point in saying anything.

She switches on the front porch light and carries her one bag to the car. As she backs out of the driveway, she pauses to look at the home she's leaving. It's just a big yellow box. It's amazing she's lived in it for eighteen years and can't think of a thing she'll miss except for the blueberry bushes in the backyard.

She parks at the bus station and leaves the key under the driver's seat. Greg can pick up the car if he wants it. Eventually she'll write to him and let him know where it is. She buys a one-way ticket to Logan Airport and gets off at Terminal A, just a short walk from the Hilton.

At the hotel reception desk, she's tempted to take a suite but decides a double is more practical, and there's no need to waste money. No need to be like . . . But she stops the thought. Let go of the bitterness.

Her room overlooks the control tower that pulsates with red and white bursts of light. She unpacks a couple of things. When she puts her toothbrush and toothpaste on the countertop next to the sink, the room feels officially hers for the night.

And then her fingers begin to tingle a little. At first the sensation is stronger in her left hand, and she thinks it might be a sign that she's having a heart attack. But soon the sensation is in her other hand as well. The decision to leave Greg had come relatively easily, and she had naively expected the blush of confidence to last. On the ride to the airport, she imagined the peaceful solitude of an anonymous, temperature-controlled, sterile room. She did not plan for her nerves to suddenly kick in and her head to feel as if it were stuck in the static between radio stations. Electrical disturbances pulse like jagged peaks of interference.

She leaves her room and takes the elevator to the lobby, where she finds the hotel lounge. A few people dotted throughout scrutinize their phones or iPads. Lizzy has a moment of panic. What if she needs to get in touch with someone? What if someone needs to get in touch with her? But after a moment, sadness replaces the unease. There is no one that important.

She asks the waitress for a cranberry juice and vodka. The first few sips taste cool and refreshing. The static lessens. A couple walks in, and although the woman touches the man's arm as he leads her to a table, there is something terse about her, and Lizzy wonders if she's a hooker, and if the man is a sex addict.

She orders a BLT and another drink.

A man who appears fifty-something, with dark, hooded eyes, nods at her. She pretends to look for something in her purse, then stares at the round table. A few moments later, she glances up. He's paying the bartender. Of course she didn't want him to come and talk to her—what would she say? But she feels let down. He's wearing a gray suit that has an expensive way of hanging. It seems he's about to leave, but then he turns to look at her. She's caught watching him and lowers her head, giving him time to walk out in privacy.

Instead he approaches her table.

"Carlos." He extends a hand.

"Hi." She shakes his hand quickly, not wanting to seem eager or over-personal.

"May I?" He points to the chair across from her.

"Sure." Her smile is as quick as her handshake. "I'm Lizzy."

"On your way to somewhere?" he asks.

"Yes. And you?" She finishes her drink. Two is her limit, three will give her a migraine, although at the moment she doesn't care.

"Back home." His short gray hair, spiked with gel, reminds her of a hedgehog.

"And where is that?" she asks, playing with the stirrer in her glass.

"Madrid," he says. "May I buy you another?" He glances at her drink.

"Yes. Why not?"

He raises his hand. "A whiskey for me, and another for the lady. Whatever it is she would prefer."

"The same," Lizzy tells the waitress.

"So, you did not say where you are going to." He has sleepy eyes, no wedding ring, and just enough of a belly to suggest he's not into any sort of extreme workouts.

"Peru. The jungle." She likes the way it sounds. The waitress comes with their drinks, and Lizzy feels herself relax.

"For pleasure? Research?" he asks.

"To help build a school."

"You are a . . . what do you call them . . . someone who does missionary work?" He leans toward her. She smells whiskey.

"No. Not really. I just want to do something useful for once." She smiles more openly.

"You do not seem like a woman who has spent a useless life."

She laughs. "No, I guess not. Maybe *change* is a better word."

"Ah." He swirls his drink. His gaze is pleasant.

For a moment she considers telling the truth, then decides that would ruin a perfectly genteel drink. "I just don't want life to pass me by and regret never having done the things I wanted to do."

"So you are the type for adventure?"

She sips her cranberry and vodka and contemplates the question for a second or two. "I guess so," she says.

"And you do this alone?" he asks.

"Yes." She wonders if it's unwise to tell a single man she is by herself. But what the hell? She needs to stop being so guarded.

"I do not know of many people who would just go off to the jungle. I think you must be brave."

"I'm not exactly doing it out of bravery—more like running away." Why keep pretending? She has to put that part of her life behind her.

"I see," he says, eyebrows raised.

She finishes her drink, liking that he didn't come right out and ask. If she tried to get up right now, she would probably stagger.

"I'm running from a bad marriage," she admits.

He nods. "I am sorry."

"I probably shouldn't have said that. It's the drinks."

"Sometimes it is easier to tell a perfect stranger, no?"

"Yes, I suppose that's true. Are you married?"

"I was once, yes. But for me too it was not so good." He tilts his head from side to side. "I traveled too much. She was bored. There was no more fire."

He looks at her empty glass. "Would you like another?"

"No, I better not. I have a lot to do in the morning."

The waitress comes to the table. Lizzy takes out her credit card. "I'd like to get this."

"Thank you," Carlos says.

It's nice he doesn't make a fuss, that he accepts her willingness to pay.

After she signs the receipt, they stand and shake hands again. This time she allows herself to enjoy his grip.

"I admire what you are going to do. I wish you luck and happiness."

"I wish you the same." Funny how she really feels that. She doesn't feel that for Greg. For a second, guilt washes over her, and the bristling under her skin returns.

She waits for Carlos to leave the bar first, but he waits for her. They smile awkwardly at each other and walk to the lobby together.

"You are at this hotel too?" he asks as they stand next to the elevator.

"Yes." She glances around, hoping there will be more people.

No one else comes. They get in and watch the numbers climb. It will be uncomfortable to have to say good-bye again. The elevator stops on the ninth floor and dings as the doors open.

"It was nice—" he begins as he takes a step toward the hallway.

"Wait," she says.

He looks at her and smiles. The doors close. He walks to her and kisses her. She doesn't hold back.

The elevator stops on the eleventh floor, and she leads him to her room. Inside, she closes the curtains most of the way. The blinking lights from the control tower flash steadily, rhythmically, comfortably. Carlos holds her shoulders, kisses her mouth, then her neck. Her lips brush against his cheek. There is a shy scent of expensive cologne.

He takes the clip out of her hair, then runs his hands through it. He tells her she is beautiful, and as the light pulses, she unbuttons her blouse. She believes him. They undress. He is gentle and confident. There is no hesitancy, no performance anxiety. The flow is natural, easy. The intimate touch of a man was something she had written out of her life plan.

She is grateful that he doesn't linger afterward. It is a luxury to be naked and feel no shame, to hog the whole bed, to stretch diagonally. After a few moments, she realizes she is submerged in silence. The ties to Greg are broken. She is simply not the kind of woman to have sex with someone else and then return to her husband.

She imagines the sounds of monkeys squalling as the sun sets on the Amazon River.

The static is gone. Sleep comes tenderly.

Hannah

Adam made peppermint tea, tried to get Hannah to watch TV, and suggested a drive, but all she can do is pace in the living room and make silent bargains with God. She'd give up anything. Her house, his sobriety.

Minutes feel like endless, horrific hours. If there is a hell, this is what it feels like. She desperately tries to push aside images of Alicia getting into some stranger's car. Adam's phone rings. Hannah stops pacing midstep.

"Yes," he says. He stands motionless, next to the coffee table.

She places a hand on her chest as she watches him.

"This is Mr. Jenkins." The left side of his mouth nudges downward. The creases on his brow grow deeper. The room has no air.

Finally, he lets out a long, audible sigh of relief.

"She's okay," he says to Hannah.

She hurries to his side, grabs his arm, and listens with him. He brushes his lips on the top of her head, and even in the midst of this crisis, she understands that he is grateful she has allowed this light kiss.

"She's being taken by ambulance to Newton-Wellesley Hospital," a man's voice states.

"We can be there in ten minutes," Adam says.

Hannah races outside, not bothering to grab her purse. Just as she's about to get into Adam's car, she dashes back into the house.

"They found her," she shouts to Sam and her mother, who are in the den. "We're going to meet her at the hospital."

Sam bolts up. "Can I come?"

"No, honey. You stay with Nana. We'll be home soon."

In the car, Hannah taps her feet on the floor. They took this exact same route when she was in labor with Alicia. Adam parks and they jog toward the bright red neon emergency room lights.

Hannah barrels through the swinging doors. A nurse in pink scrubs with her hands on her hips stands in Hannah's path.

"My daughter, Alicia Jenkins. Which room?"

The nurse doesn't stop Hannah; instead she turns and leads the way to a curtained-off area. Alicia is there. On the bed, eyes open. Alive. Hannah races to her daughter, kisses her forehead, and caresses her hair, as a doctor pats Alicia's shoulder.

"Everything looks good," the doctor tells Hannah. "We're just giving her some fluids. It was a hot night, and she might be dehydrated."

"When can we take her home?" Hannah asks.

"Soon, I imagine. But there are a couple of routine interviews for a case like this." The doctor smiles at Alicia. "You seem like a strong girl. Think you can answer a few questions?"

Alicia nods.

The doctor walks to the opening in the curtain. "I'll be back to check on her again."

Adam moves closer to the bed. He holds the metal rail.

"I have never, ever been so happy to see anyone," Hannah says. Her heart is slowing, and she can finally catch her breath. There is no blood, no bruises, no bandages. Alicia's skin is pale and clammy, but her blue eyes are clear, and Hannah feels as if her sanity has been miraculously restored.

"We were very worried," Adam says sternly.

Hannah glances at him and shakes her head just enough to show him this isn't the time to be angry.

"We're just so glad you're okay. How are you feeling?" Hannah asks.

"Scared," she whispers. Her lips arc cracked and dry. She probably hasn't had anything to eat or drink in hours.

Hannah tucks the stiff white sheet around Alicia. "No need to be frightened anymore. Soon you'll be home, safe and sound."

"Where were you?" Adam asks.

Hannah looks across the bed. She tilts her head, trying to ask Adam what he's doing, speaking so harshly. Then she glances at his hands gripping the bedrail. His knuckles are white.

"At the mall," Alicia whispers.

"How did you get there?" Adam asks.

"I walked," she murmurs.

"Adam," Hannah says, "we'll get to the details later. Let's just get her home and get a good meal into her." When she kisses Alicia's forehead again, she gets a whiff of something that reminds her of sour milk. It's the way her children smell when they're sweaty and exhausted.

"You walked from school?" Adam asks.

"Yes."

"Let's not do this now," Hannah says firmly.

"Can we leave?" Alicia asks.

"In a few minutes," Hannah replies, as a man and a woman enter.

"I'm Officer Ward," the man says. He's beefy with strained eyes and cheeks that sit too low on his face. "And this is Miss . . ."

"Theresa, just call me Theresa. I'm from DCF," the woman, who is clinging to a legal pad, pipes in. Her voice is high, her features nondescript.

Officer Ward moves forward. It's too much, Hannah thinks, all these adults hovering.

"We need to ask your daughter a few questions," Ward tells Adam. "It might be easier if we did this alone."

"I'm not leaving," Hannah tells the officer.

"Okay, then." He takes a notepad from his pocket. "Alicia, can you tell us how you ended up in Cambridge?"

"Cambridge?" Adam asks, startled. "No one told us that's where she was found."

"Sir, it would be best if we had no interruptions, if we just heard from your daughter for the moment."

Alicia bites her lip and looks up at Hannah.

"It's okay, honey. Just answer the questions honestly, and then we can go home. Tell the policeman how you ended up in Cambridge."

Alicia shrugs, confused. "I went to the mall. Then I took a bus because I wanted to go home." Her breathing is rapid as she tries not to cry.

"The person who called this in said you were on a park bench. A man was talking to you. Can you tell us about the man?" Ward asks.

She shakes her head no.

"What kind of man?" Adam asks.

"Sir, I am going to ask again that you not interrupt."

Adam's mouth draws into a tight line.

Hannah thinks of how calm he was all afternoon, how she was the one flipping out, and now that she's grounded and rational, he's losing it. But he can't do this in front of Alicia.

"Alicia," Officer Ward begins, "we don't think the man did anything wrong, but we just want to make sure you're okay. Did he say or do anything that felt threatening?"

Alicia looks up at Hannah, puzzled.

"Did he say or do something that didn't feel okay?" Hannah clarifies.

"He said there were a lot of bad people." She clutches her mother's hand.

"Did this man approach you, or did you approach him?" Ward asks.

Hannah wishes they would all leave. They're only making this harder on Alicia. She's fragile and overwhelmed at the moment. "Who was sitting on the bench first?" Hannah rephrases. "You or him?"

"Me."

Adam draws in a breath. Hannah glances at him, trying to tell him to stay calm.

"Did he try to hold your hand or touch you in any other way?" Theresa asks.

Alicia looks up at Hannah again.

"Did the man want to touch you?" Hannah asks.

She shrugs. Tears well in her eyes. "I don't know."

"It's okay," Hannah comforts. "You don't have to remember everything right now."

Officer Ward flips his notebook closed. "Well, I think we have what we need for the moment. I'll let . . ." He looks at Theresa. "I'll let DCF take over from here."

"I certainly hope you are questioning this man," Adam says to Ward.

"We will keep you informed."

"I think—" Adam begins.

"Thank you, Officer," Hannah interrupts. Adam getting cantankerous isn't going to get Alicia home any faster.

Ward nods at Hannah, then looks at Alicia. "Good to see you're okay." He taps the foot of the bed and walks out.

"Alicia," Theresa chirps, "I have a few questions for you now."

"I think it's been enough," Hannah says. "Perhaps another day. She needs to rest and eat."

"I understand. But it's protocol for runaways." Her thin hair is slipping out of its ponytail, but her gaze is direct and unfaltering. Commanding even. She softens when she turns back to Alicia. "Can you tell me why you went to the mall?"

"I don't know," she mumbles.

"Was there a reason you didn't want to go home?"

"I think she's exhausted," Hannah says. "It's too much."

"I know it's hard," Theresa says to Alicia. "But can you hang in there for a few more questions?"

Alicia nods.

"Good girl." She touches Alicia's hand. "Did you want to go home after school today?"

"No," Alicia answers.

"Can you remember why?"

"I . . . I don't know. Because Daddy is sick and I didn't want to talk about sex," she blurts.

"Why would you have to talk about sex?" Theresa asks.

Alicia looks at her mother. "Because that's what Mommy said, and because Daddy's a sex addict."

"Right." Hannah caresses Alicia's hair. "Because you overheard some things that were for adults only."

Theresa clears her throat. "I think it's best at this point if I speak with Alicia alone."

"Why?" Adam asks.

"It's protocol in this type of case," she says quietly.

"What is that supposed to mean?" Sweat beads on Adam's forehead.

As much as Hannah doesn't want to leave Alicia's side, she can see that the best thing for everyone right now would be to take Adam out of the mix. They have done nothing wrong, and interrupting and commenting on everything Theresa says may only make them look guilty.

Hannah strokes Alicia's arm. "Daddy and I are going to step out for just a couple of minutes. Answer the questions as best you can. If you can't remember, just tell her that." She leans down to kiss her.

Hannah walks to Adam, tugs his hand, and leads him to the waiting room. Two square vinyl armchairs with plum-colored cushions sit in a corner. A round wooden coffee table littered with various magazines stands next to the chairs. Hannah points and Adam obeys her gesture to take a seat.

He shakes his head, then covers his face with his hands. Hannah sits next to him.

"You have to calm down," she tells him.

"Why? Why would she do that?" he asks. "Walk five miles to the mall?" He drops his hands and stares at her.

She puts a hand on the armrest of his chair. "We'll figure out all the whys. At the moment we just need to be calm and show her we're not angry, and that home is a safe place to be."

"I just don't understand. She knows better."

"She didn't want to go home. That's all. Don't read more into this."

"That's all? She left the mall and somehow ended up in Cambridge where some man sat on a bench with her. God knows what he did."

She moves her hand to touch him, but withdraws it. "It doesn't sound as if he hurt her."

"We don't know that. She might be too terrified to say anything. He could have told her something horrible was going to happen if she talked."

"Adam, she'll tell the truth."

He shakes his head. "Children don't in these situations. They get scared. An adult makes a threat. Says he'll hurt her family. She doesn't know what's true or not." He looks at Hannah, his eyes searching for answers she's not sure she has.

"Is that what happened to you?" she asks. "Is that what your uncle made you believe? That someone in your family would get hurt?" She's never pressed him for the details about his uncle, and now, as she looks into his eyes that she thought she knew so well, she notices gray specks— fault lines.

He stands and takes a few steps, then turns back and glances at Hannah. "It's just that . . . It's so easy to snap. Someone tells you something. You don't know what to believe. And it's gone. Your former self. You're never the same, not really. And . . ."

She pats the plum-colored back of the chair. "Come sit."

He doesn't. He stares at the dark window and seems surprised to see his reflection. "It doesn't take a lot. Not really. Children are sensitive. They blame themselves, then their thoughts get confused, nothing is right anymore, but you don't even realize it. You think it's normal to obsess about sex. Normal to lie and tell the guy at the counter you're buying the porn for your dad. Your mind becomes a demented maze. There's no getting out."

244 • sylvia true

"Adam, it's okay. She'll be okay. You'll be okay. Come, sit. Please."

He acquiesces, then knocks the wooden armrest with his knuckles. "It's about a power imbalance."

"Adam, stop. We're not going to let anyone take away Alicia's power."

"I'm not. I would never . . ." He looks at Hannah. "I would never hurt my children."

"I know."

His shoulders round. "I never meant to hurt you."

"I know." And right now, she does know. The tall, sturdy man, her anchor, the man she wanted to believe would keep her and her children safe, is just a child himself.

"Every day that you don't leave me, I thank God." The rims of his eyes are pink.

"It's okay," she says quietly. "We don't have to talk about us right now." Again she reaches toward him, but again only touches the arm of the chair.

"I don't have a right to say how I feel. But—"

"Of course you have the right. All people have the right to talk about how they feel." She believes what she says, even though she knows that there were many times when she didn't want to listen to him, didn't want to hear all the reasons he chose to have sex with male prostitutes.

"I was so scared today. So unbelievably scared. And it made me realize how scared I am all the time." He pauses. "I'm not asking for forgiveness . . ."

"I know." She looks at a *Good Housekeeping* magazine on the table and wonders what secrets the perfect-looking wife on the cover keeps.

"When I drive home from work, I get so anxious, thinking that this will be the night you finally tell me you just can't take it anymore. Sometimes I imagine you'll have all my stuff on the front lawn in big green garbage bags."

She wants him to stop talking, to stop telling her how frightened he is. It's not that she doesn't care, it's that it occurs to her that they are both terrified, both unanchored. They have melting points, breaking points. They have the ability to come undone.

"It will be okay." She's the one doling out the platitude this time, only it doesn't feel trite. She means it, and it occurs to her that Adam might be equally sincere when he tries to soothe her.

Theresa finds them.

"Everything seems to be all right, but I will need to follow up with a couple of home visits," she tells them, glancing from one to the other.

"Can we go back in?" Hannah asks as she and Adam stand.

"Yes. But I would like to say something, if you don't mind." Theresa's small mouth curves downward.

Hannah does mind. "Go ahead."

"I don't think it's wise to talk to children about sex until they're ready."

"We know." Hannah glares at Theresa. "We also know—"

Adam gently pulls Hannah away before she says something she might regret. He is transformed back into the man she needs him to be.

This time, when they walk into the room that smells as if it's been doused in bleach, Adam greets Alicia with a kiss on the cheek.

"We're going to have the biggest, baddest sundaes ever," he tells her. She smiles. "Can we go home now?"

"As soon as the doctor says it's okay," Hannah says.

"I'm sorry," Alicia whispers.

"We're sorry too," Hannah tells her as she figures out how to lower the rail. She climbs onto the bed and gathers Alicia into her arms.

Bridget

Bridget's shift is nearly over. She should be finishing her notes, but she can't concentrate. She keeps thinking of home, of how no one will be there. She doesn't know how she's going to make it through the night without Michael. It's weak and pathetic, but she needs him there. Just for a few more days, until she gets used to the idea. She promised herself earlier that she wouldn't call him, but now that the end of her shift is only minutes away, she's starting to panic. If she texts him, he can get there before her. Maybe she is a co-addict, or codependent, or whatever anyone else wants to fucking label her. All she knows is that she's a terrified pregnant wife. She takes out her phone and stares at it.

Hannah never called back. Bridget hadn't pegged her for a cold person, but maybe Bridget's intuition about people is screwed up.

After all, she thought Michael was a good guy, honest to his toes. She thinks about the time, a few years back, when they went out with Janice and Janice's boyfriend. The boyfriend went to the bathroom, and Janice checked his phone. Michael shook his head, disgusted, and said he and Bridget didn't play those sorts of games. Bridget snuggled closer to him, thinking she was the luckiest girl in the world to have someone so decent and respectful. It still shocks her to think that so much of him was just a scam.

Lizzy didn't call back, either. Gail was the only one who replied. It almost seems funny now, how much Bridget couldn't stand Gail when they first met.

Hey, can you

she begins her text to Michael, then erases it. She needs to hold on, make it through at least one night.

Hector, the other nurse on duty, joins her at the desk that sits behind the huge glass shield. The patients are all in bed. The quieter the ward, the more agitated Bridget feels.

"Outta here in fifteen," Hector says as he glances at a clipboard. He's a no-bullshit kind of guy, and for the most part, she likes working with him.

"Yeah, thank God," Bridget replies, stuffing her phone in her pocket.

"You okay?"

"Yeah, why?"

"You're usually swearing up a storm by this point."

She shrugs. Michael didn't even text her to see if she was all right. It just feels unreal. How can the man who she believed read her every thought just be out of her life?

The desk phone rings. Hector picks up. "Floor ten." He nods. "Now? Can you wait like five minutes, until the next shift?" He nods again. "Yeah, of course. Bring him up." He hangs up.

"A new intake?" Bridget asks.

"Yep, in a full-blown psychotic state. Should be fun. I say we get him into the back quiet room and let the next shift do the rest."

"No, I'm up for it. What did they tell you?" she asks.

"Name is Marc Backstram, but I guess he likes to go by Saint Bartholomew. They checked him at the hospital. Seems fine physically. Gave him some Thorazine to calm him down."

She watches as two attendants carry in a thin man with long hair and a scraggly beard. A cop shuffles at the rear. Marc's arms are restrained by a white jacket. It doesn't matter how many times she's seen it, or how many times she tells herself that the cloth restraints are painless and safe, it still gives her the chills. They carry him around the corner. She follows.

Bridget signs the paperwork. The attendants leave.

"Why you here?" she asks the large, burly cop.

"He caused a scene. Was with some kid, who might have been running away. We just gotta make sure nothing happened. You know?"

"He probably just freaked the kid out. Happens with schizophrenics." She glances at Marc. All she wants now is to lose herself in someone else's fucked-up world.

"Can't say I know that much about the disease," the cop remarks.

"We like to calm patients down, and it's normally best if there aren't too many distractions. It would be better if you wait outside. Let me talk to him."

"Fine by me. But I gotta listen."

"Grab a chair." She points down the hall. "And there's coffee at the nursing station."

Marc is flat on his back, staring at the ceiling. The pale room is furnished with a mattress and one hard plastic chair. She doesn't use the chair. Instead she sits cross-legged on the floor next to him.

"My name is Bridget," she says softly. He stares at the ceiling and shivers so violently his teeth chatter.

"I'm going to stay here and talk to you for a little."

He turns to her. His skin is thin and papery, his eyes bloodshot.

"Can you hear me?" she asks.

He doesn't respond. He could be catatonic. They probably roughed him up good when they brought him over.

"Marc, I'm here to help. I want you to know you're safe."

"Whore," he hisses.

"Good to hear you talk," she replies.

"Whore," he says again.

"Do you know where you are?"

He glares. "Inside a spaceship."

"You're on a psych ward in Jamaica Plain. We're going to help you get better."

"Free me or you'll be damned." He kicks his legs. The cop pokes his head in. Bridget nods, signaling all is fine.

"You're not a prisoner here. No one is going to hurt you."

"You come in the middle of the night and take out people's brains. I was trying to help that girl. Now she's gone."

"She's safe."

"You're a liar and a whore." His breathing is jagged. "My name is Saint Bartholomew, and I am without guile."

"I like people without guile," she tells him.

He looks at her again, and although his eyes are still wary, she can see she has an opening.

"I am without fear. I will be skinned alive and nailed to a cross."

"That sounds frightening." She reaches over and touches his shoulder.

"I live without guile and without fear."

"Wish I could do that." She likes this man, this Bartholomew without guile.

"The earth will end in a great fire. Sin will taint all the lovers, and they will burn until their skin is charred and their eyes melt."

The cop steps in. "There a place to order takeout around here?" he asks.

Bartholomew snaps to sitting. "Go to hell," he shouts.

Bridget glares at the cop. He backs up. "He's leaving," she says to Bartholomew.

"You whore. You tricked me. I see what you're doing. I see through your glass eyes." He tries to free his arms but can't. He twists and grimaces.

"I'm not trying to trick you," she assures him.

He pulls up his knees and drops his head. His breathing becomes labored again. She will stay with him and give him all the time he needs. She guesses he's in his fifties, although he looks much older. And in another way, much younger. As she watches him begin to rock, she sees herself, stubborn, fighting battles she can't win, never wanting to put down the sword because the surrender, the pain that comes with it, is distilled, pure loneliness. For thirteen years, since her mother died, she's been trying to run from it, and now here it is, pressing fiercely on her chest.

"Saint Bartholomew," she whispers. Her voice falters.

He glances at her. His eyes are sad. For a second she feels as if the two thin threads of their universes entwine.

"I am without guile," he tells her.

"I admire that," she says. And she does. As sick and psychotic as Bartholomew is, she knows that he is never dishonest, would never purposefully hurt or deceive.

"You're a whore. Your mother is a whore."

He lies down, faces the wall, and curls away from her. She leans toward him and strokes his snarled hair. "You are not alone," she whispers.

After he is asleep, she stands to leave. On her way out, the cop stops her. His eyes are compassionate. "Tomorrow will be a better day."

Her lips quiver. She forces a smile. "It fucking better be," she says, trying to get some of the old Bridget back.

Outside, it's still as muggy as it was at two in the afternoon. But she doesn't care anymore. She can handle it. Not once when she sat with Bartholomew did she think about calling Michael or wonder why he hadn't called her.

SESSION EIGHT

Alicia stayed home from school with Hannah today. They slept late, watched *Beauty and the Beast,* and looked at old photo albums.

Although Hannah is wrung out from yesterday's ordeal, she isn't about to miss group. It's time to talk about herself. She arrives at Kathryn's office at exactly seven. Gail, who is already settled, smiles perfunctorily.

"It's good to see you," Kathryn tells Hannah.

She sits on the wooden Windsor chair. "I'm sorry I missed last week. I needed to—" She stops when Bridget traipses in, wearing jean shorts and a tight green scoop-neck T-shirt that shows off her baby bump.

Bridget settles in her usual seat, the armchair to Kathryn's right, and crosses her arms in front of her chest. She smiles at Kathryn and Gail, avoiding Hannah.

Lizzy is next to arrive. She is buoyant, her face glowing. Life has found its way in, Hannah thinks.

"Would anyone like to begin?" Kathryn asks.

Lizzy pulls a tube of toothpaste from her bag. "I will," she says. "Last week when I got home from here, Greg was grabbing some things. He went to put the toothpaste in his bag, and I snatched it." She sits taller and smiles. "I know it's silly. But I took something for myself."

"That's not silly," Bridget says.

"Did Greg leave?" Hannah asks.

"I'm sorry," Lizzy tells her. "I guess I jumped in a little too fast."

"No, it's my fault. I missed last week. I'm sorry."

"Enough with the apologies," Bridget quips. "Tell us what happened. I could use some good news."

Lizzy looks at Hannah. "Brief recap. Greg got fired from work for watching porn. People in the town where I work, same town he works in, found out. Some parents got nervous and thought . . . who knows what . . . Anyway, the result was that I was asked to take the rest of the year off."

"That's horrible," Hannah tells her.

"It wasn't one of my better days. Greg and I fought. He left. And then he shows up last Wednesday trying to sneak out some of his stuff. He thought I wouldn't be home until later." She waves the toothpaste. "Anyway, during the past week, I feel like I got my act together. I went to the bank, set up my own account, and decided to leave him." Years have melted off her face.

"Where are you staying?" Kathryn asks.

"For one more night, at the airport Hilton. I'm flying out tomorrow. I'm going to help build a school for children in the Peruvian jungle."

"You're not serious?" Gail fans herself.

"Yep. I am. I unplugged myself. I have no phone, no computer, just a ticket. I paid the mortgage for the next three months so the bank won't take the house if Greg doesn't pay." She extends her arms. "I'm free. I keep waiting for Greg to call, to apologize, to make things better, and then I remember he can't call, and even if he could, I can't do anything to help him. So why should I sit around here and grow bitter?"

"I'm so frigging proud of you," Bridget says.

"Me too," Hannah agrees.

"It seems a bit sudden. You don't want to think it over more thoroughly?" Gail asks.

"No. I've been wanting to do this for a while, but I always thought it was selfish to just leave for the summer. Not be there for Greg." She laughs. "As if he wanted me."

"So you're coming back?" Kathryn asks.

Lizzy shrugs. "I plan to. But I'm open to whatever happens."

"It's wonderful that you are taking a very difficult and hurtful situation and turning it into something positive," Hannah says.

"I wish I could go with you." Bridget rubs her belly. "So is that why you didn't call back? You had no phone?"

Lizzy's smile fades. "I'm so sorry. I would have. But I didn't know you called. Is everything okay?"

"Yeah. Well, no, actually." She stares at Hannah. "I called you too."

"I know," Hannah replies. "Honestly, I was going to get in touch, but yesterday was really crazy."

"Of course," Bridget snaps. "What, a busy day taking the kids to play dates?"

Hannah leans forward. "Alicia ran away. We had to call the police. They didn't find her until last night. I wasn't trying to avoid you."

"Oh my God." Lizzy covers her mouth.

"It was the most harrowing day of my life. I thought all this stuff I've been dealing with with Adam was bad, but honestly, in comparison, it was nothing." She looks at the rug and shakes her head. "The thought that I might have lost a child . . ."

"Do you know why she did it?" Gail asks.

"Basically she overheard Adam and me fighting. I said something to the effect of maybe I shouldn't have had kids."

"I'm sorry," Bridget murmurs.

"Right now I feel like the luckiest person in the world. That she's home and safe."

"I'm glad she's okay," Lizzy says.

"Me too," Bridget seconds.

"I didn't want you to think I was ignoring you," Hannah says.

"Whatever." Bridget shrugs. "Gail was there."

Gail stands, moves her chair closer to Bridget, and resettles herself.

"You can tell them," she says, placing a hand on the arm of Bridget's chair.

"Michael left me."

Lizzy gasps.

"Yep," Bridget says. "For my own fucking good." She attempts a laugh.

"It's all right to be upset," Gail tells her.

Bridget shakes her head. "I know. It's just so wrong. Him leaving me. He says I need space to heal and I can't do that with him around. Isn't he so kind and magnanimous?"

Gail sighs. "I'm in no way defending him. But sometimes space can be a good thing."

"Yeah, except all I want to do is call him and tell him to go to hell and get the fuck out of my life, and then I remember, Oh yeah." She throws up her arms. "He is out. How messed up is that?"

"It's not messed up at all," Hannah says. "You're hurt and angry. You have every right to be."

"I feel like the goddamned addict. You know how hard it's been not to call him? And why hasn't he called me? You'd think he'd feel just a little guilty. You'd think he'd want to check on his pregnant wife."

"Why do you think he hasn't called?" Kathryn asks.

"I don't know. Sometimes I think he only gives a shit about himself. But . . ." She sighs. "I guess we kind of have to stop the cycle we're in. It's not like we're getting anywhere good." She crosses her arms.

"You have to focus on the fact that you haven't called him since he left." Gail leans closer to Bridget. "That's taken tremendous strength. Keep reminding yourself that some distance can bring clarity."

"I've barely managed. I keep calling up his number."

"But you haven't hit send," Gail says.

Hannah wishes she would have found a moment to call yesterday.

A tear rolls down Bridget's cheek. "I don't know if I can make it another day."

"We're here for you," Gail says.

"We are," Hannah tells Bridget.

"I'm so sorry that I'm leaving," Lizzy whispers.

"Just promise me something." Bridget brushes away a tear. "Promise you'll stop apologizing for yourself."

Lizzy smiles. "I'll try."

"Is there anything anyone else wants to say about Lizzy leaving?" Kathryn asks.

Lizzy blushes and holds up the toothpaste. "No, it's fine. You don't need to spend any more time on me."

Hannah glances outside at a tree that stands near the window. The new buds, the first of the year, strike her as brave. "I'm so impressed. Why not go on an adventure? It sure as hell beats stagnating."

"Do you feel as if you're stagnating?" Kathryn asks.

"I think I was. I've been so focused on Adam changing, I think I missed looking at my part in the equation."

"It's not your fault," Lizzy says.

"I know. I didn't mean it like that. Just that there are things I can do for myself. To help myself." She glances at the tree. "I feel so ashamed. I get that I didn't do anything, but . . . it's humiliating. To have this life. I don't know how else to say it." It feels as if there's a hot coal sitting in her stomach. Although she realizes she's barely shared anything, it's as much as she can do tonight.

"I used to feel that way so much of the time," Gail tells Hannah. "But talking truly does diminish the shame. Keep coming, keep sharing." She looks at Bridget. "It gets easier. I promise."

Hannah wishes she could believe Gail.

Kathryn talks about the importance of group fellowship and trust.

Gail keeps a watchful eye on Bridget, and Hannah looks at Lizzy. Next week that faded, sagging couch will be empty, and the two remarkable, brave women who shared it will be in other parts of the world.

Hannah

✤

For the second night in a row, Hannah, her children, and Adam share the same bed.

At two in the morning, Alicia is cuddled into Hannah. Sam's legs move softly. His face twitches, and a small smile appears. He is a happy dreamer. Hannah kisses the top of Alicia's head. Adam's arm drapes over Sam and his hand touches Alicia's arm. The family nest is tranquil. Yet Hannah is anything but tired. Once again she relives yesterday's events. The relief when she saw Alicia at the hospital, the gratitude, the joy, were the purest emotions she'd ever felt. She still feels those, but now other things are rustling—the remembrance of fear, the terror of loss.

Hannah strokes Alicia's hair, then carefully slips out of bed and tiptoes to the glass door that opens onto their bedroom patio. The air is still heavy and humid. She sits on one of the Adirondack chairs as the rustling inside of her grows stronger. A few stars manage to fight through the haze. The boundaries of light from one collide into another. On a clear night, there would be thousands of lights, millions of points of intersection. Minutes later, the glass door clatters quietly on its tracks, and Adam joins her. He sits on the matching wooden chair.

"Do you want to talk?" he asks.

She glances at him and smiles. "I've been focusing on all the wrong things."

"You can't blame yourself."

"Wouldn't that be simple, to blame or not to blame? But it's not one or the other. I have to take responsibility for how my behavior played a role in what happened, just as you do. The funny thing is, I'm not angry. Not at you or myself. Just sad that it had to come to this for me to see how narrow my vision has been."

"You're hardly close-minded."

"Maybe not in some vague theoretical way, but the thing is, I really have been close-minded. I've been so fixated on your recovery, waiting for some magical moment that would assure me that I could live again. As if that could erase the past and somehow return everything to what it's never been in the first place."

"It hasn't been all bad."

"Of course not. But all my rules, trying to order things into neat lines or put them into pretty boxes, isn't going to make my life something that it never was to begin with. I married you knowing the problems, yet I still closed my eyes and thought if I kept them squeezed shut tightly enough, somehow we'd be the fantasy that was never real to begin with." A few stars shine boldly through a small break in the haze.

"Reality isn't always fun to live with," Adam says.

"Life is so strange," she replies. "How we end up where we do. How much is just plain chance?"

"Probably more than we'd like to believe."

"Certainly more than I'd like to believe. Then again, maybe it's all beautifully scripted, every detail, so that in the end we'll all have played our roles just as we were meant to play them." The haze in the sky returns.

"I just hope like hell I get to keep playing your leading man."

There is a pause in time, a stillness that comes with an acute awareness that for every gift there must be a sacrifice. The moment passes. Hannah feels a fleeting chill and rests a hand on top of Adam's.

Gail

Thursday evening, as Gail listens to Schubert and prepares dinner, she thinks about the group and how lucky she is to have a man who is honest, dedicated, and willing to stay the course. Not that she has ever taken Jonah for granted, but last night as she listened to the others, she became sharply aware of how delicate marriages are, how much care and attention should be given to them. This evening's meal, with its Irish theme, will show Jonah that their relationship is her priority.

The salmon is fresh, as is the lettuce and asparagus. Two weeks ago she had place mats and coasters made from pictures she found on the Web of the different places they're visiting in Ireland. Their trip is in eight weeks, and she plans to make it a second honeymoon.

She lays the table, giving Jonah the place mat of Dingle, her favorite, with the sheep grazing in front of the blue sea and mountains. A piece of heaven. The champagne sits, chilled, in the silver ice bucket.

At seven-thirty, he isn't home. Not to worry. In the bathroom off the dining room, she applies another coat of red lipstick and runs her fingers through her hair, which could use a fresh trim. But she's been too busy. At least she had time for a manicure. She chose a soft peach polish.

He arrives at eight. She meets him in the foyer and sees immediately that his shoulders are slightly curled, weary.

"Here, let me take that." She reaches for his briefcase. He doesn't let it go.

"It's fine. I can manage."

"Long day?" she asks.

"Very. I'd really like to just relax in the study for an hour."

"I made dinner," she tells him.

He sighs. "The weather has left me with no appetite."

"It's light." Her hands clasp in front of her chest.

"May I get by?" he asks.

She's suddenly intensely humiliated. She hadn't meant to be blocking his path. She plasters herself against the wall, holding in her stomach.

"What about a nice cold glass of champagne?" she asks.

He glances at her, his light eyes panicked.

She laughs. "Don't worry, you didn't forget our anniversary."

He places a hand on his shirt, which is coming untucked. He's such the intellectual, no care in the world about clothes or appearances.

"Why the champagne?" He walks slowly toward the staircase.

"I wanted to do something nice for us. We've both been so busy, I thought this would be a treat. Come in the dining room. Have one glass with me."

He nods, still facing the stairs. "Let me wash up. I'll be down in a few minutes."

She puts their salads with cranberries and goat cheese on the table, then sits. She looks at her place mat, which has a picture of Donegal Castle, another one of their destinations.

The candied pecan that sits on the top of her salad is irresistible. She picks it off and enjoys the light crunch. Then she glances around, making sure Jonah isn't in sight, and takes a pecan from his salad. They had both started with six; she wants to keep the numbers even. Ten minutes pass. She nibbles on four more pecans.

After ten more minutes, he joins her in the dining room. He's changed into a white shirt and jeans. She can't remember when she saw him last in jeans. Possibly never.

"New clothes?" she asks.

"Actually, most of the professors are wearing this type of thing. I thought I'd give it a try." He sits at the head of the table.

"I never thought you'd be one to notice fashion trends," she says.

"I have the occasional enlightened moment."

"As long as it's not more than occasional," she teases.

"No need to worry about that." He glances at the salad. "Looks good," he says.

"I know you're not hungry, but this is light. Would you like to open the champagne?"

"I think I'll stick with water for tonight."

He'll change his mind after the salad. "Take a look at your coaster." She feels like a child unable to contain her excitement.

"Nice," he says. "Are they new?"

"I made them. Not actually made. But I found pictures and then had one of those photograph companies do it. That one is of a little bay in Inishbofin."

"Where?"

"Inishbofin, the island we're going to. Off the west coast of Ireland."

He picks it up, turns it over, spends more time studying the cork on the back than the picture. "It's nice," he says.

"I can't wait to see it. Your place mat is Dingle," she says proudly.

He moves his salad plate to the side and looks at the picture of the sea and the cliffs. "It's nice," he says again.

"I'm so excited." She takes a bite of her salad.

He glances at her, his gray eyes strained. "Gail," he says, then picks up his fork and uses it to push around one of the few pecans that is left.

She wants to keep showing him all the other coasters. Under his water glass is a picture of a puffin from one of the Blasket Islands. She has different coasters for the Baileys she has planned for after-dinner drinks. But she restrains her enthusiasm and wipes her mouth with the linen serviette. The red lipstick stain is prominent.

He sighs, putting his elbows on the table and his head in his hands. His round bald spot looks well polished.

"We should talk," he mumbles.

The words themselves wouldn't be so terrible, but combined with his body language, she can't ignore the feeling that she walked right into a stomach punch.

"Go ahead." She folds her napkin so the red lipstick is hidden.

"I don't think I can make the trip."

She tends to steer away from ratings, but right now, on a scale of one to ten, this is about a five. He's got a conference. He's too busy working on an article. The trip will be postponed, but all will not be lost. This is manageable.

He pushes the place mat away and sighs again, this time more emphatically. "I'm sorry." He lifts his head. His eyes are glassy with a slight blue haze that makes her wonder if he's getting cataracts.

Although her heart is heavy, it has the ability to race rapidly, knocking against her rib cage.

"Work?" she asks.

A deep breath followed by yet another sigh. He shakes his head no.

"Is someone in your family sick?" It's a silly, hopeful question, and she thinks of her demeanor in Dr. O'Reilly's office, how strong she was. But sitting here, her deepest fear near the surface, makes her feel weak and withered.

"I've been trying to talk about this for a while now. I just couldn't find the right time."

She squares herself, holding the edge of the table. "You've had a slip?" She can manage a slip.

"I wish it were that simple." He looks at the oil painting of the bowl of fruit. She bought it years ago in Italy. It was much too expensive.

"A relapse?" The letter from April makes a dot in her thoughts.

"No. I've been talking to my therapist, and we've decided that I'm not actually a sex addict."

She stares at him. He's not making sense. "Of course you are. How can he say that?"

"Because my behaviors don't fit the addiction model."

"Then what does he think is the matter?"

"I'm not sure he thinks anything is necessarily wrong with me. It's more of an identity crisis than any sort of disease."

She picks up her glass of water, but her hand is too unsteady to bring the drink to her mouth. "He told you that you were a sex addict. How could he not know that? It's his job to diagnose people."

"He made a mistake."

"I hope you're thinking of switching."

"I don't think it was entirely his fault that he misjudged. I may have led him to believe my behavior was addictive." He looks away from the painting, scans the room, and then focuses on the place mat.

She flushes. Her heart continues its heavy pulsating. Her blood pressure must be soaring, and she didn't take her medicine today. She didn't want it to interact with the champagne.

"You're just trying to give him an easy out. If he's a good therapist, he would have picked up that you were skirting the real issue."

He pokes his fork in the place mat. She wants to take it away from him, to tell him he's going to ruin it.

"I'm in love with April."

"Oh, don't be ridiculous," she says, and waves her hand in the air. "She's a student. She's young."

"She's not that young. She's thirty-one."

"You're almost fifty-five."

He keeps poking at the place mat. There are indentations in the blue sea. "I stopped seeing her for a time. I thought maybe I did have addictive tendencies, but I kept thinking about her. She returned to Harvard and we began meeting."

"So you lied about not knowing she was back?"

He nods.

She can't breathe. She looks at her place mat, thinking about the suite she reserved with the plush furniture and the binoculars. The simple touch of binoculars to enable guests to bird-watch convinced her to book that hotel.

"I know this is difficult. But I couldn't keep up the lies." He touches her arm.

"But then . . . I mean, what about the other women? It wasn't just April."

"There was actually only one other woman, and it was after April left the first time. I was desperately trying to figure out what was wrong. I wanted to believe I was a sex addict. I really did." He looks at her now, his eyes clear.

"You are a sex addict," she says.

"No, Gail, I'm not. I'm in love with April. I have been for over two years now. I've tried to stop seeing her. I wanted to make our marriage work."

"You need another opinion. You can't just rely on this one therapist."

"It doesn't matter what another therapist says, it matters what I know in my heart to be true." He puts a hand on his chest.

"But it's not true. We've worked through so much. You can't just throw it all away."

"We have worked through a lot. And you're a wonderful, intelligent companion, and I will always deeply love you."

"But . . ." She feels as if she can't swallow. She puts a hand on her throat.

"Would you like me to open the champagne? Maybe you need a glass."

That seems cruel, a glass of celebratory champagne as an elixir for her broken heart. "No, thank you."

"Perhaps you should eat something."

All she wants is the Hostess cupcakes that are hidden in her closet. "No, thank you."

"Gail, I couldn't keep up the lie. I couldn't go on a trip with you when I knew that I was betraying you."

"We can still go." Her heart, which has continued to beat ferociously, feels lighter.

"That wouldn't be wise."

"I have all the places booked. We'll go as friends." She doesn't really want to have sex with him anyway. Not because she's not attracted to him, but because she always feels so ashamed of her own body. "We can have fun. Be companions." She's convinced he'll see this is a good idea.

"I don't think you'll want to be with me once this sinks in."

"April's a child. She's a fling. You can see her if you need to. We're meant for each other. We're equals intellectually." She reaches for his hand. He puts it in his lap.

"No. She's not a child, and it's not a fling. I want to be with her."

She needs to make herself clearer. "We'll share this apartment. We'll still have our life together. You'll just see April when you need to. We're compatible and that's what's really important in a relationship."

"Gail." He sighs. "We're not really compatible."

"Of course we are. We like the same things. We enjoy each other's company. We don't argue."

"I'm sorry." He sighs again. "I can't do it. I can't live here."

"But all your books are here. And we've decorated together . . ." She wants to continue, but she looks into his eyes and sees resolve. She has lost this last desperate attempt. On her lap, she unfolds her napkin and looks at the red lipstick stain.

"When I'm gone, you'll feel better," he says. "You won't have to worry anymore about what I'm doing. You'll be free. It will be like a burden has been lifted."

Perhaps the shade of lipstick is too red. An orange tint might be more suitable. She stretches the fabric, studies the stain.

"I understand you're upset," he says. "But it would be terribly unfair of me to stay. You deserve to be loved."

She moves her salad plate, places her napkin over the place mat, and compares the red to the color of the apple in the painting. The apple is more subtle.

"Gail?"

Color is so important. Color is everything. She's spent much too much time ignoring the color of things. The shades in the room have too much green. Why hadn't she seen that until now?

"I'm going to go out for a while. Let you think about this. All right?" he asks.

At least she chose her nail color wisely. Yes, peach is almost always right. Pinks can be good as well. It's just that they have the danger of seeming girlish. Someone told her mental hospitals had pink rooms. It calms people, supposedly.

"If you could become a color, what would you choose?" Her voice is curious.

"Please, Gail. Stop playing these games. It's not going to help either one of us."

"I think you'd be blue." She imagines him encased in a block of ice. Vine-like fissures entangle him.

"I'm not doing this." He stands. "If you want to talk seriously, that's fine. But I don't have time for this nonsense."

Jonah walks away. His aura isn't blue, but dirt brown. How did she manage to misjudge him so drastically?

The front door closes. She opens the champagne, pours herself a glass, and studies the liquid. It's the color of empty.

He's been gone for two hours and thirty-six minutes. She's eaten a box of Hostess cupcakes and three candy bars. All the sugar in the world isn't going to help, but she needs to restock. There is no possible way she will make it through the night without snacks. Actually, she can't imagine making it through the next hour. Her heart races, and as a cautionary measure, she takes out the blood pressure cuff that she bought at Walgreens a year ago. It reads 220 over 150. She stares at the numbers until they blur. Her blood pressure has never been that high. She takes four Atenolol. Twenty minutes later, the numbers are down only a few points. She takes three more pills.

She must have sounded as if she were out of her mind, talking about colors the way she did before he left. She should have negotiated, reasonably, asked for a six-month trial period, time to see a new couples' therapist, time for her to work on her weight issues, time for him to reconsider. Why does she have to become such a weak, insecure woman around him? Where does the formidable, competent Judge Larson go?

Her therapist would tell her this is the time to call someone for help, but what would she say? That her husband isn't even a sex addict? How ludicrous would that sound? She holds the banister as she descends the stairs. She wheezes. Her asthma is acting up. Why hasn't he returned yet? What if he went to April's to celebrate? Would he be that callous? She searches for her inhaler and absentmindedly picks up her car keys from the kitchen counter.

Outside, standing on the sidewalk, her legs feel water-logged and swollen. She's probably retaining fluids again. Nothing a diuretic won't cure. The yellow street lamp gives her car a green hue. Just as she puts a foot on the road, a teenager, smoking a cigarette and not watching where he's going, bumps into her. Her ankles, thick with water, wobble, and she falls slowly, first to her knees. Her left elbow bangs the pavement, her pocketbook flies out. Loose change rolls away as she lies prostrate on the sidewalk.

"Are you okay?" The young man's voice sounds as if it recently dropped.

Gail manages to sit. The boy drops his cigarette and stomps it out.

"Just get me my purse," Gail says.

He does as he's told, then lingers.

Gail glances at her torn stockings and sprawled legs. "Help me up." She extends her good arm.

The boy pulls. Gail rocks a bit, but she's stuck. The humiliation is unbearable. "Go away," she shouts. He does.

She knows what she has to do to get up, and she doesn't want anyone bearing witness. Gail maneuvers herself so that she's on all fours. A pebble grinds into her palm as a few raindrops splat in front of her. Carefully, she moves her hands a little closer to her knees. She places one foot, then the next onto the sidewalk. In stages, she pushes herself up.

She's grateful that it's dark and the holes in her stockings are hidden by her skirt. She hopes to God no one was watching. To have to display oneself like a dog in front of one's house is as degrading as life can get. Then she remembers Jonah left her.

She hobbles to the car. As she slides in, every bone aches, and her left elbow throbs. She moves the seat back in order to get some extra breathing room, even though that means her feet can barely reach the pedals. For ten minutes she sits, catching her breath, regaining her bearings. The light rain patters and glistens on the windshield. The heat will soon end. She massages her elbow, rubs her scraped knees, and feels old and decrepit. Certainly she can't go to the local convenience store looking like this.

Finally she starts the engine and decides to take Storrow Drive. Her extremities still ache, but a deeper pain in her chest begins to take over. She feels as if she's been shot.

On 95 North, her breathing is still wheezy, but her heart isn't racing quite as much. Deep breaths hurt, so she takes shallow ones and grips the wheel. A large green sign for Gloucester hangs above. For a moment the pain disappears as she thinks about Long Beach and the cottage there. She can hear the lapping of the waves and the cries of seagulls. She drives north. Home is toxic, a mocking reminder of the lie her life has been. She rolls down her window, lets the breeze caress her face, and thinks of how worried Jonah will be when he comes home to an empty house.

The parking lot is deserted. Gail leaves her purse and the keys in the car. No one is around. Nothing will get stolen. Her feet are still swollen, but her elbow is what hurts the most right now. She can barely bend it. Tomorrow she'll get it checked out. The beach is only a few feet ahead. Her body feels odd, leaden and heavy, tired and at the same time feathery, as if she is filled with helium. It must be the Atenolol.

The air smells thick with salt and seaweed. Soft rain drizzles as waves spill onto the sand. The heels of her shoes sink, and so she steps out of her pumps. The sand is pleasantly damp and cool. If only she wasn't wearing stockings. She lifts her skirt and begins to roll down her nylons, but when they're close to her knees, she recognizes her mistake. She's unsteady, and the best course of action will be to plop down right here. Her tailbone sustains a hard knock. Nonetheless, she's managed to sit and remain in one piece. She finishes taking off her stockings, then lies on her back, stretching out her arms and legs. She closes her eyes. Rain falls on her face, her lips. She licks a few drops, but soon her blouse is wet, uncomfortably sticking to her. She sits up, takes it off, then works her way out of her skirt.

It's heavenly not to be so restricted. She glances around. Behind her is a cement retaining wall. To her right and left, there's just beach, and in front of her the ocean. It's not easy taking off her camisole with her bad arm, but she manages. Finally, she unhooks her bra and pulls off her underpants. She can breathe again. She thinks of floating on a raft, of the sun warming her, the water sparkling around her, the waves rocking her.

She wants to feel lighter, freer. She rolls onto her side, once again gets onto all fours, and pushes herself up. With open arms, like wings, she walks toward the water.

Her feet sink in the wet sand. The first wave that crashes around her ankles feels like ice. But soon her feet are numb, blissfully devoid of any feeling. Inch by inch, methodically, she numbs her legs until there is no sensation. The water is at her thighs. She looks at the twin lighthouses on Thacher Island. The rain has stopped momentarily, and she can make out a cloud, a wisp of a thing, between the two lighthouses. They look as if they are holding hands, one watching out for the other. She will always be Jonah's lighthouse, and he hers. A wave comes in. The water swells to her belly. It's shockingly cold, but she doesn't mind. As it ebbs out, she feels the grip behind her knees. Her body falls forward, her head plunges into the sea. She extends her arms, pushes down on the water, and reaches air for a moment. She exhales but is pulled under before she has time to take a breath.

Time slows. She can hear raindrops hit the water. Then they morph into beautiful golden orbs, suns. All around her, fire falls. Balls of orange, the color of autumn, dapple her world. Just as she feels safe, cradled in a womb of salt water with the two towers beaming their lights above her, another wave pulls her to the surface, and she gulps at the air.

Kathryn

Friday morning, the heat has broken. Outside, it's that perfect temperature that licks up sweat the moment it appears. Kathryn finds her running pace. The sidewalk feels as if it has extra give this morning. Seeing Hannah return to group was a huge relief. Losing Lizzy was unexpected, but Kathryn feels good about the choices Lizzy is making. People really do change. The group will go through stages of growth, but it will not end. Last night Kathryn sent an e-mail to a number of colleagues informing them that she had a few open spaces. She is sure there are women who could use the support and wisdom Gail, Bridget, and Hannah have to share.

The moment Kathryn opens her apartment door, she hears the phone and dashes to pick it up.

"Kathryn Leblanc." Her voice is alert, ready. She expects it is someone querying about the group.

"It's Bridget. Did you see the news?" The words race out.

"No," Kathryn answers. Her first thought is that there was some sort of report on missing children and Hannah's daughter was mentioned.

"They showed Gail. A picture of her face."

It's likely some high-profile case, and Gail's occupation will no longer be a secret. "What did they say?" she asks, beginning to stretch out her calf.

"She was found lying on some beach, naked."

Kathryn mouths, *What*, but no sound comes out.

"They took her to a hospital. She may be dead," Bridget shouts, then begins to cry.

"Did they say what hospital?"

"No."

"You said you saw her picture? Are you sure it wasn't someone else?" Kathryn asks.

"I know what Gail looks like."

"Of course. I didn't mean it like that. I was only wondering . . ." But she can't think clearly. She doesn't know what she was wondering. Just that Bridget must have the facts wrong.

"Did you know she was a judge?" Bridget asks.

"Yes." That piece of information virtually confirms Gail's identity.

"What are we going to do?" Bridget sounds desperate.

"First, I'm going to make sure it was actually Gail." She puts a hand on the front table to steady herself. "Then I will find out if she's okay."

"I know it was Gail. It's not like I wouldn't recognize her."

"Can I reach you at the number you're calling from?" Kathryn closes her eyes for a second. Shadows reach out to her.

"You need to find out what happened," Bridget says.

"I'm going to make a few calls right now, and I'll get back to you."

"Hurry." Bridget hangs up.

Kathryn looks at the phone, not making a move. She knows she should be thinking of more logical, rational, concrete things, but her brain isn't working the way it should. Was there something she should have done differently? Something she should have paid more attention to?

Dazed, she walks to her study, sits, and stares at the bookshelf. Minutes pass. She opens her laptop and types *Judge Larson* into her search engine. A picture of Gail fills the screen. Underneath it, Kathryn reads *North Shore, esteemed judge, possible suicide attempt.*

Hannah

Eleven-fifteen, Friday morning, Hannah is driving to Kathryn's office. It's the last thing she imagined she'd be doing today.

It doesn't seem possible, what Kathryn said on the phone. Fragments circle, as if they're outside of her, unable to settle. *Sad news. Found on a beach in Gloucester. Almost drowned. In ICU at Beth Israel.* She glances at the speedometer. It reads seventy-five. She should slow down. It's not as if getting there sooner will change things. Details probably won't help either, yet she feels that's what she needs. Details and answers.

She takes a sharp left into the small parking lot across from the Victorian house and dashes in. Bridget is already there, her eyes red and swollen. Kathryn's face is drawn. Her hair is pulled into a ponytail, her bangs pinned up. She looks frail.

Hannah walks in and sits on the couch, where Flavia used to sit. The hard Windsor chair, her usual seat, seems hostile.

"What about Lizzy?" Hannah asks.

"I tried the hotel," Kathryn replies. "But she checked out yesterday."

Hannah lays her hand on Lizzy's empty spot on the couch. "Maybe it was meant to be, that she didn't have to find out. If she knew, she'd be pacing in the hospital lobby."

"I can't fucking believe it." Bridget stands, then sits again. "I mean . . . when I saw that picture of her on the news, I thought maybe she had a twin or something."

"Do you know what happened?" Hannah asks Kathryn.

She fiddles with a paper clip. "I called the hospital. Her husband was there. I spoke to him for a few minutes, but . . . it wasn't the time to ask for specifics."

"Did he reveal anything?" Hannah takes off her blazer, but then feels chilly and puts it back on. She can't get comfortable.

"He said she was distraught. Not acting like herself. He thought it could have been some sort of breakdown."

"Yeah, I sure as hell wouldn't believe anything he said. For one, Gail wouldn't have had a nervous breakdown. She wouldn't allow it," Bridget says.

"It's very hard to hear distressing news about people we care about." Kathryn glances from Hannah to Bridget. Her shoulders look bony in the silk blouse she's wearing.

"You said she was in ICU," Hannah says. "Do you know any more?" Answers would help her nerves.

"I'm afraid all they could tell me was that they were getting her stabilized."

Bridget stands. "Then I say we go to the hospital and find out. If he knew she wasn't okay, and he let her drive . . ." She faces the door.

"They only allow family into ICU," Kathryn says. "I think it would be best if you stayed and talked about how you're feeling."

Bridget spins around. "How I'm feeling? Seriously. How the hell do you think I'm feeling? Angry, guilty, and fucked-up."

"That sounds frightening," Kathryn says.

"Can you not be a therapist for once, and just be human? Gail might be dying, and you're just doing the talk. *Perhaps you should think about how strong you are*," Bridget mimics. "I'm not strong. I feel like my insides are corroding in acid."

"I'm sorry you're in so much pain," Kathryn says.

"Jesus, there you go again, stating the obvious. Maybe it would help us to know how you're feeling about this."

"I'm shocked and deeply concerned, as you are. But what's important in here is how you're feeling," Kathryn replies.

"Wow." Bridget shakes her head. "You really can't stop."

"Bridget." Hannah gets up and walks toward her friend. "She's trying. She's upset too."

"I say we go to the hospital," Bridget says.

"I don't know," Hannah replies. "Maybe we should talk a little more first." She rests a hand on Bridget's arm.

"I think we should find out if her husband cheated, and if he did, we should . . ." Bridget looks ready to fight.

"Let's stay here for a little longer," Hannah suggests. Bridget causing a scene in the hospital won't help anyone.

"Whatever." Bridget walks to her chair. Hannah takes the seat next to her. When she realizes it's where Gail usually sits, she feels dizzy, as if the world is spinning the wrong way.

"When you described how you were feeling, one of the words you used was *guilt*. Can you talk a bit more about that?" Kathryn leans toward Bridget.

"I feel like we should have known more. If we were her friends, like we said, we should have known what was going on in her head. We could have done something. I mean, I kind of made fun of her for her life being so hunky-dory with a sex addict. It's like we never took her totally seriously. And when she really needed us, she probably didn't think we'd be there."

"I think you found a way to connect with her that she really appreciated. Sometimes, when someone isn't thinking rationally, they don't make the best choices. I don't think it has anything to do with her not feeling your support," Kathryn says.

"Not enough for her to call when she was in trouble." Bridget runs a hand over her belly.

"I know we're not supposed to blame ourselves," Hannah says. "But remember what I said to Gail a couple weeks ago? About how getting letters from her husband's girlfriend didn't exactly promote confidence?" Acid rises in her throat. She feels as if she's going to be sick. "What if she took that to heart, went home, and started questioning Jonah? What if . . ." She's warm again, but taking her blazer off would mean she'd have to shift, and right now even small movements would upset her stomach more.

"Doesn't matter," Bridget tells her. "If she went home and found out he was a liar, that's not your fault."

"She's right," Kathryn adds.

"I shouldn't have said that though." Hannah stares at the window behind Kathryn as a focal point to settle her nausea. The glass looks as if it's rippling.

"You can't go down that path. None of us can. I know I started all the 'It's my fault' shit. But it's not." Bridget looks at Kathryn. "And it's not yours either. You've been good at this. At dealing with all of us. I know I just yelled at you, but that wasn't really about you. You've done everything you could for us."

"Thank you," Kathryn replies.

Hannah fiddles with the button on her blazer. Right now she would like nothing more than to be out of this room. To never talk about sex addiction, or hope or support or guilt or blame. To never think about what Gail did. But she also knows she can't keep pushing things away.

"When I was driving here today, I thought about facades." Hannah's face feels hotter. "I thought about how Gail seemed more together than the rest of us. God, I hate to say this, but I think I haven't been far from teetering on the edge of a breakdown of my own, and if I don't start getting it out there . . ." She stops. The second hand on Kathryn's clock ticks.

Bridget places a hand on the arm of Hannah's chair. "Keep going," she whispers.

Hannah takes a deep breath and focuses on the window. "I . . ." she hesitates.

Taut silence follows.

"I hate Adam sometimes. I love him too. I don't know if it would bother me more or less if his addiction was with women, but I do know that what hurts is that his attention wasn't on me or the kids. Sometimes I wake up in the middle of the night, and I spend hours imagining all the things he's done, all the lies he's told me. I think about stupid things, like the fact that he probably spent ten minutes picking out a birthday present for me, and three hours planning a hookup. Then I tell myself to stop being petty, to get over it and move on. I should be grateful for the things I have. And I am. It's just that I still get so angry, and I'm afraid I'm going to get old and bitter."

"Does the anger frighten you?" Kathryn asks.

Hannah takes a moment to think about the question. "I guess. Yes. But it's more than that. It's the hurt. Mostly the fear. That just when I get complacent again and think everything is fine, I'll discover that Adam's still being unfaithful. That my whole life is a lie. So I keep myself guarded, like I'm afraid to really live, and what kind of life is that?"

"Talking about all these things might help," Kathryn says.

Hannah chuckles. "Funny, I hear myself tell that to other people all the time. Might be good if I listened to my own advice sometimes."

"It can be hard to take care of ourselves." Some color has returned to Kathryn's cheeks.

Hannah nods. She agrees, but what she's feeling at the moment is relief that Kathryn looks healthier, sturdier.

"We have to look out for each other, too," Bridget says. "I mean, if we don't, then who's going to be around to help us? If Gail doesn't get better . . ." She lowers her head.

"Why don't we go to the hospital and see," Hannah suggests.

Bridget grabs her bag and looks at Kathryn. "You coming?" she asks.

"I think it's best if I don't. But please call me and let me know how she is."

The tree outside of the window is now sharply in focus. A bud looks ready to burst open. Hannah stands and walks to her therapist. It might be against the rules, but she doesn't care. She hugs Kathryn, who returns a warm embrace. And for the first time Hannah feels completely sure that she will be returning to this room.

Acknowledgments

I have been a teacher for so long, I had almost forgotten what it was like to be a new student. The process of getting a novel published, with its excitement and challenges, put me right at the beginning of the learning curve. Without the help and support of some wonderful people, I could not have managed this journey.

My agent, Joy Harris, has been a truly phenomenal teacher. Her patience, her intuitive understanding of me and my work, her cheerleading, and her warp-speed replies to my endless questions have reminded me that really good teachers are great coaches.

A huge thanks to Jennifer Weis and her team at St. Martin's Press for helping to shape and edit the novel. Jennifer's clarity about how and what to change was remarkable.

To Caroline Upcher, for reading through rambling drafts and always pointing me in the right direction. Also thanks to Bonnie Hearn-Hill, an extraordinary instructor, for teaching me the foundations and the essence of a scene.

I am truly blessed to have supportive friends, who were willing to read and reread, and give honest feedback in a way that didn't make me feel as if I should use the pages as kindling. Thank you, Randy, for the hours and hours of phone calls. Thank you, Caryn, Anne, Barbara, and Amanda, for always being there. To my sister, Anne Lutz, a psychiatrist, thank you for answering many of the specific and technical questions. And to all the people who generously shared their stories of struggles with addiction, you are courageous.

To my husband, whose critical eye helped keep this real.

And lastly, to my adventurous and eccentric daughters, who jump into life with both feet, you motivate me.